L.A.

TALES FROM THE
SUBURBAN SIDE OF HELL

SCOTT SHAW

BUDDHA ROSE PUBLICATIONS

First Edition 1990
Fifth Edition 2026

ISBN 10: 1-877792-18-7
ISBN-13: 978-1-877792-18-2

Library of Congress Control Number:
2011940174

10 9 8 7 6 5 4 3 2 1
Printed in the United States of America

L.A.

TALES FROM THE SUBURBAN SIDE OF HELL

CONTENTS

INTRODUCTION

Some people live life. Some people prefer to simply read about the life others live. That is why some of us, myself included, must take this existence to the extreme—you know, like so others can read about it...

*   *   *

My *Main and Current L.A. Babe,* she asked me today, if Chandler, if Spillane were influences of mine. She inquired, for she has recently been required to read their writings for a university class she is taking.

She is not the first to mention this to me. But, aside from the fact that I really have no influences, I actually have never read a word either of the men have written.

I, of course, know of them, due to the movies and the T.V. shows that have been based on the characters they have created. And, in a roundabout way, I understand where they are *a-comin'* from.

I think I must change that though. I must read their works—understand what she, my *Main and Current L.A. Babe,* and the other people are *a-talkin'* about. Or, maybe not...

Anyway, she, my *Main and Currently L.A. Babe,* (a decade or so younger than I), said that the attitudes of their central characters reminded her of my books and when they were discussed the writing style of these two men in her class, *"The tough guy approach,"* was the title given it.

She, my *Main and Currently L.A. Babe,* told me that she kept wanting to yell out and insert into her class discussion, *"Hey, that's just like my boyfriend! Sexist! You know, no respect for women—thinking that they, (the women), have only one purpose and that is for sex, but expecting them all to be good little virgin girls."* She says I am just like the, *"Tough guy,"* character(s) in Chandler and Spillane's books—living life outside of the mainstream.

"Yeah," she said, *"That's just like you! You and your work. It's Studly."*

'Studly?' What a funny word, I thought...

Awh, the exuberance of youth. She's only twenty...

But yeah, I guess I am sexist, and I do play things according to my own rules, following the, *"Tough guy approach."* But, like hey, I just feel like that is the way things are supposed to be.

But, as I have long realized, I wouldn't want the babes to do to me, what I have done to them. ...To treat me, the way that I have treated them. But, in fact, and in actuality, I guess that's beside the point... For I have lived as I lived. I have done what I have done. And, that is that.

8

But, back to the subject at hand...
After her initial discourse, I exclaimed,

"What! You don't think that my work is erotica?"
"No, just studly," she answered. *"And, if I didn't know you and love you, I would think that you were a real asshole."*

Well, maybe she's right. It's for you to decide...
As for a charter name, in association with this book, just call me, Mr. Studly; Sam Studly...

*   *   *

Concerning this book... It's just another example of my living life so others can stay at home and be good *family-men* and *business-people.* It's a dirty job but somebody has got to it...
Also, the same lady, my *Main and Currently L.A. Babe,* the one that will, more than likely, be on the serious side of history by the time you read this, she tells me,

"What you really are is a historian. You are depicting an age and an era in your writing."

Sounds good! We'll stick with that!
So, for whatever it, (and this), is all worth—here's another chance to read about my experiences in this age and of this era. Read

about it, so you won't have to live it. Read about it, so you can learn from my mistakes. And, read about it, to possibly even gain from my realizations.

Oh yeah, and as I am frequently reminded, I need to mention that things are never quite what they seem in my writing(s). So, in all of these words, there is a story within the story. Remember, read between the lines.

Live on, dream on, read on. Feel the perfection and live the mysticism. So says, Sam Studly.

S.
31 March 1990
Redondo Beach, California

L.A. 1

7:30 AM. The mystic music of the alarm clock rings. It's for her. Not for me. She, who has to rise and has to go to a job to pay her bills.

"I am so broke," she tells me. *"I would love to stay with you. Sleep late, drink cappuccino, walk along the beach. But, you don't give me any money! You don't even give me much love! So, I have no choice, I must go!"*

As the abstraction of the reality takes hold, there's no place left for me to run. I'm awake. Awoken, to the sound of the fading old wave/new wave music coming home into the tale end of the 1980's.

I turn off the sounds from the alarm clock/radio, for it's closest to my hand. She climbs over me. The window/the ocean, on her side. I follow her up/I follow her out into the realms of my small beach apartment.

I get up, because I trust no one. Call me a borderline paranoid...

But, more importantly, where did it begin?

This morning... Yes, I know... It began this morning.

But, *"It..."* Where and how was the *starting-point* for this, *"It?"*

Insanity—its inception into the melodrama from where it rose. Can I even recall?

Well, yes... Yes, I can.

It was I who said, *"Good-bye."* Yes, it was I.

After being awoken for another morning—way too early. Being awoken due to someone else's karma someone else's destiny someone else's bills to pay, I told her that after this AM/after her current exit, she would only have my telephone answering machine to speak with—she would never see me again. It was over. OVER! Yes, I wanted it that way!

She never took/never takes things lying down. Chinese... She's Chinese. As per her culture, she is very-very forward.

She knows what she wants. She knows what she's got. And, she knows how to use it. *"It."* Yes, this is where, *"It,"* began.

*   *   *

She would raise her voice. I would ask her to please keep it down. For a second, she would—perhaps two, maybe even three. Then, the amplification. Volume to maximum output capacity. Her voice, it would rise again—full blown level.

From yelling to tears. If one, (the first failed), then switch to number two. Then, again, try the other—the other one.

She... She had maximum money in her childhood affairs; one leads to the other, one leads to two, and you always get what you want, if you play the game long and loud enough.

12

Yes, she... She came from maximum money. When you come from that, it makes you who you are/what you are. It's one of those blessings/one of those curses that can/will never be forgotten.

She yells. She cries. I ask her to please be quite for all the neighbors they can hear. She does not care. *"I have no shame!"* she screams.

I guess that goes along with being Taiwanese/Chinese: (the forward), the mega money; limousine(s) to kindergarten and all...

All equaling what, is the eternal question—in an adult life with no money? Where she has to go to work to pay the bills.

"I love you!" She screams it.
"Yes, I know. Many women have loved me. I have loved many; such as my love goes..."

To be blatantly honest, many have loved her, as well. Too many in my mind.

"I love you."
"Yes, I know."
"Don't leave me."
"Why?"
"I'm so afraid of being without you. I'm so afraid of being alone. I love you so much."
"So what?"

I do not mean to be unfeeling here. I do not mean to be cold. But thoughts, they built up in the mind of nowhere. And, when love is the

only answer to being alone. I don't know...
Then love, it is for suckers.

I even remember this one love. This one
love of mine. One, a long time ago... No, not
this one—another one.

Let me see... It must have been deep in
the Indian country of New Mexico. Her, she
and I; we were driving. Well, I actually was at
the wheel. We stopped at a little sales shop on
an Indian Reservation. She, her and I.

Nothing much: a blanket or two for sale
and some ugly turquoise jewelry. I hate that
shit! So-so, in the so-so category and
departamento.

A blanket; an Indian, (American Indian),
blanket caught her eye, however and etcetera.

"Do you want it?"
"I don't know."
"I'll buy it for you if you want it."
"I'm not sure..."

Not knowing and unsure; we left. We
took a walk. The statues of New Mexico's
natural art—rock formations, they rose into the
crystal blue approaching evening sky.

"Do you want it?"
"I don't know."

We drove off, thirty miles onto a
horizon, on the framework of the mind.

"Do I want it?" She asks me.

14

I don't know?" I answer.

I turned around. Drove her back. Let her make a clearer visual decision. Inside the shop, Indian eyes, (American Indian eyes), look us over/look at us again. In the middle of nowhere/nowhere from here.

"Do you want it?"
"I don't know."

Into/onto the highway, off into the realm of the real again—we drive fifty miles. The evening, it was quickly closing in.

"I think I want it."

I drove back. Again, Indian eyes, (American Indian eyes), wondered of our scene. Money exchanged. The blanket in the car. It was hers. She now owned it. The deep night in/of New Mexico upon us. We drove... She said,

"It was just a whim. I don't know if I really wanted it."

I smiled... This/that situation so perfectly depicted my life—giving but never receiving.
This morning; not then. The morning in question/of question. She, not that one, this one; yells—continues to yell.

"Please keep it down. The neighbors can hear."
"You care more about them than me!"

That not being the case, it's just that my business is not their business and I have to live here and see them again and again and again and again... And, for a woman who spends my money, spends my time, cooks my energy for breakfast, and then spits it out wanting more— more love, more time, more gifts, more money; and with nothing to give in return... I'm sorry, the business of trade, it's just not worth the cost.

"Well, if you are not going to answer your phone then I am going to take your favorite Rolex."

She grabs it. This is *no-go* in my book. Give it back, jack!

The screams, the tears, the arguing, the complaints go on and on and on and on and on. Really, I don't want to hear them anymore!

I hear my upstairs neighbor. He begins to sing his good morning groans/chants. They're almost operatic, almost Zen.

No, they are not voice training. I don't really know what they are. Weird, that is what they are.

If I can hear that. They, the ones around us, can hear her/us. Fighting for no reason.

She just will not leave me alone. Days of letting the answering machine handle it, and then she knocks upon the door.

Yes, I am a fool. Yes, I let her in. Deep addiction. Like a needle in the vein.

Alone and thirty, alone in a world that does not care. I want to return to Asia. I want to live, where the living is good. I want to write my books, my poetry there; paint my painting there. But, that is all known fact, cast to the realm(s) of the *devis*. Known is known; so I won't go into those abstract musings of desire here. Back to the story at hand...

Post the point of the other aforementioned yelling and screaming attacks and nothing, equaling nothing—her not getting her way... Out of nowhere, (literally), out of no-where, she screams,

"Don't hit me!"
"Do you think that you yelled that loud enough? Do you think that you have embarrassed me enough? I don't hit you. Do I? I have never hit you. Have I? Maybe I should? Stop yelling, you are really embarrassing me!"

She screams again/cries again/yells again. Alphabets confined in a mystic world's mind.

"Okay then, I'm going to take this album that I gave you," she shrieks.

17

A rare, hard to find abstract piece of vinyl.

Pushed too far. Smash! I take it from her hands and up against my record player it goes—hard/fast. I break it. No more record. No more vinyl.

"Now just go!" I give her a slight push in the directions of the door.
"Don't hit me!"
"I'm not hitting you."
"Don't push me!"
"Just leave then."
"No!"

The morning, 7:30 AM; awoken to the sound of music, post punk, post new wave, dance beat on the radio. I turned it off. I was the closest. It was for her to wake; to go to the/her job.

Now, her fourth and final tactic—when all else has failed: hit and kick. She hits and kicks me.

If it/this had been at her pad, if it/this had taken place there, I could have screamed; screamed as she has screamed, *"Don't hit me!"* But it was mine. Mine, in all of its embarrassment of the *Soap Opera* for the morning neighbors to hear. They must think I am one serious woman beater as she has made these cries before.

I turn. I start to walk away... As I do, *Bap!* She halls off and hits me from behind. Hits me in the side of the face.

18

Reaction, I slick a back-fist near the side of her head. No contact, just a calculated blow, caught in mid-air from a lifetime of martial art training. She screams, literally screams accompanied by,

"Don't hit me!"
"I didn't hit you."

Two children at their game...
Now, we are in the kitchen. The kitchen *en route* to the door. She yells,

"I'm not trained not to flinch. I'm not trained in the martial arts."

Actually, let us call a spade a spade, in this moment of our lives. She has had many; many before me... She wants to add me to not only her *dick-list* but her *live-in-list*, as well. She claims, I am the only one for her. That she loves me so much more than all the rest/all those before. Though she has lied much, at the doors to the gates of hell, her story has proven to be somewhat sound.
Sound as it may sound. But sorry, no brass ring, (or gold band), as it were.
Lies... I don't trust her. But, attachment runs deep—deep as the deepest river. Deep as the deepest ocean. Deeper than deep. And she is only attachment deep.
Dudes; the dudes before me, they took a hand to her more than once. More than one:

dick-list, live-in-list. Basically, I think that she probably deserved it.

Deserved it; as it may be... Me, in my old age; thirty, I have chilled. Maybe more secure, maybe more of a fool. But, what fun is there in beating someone that you know you can beat? What fun is power and control, when there in none that you want? Me, I prefer enlightenment.

In the kitchen, the please/leave... The yells. The screams. The asking to please keep it down; someone is going to complain. Right there/right then came a knock upon my door. I looked at her/she at me. *'Fuck,'* I thought. *'When I opened the door, there will be Mr. Uck, the overzealous AM security guard.'*

I looked at her. She looked at me. I go to open the door.

"Hi, I forgot my keys, can I climb from my patio to yours?"
"Sure."

My next-door neighbor; a girl. A girl I do not even really know—one year and half later. She moved in a few days after I.

Blonde, she is blonde. Blonde like I. Dudes, I have seen more than a few out there upon her good morning, post the night of a love, patio. But me, I don't care. *Nada* to me. She's just not my flavor.

I swing the door open. Sure footed she makes her way towards the light. The light that hides the darkness from the night.

She moved. No vision to her left. No vision to her right.

She moved past two of my Italian racing bicycles, which hang on a rack in the hallway—no comment. She moved past my lady who stood there in the kitchen, tears in her eyes—no comment. She moved past my wall of books—no comment. She moved to the moving onto the light—no comment. She moved, stepping over my leg-stretcher. (Hey, I am a martial artist. I must keep my full-splits *comein'* on); which sat mid-way, mid-floor, against my couch—no comment. She moved past and through the mess which makes up my apartment—no comment.

To the door. The sliding glass door. The morning curtain(s) still drawn. I pulled them back. I slid the screen door. She steps out. Finally, with a comment,

"We have an artist here, I see."

A drop cloth. A rusting metal easel. Everything metal rusts at the beach... Plus, paints, brushes out there by the sea; upon my patio.

"Or something," I answer.

I smiled. I was all smiles. I can pretend real good!

I smiled. I did not feel like smiling. The situation; the condition in which I live. Too small of a space for an artist, (or something), to live in...

I smiled. I did not feel like smiling.

She had to have heard. They, the other neighbors, had to have heard. I smiled. But, I did not feel like smiling. I was ashamed/embarrassed/humiliated.

If I had some money, I would have run. I did not/do not; not yet anyway...

An exchange of the, *"Now are you happy(s)?"* To my love of no love. And, the dance, in the guilt; the guilt on both of our parts. An exchange of unhappiness. A yell again. A scream again, or two... On her part of course; not mine.

A speech of how I always make her mess up her jobs; now she will be REAL late. I respond with a lecture of/about all her lies and all her deceptions.

"You have a lot of making up to do," she tells me.

I laugh at her. Talk is cheap!

"Will you walk me to my car," she inquires.
"Sure, let me find my shoes."

I'm always a gentleman...
Shoes on. Shirt on. Outside we walk.

"I'm going to kill myself," she says.

22

"Good, that will solve both of our problems. The world would be a much better place." I conclude.

She got into her car. Started it. Revved the engine of her 1986 hardtop *Suzuki Samurai*. She madly drove off.

Psychological anger, give it to *'em*—make *'em* too angry to kill themselves. So it says in the textbooks. So I have seen it spelled. All my paranoia came up though. I worried. I wrote the tale in my journal—covered my ass.

Back to sleep, 9:00 AM. What a morning of nothing but this vague poetic literature which means nothing to no-one.

Sleep/dreams... I was in a building. The building was a big one—tall. A skyscraper up in the sky. I was with a babe. It is/was foggy. How/why, I don't know? But, she was there with me. This beautiful white chick with long flowing brown hair. We looked at this very large aquarium *to-get-her*. Then, it moved. The dreamed moved. There I was. I saw my long blond hair, a growing out, three-day old beard. Though the scene had changed, I was still in the building. Up—up there high. I was with two others: a man/a woman. They suggested that we must leave. Me, I did not see the need, but I left anyway. Something they said/something they did, made me somehow believe. Down the stairs we raced. The elevator before our decent had become stuck/trapped with people inside of it; trapped, *none-the-less*.

Down a stairwell. A painted stairwell, with a white/metal banister. Somehow, I was in front and I taught them, the other two, how to almost fly in the sliding down. As we approached the bottom, the ceiling plaster began to fall—a major earthquake. The building was breaking down.

To the bottom. To the out. The structure was bent/tilted—inclined halfway.

We had made it out. I had woken up. I leave it to you, the dream interpreter(s), to figure out the meaning—what it meant... And, may all the character(s) of my AM dream; all the ones who I have forgotten to mention forgive me for not describing them more clearly.

11:30 AM. What could I do? Jump back into the addiction, the addiction that I had run so far away from? I answered the phone. It rang. She called me from her place of employment—extension 5304.

"Would you like to go to lunch? I'm sorry for this morning! I love you so much!"
"Thirty minutes, I will be there. Thirty minutes maybe more." Was my answer...

Lunch it was her choice. My stomach not really in the mode/mood. A midnight session of two double chili cheeseburgers from *Tommy's*. *Tommy's,* (the real one), off of Alvarado.

One for her. One for me. She wouldn't eat hers. The un-bohemian brat that she is. Me, I had to eat two...

24

Post her day of/on the job junk food snacking; she picked the place. She is a real junk food eater. I am not.

Lunch, rang me up at forty dollars, for two salads. You know the kind of *shi-shi,* overpriced for nothing place.

We spoke as the waitress, obviously cute and from the south, brought us our poison. We discussed the abstract, the surreal quality of the day that had preceded us.

I took her back to her temporary employment at a major motion picture studio. They said she could not take a lunch—too busy. She took it *any-way.* That's just who/how she is...

I, well me, post all this/that, I went out looking for another copy of the record I smash in the AM. It seemed all so important to me at that moment.

I went out, out in the fading summertime—coming autumn; Thursday heat. I searched everywhere. I found it naught.

The freeway heat. The freeway traffic. Three o'clock high. I headed from the central city to the South Bay of L.A.

Home and at the beach. Home and into the ocean—my summer wet suit on; board in hand; a green one—custom-made by a friend of mine's brother. Tossed and turned. The ocean it was choppy as I tried to get in a little aerobic; burn some, too many calories, dinner late and lunch early.

In the surf, I asked,

"Heal me Divine Mother Ocean. Heal me, like Tokyo heals me."

As I doddled in the water, trying a catch a wave in the choppy surf, I could not help but think how it had been my mistake to not meet my sweet Singaporean princess in Tokyo—the plan(s) we had made almost a month ago.

Me, I stayed for this woman—the one this story is about. But, as is always the case, hindsight is twenty-twenty. You don't know then, what you didn't know then...

Home/inside, six o'clock in the PM. The telephone it rings. She, the girl/this girl calls me from the office,

"Do you want me to come over?"
"Okay," was my answer.

"Okay," though I did not really mean okay. *"Okay,"* I said it anyway.

She calls me from her home a bit later on. I make problems from this and that and other things. All in the this. The this of the that. The way in of no way out. She is still to come over.

I watch a repeat on the television station; on a repeat channel, in a repeat time.

The show was of/about this writer; of this traveler, of this adventurer who had lived, long and hard. Number up. His time came to die. The doctors knew it. They gave him his countdown. He was to make the jump; hang glide from Oahu to Molokai. Certain death. An

26

impossible flight. Death, his time/his style/his way. He yelled back—back to the star of the T.V. series,

"With my luck, I will probably make it..."

Hit a little too close to home.

Post the show, I moved over to these keys. I typed away. A telephone call, it does come in. A call from a pay phone in the city,

"I am so dizzy. I keep blacking out. I am sick. I am going home."

No problema in the *no problema* sense of the word. I really wanted out anyway. It was her/she/the one I write this tale about.

It is alone and addiction that holds me too tightly in. But now, now I was/I am free.

I thought about continuing to write. But, *"No,"* I could now go to the Huntington Beach Health Spa and see this little Vietnamese/Chinese girl who awaits my Tuesday and Thursday night arrival(s). The other nights of the week I hit the one over here; South Bay Way, on Hawthorne Boulevard.

Life in its perplexities. I forever chase the ones I do not really want. I guess it is just that I never meet the ones I do want. Just the ones that are not all that worth chasing. Call me a fool. I call myself one...

A call from the girl; the same girl, the one I am speaking about. It puts my typing fingers to rest. Put to rest, I got dressed—

27

workout clothing in my bag, I was almost out the door. The telephone rings again. Again, it is her/her from her home,

"What are you doing?"
"About to leave for the health spa. Go and pick-up on some sweet young thing; something/someone who has much more to offer me than you."
"You are so mean."
"Are you feeling better?"
"No, not really. I feel sick and I am so tried."
"But, not too tired to go to work tomorrow, right? I don't like your priorities."
"But, I'm broke and you don't give me any money."
"Just dream...Goodbye."

I hang up. I'm out the door, 8:15 PM. Twelve hours plus since my initial rise in the AM.

Out the door. In my *'64 Porsche 356 SC.* Down the street/down the freeway— Huntington Beach. Four miles on the track. Into the jacuzzi. Immediately, I am attacked by a *white-bread/white-trash,* a little over in the pounds *departamento,* female.

"Where are you from," she inquires.
"L.A. Born and raised."

From there, the conversation moves on and into the everywhere of *no-wheres-ville-daddy-O.*

28

A social worker from Ohio. A brain tumor, cut out. We compare bowling ball holes in our heads. Hers from her too many birth control pills—so she says/said. Mine, from introducing face to pavement; *Street Pizza,* caused by a brand-new *Mercedes* meeting my bad scoot head-on and sending me flying, head-first, through the air, onto the ground off of my motorcycle.

She wanted to feel mine. I let her. She guided my hand to hers. Personally, I didn't really care.

A talker. She talked forever. Tried to drop names of poets, of writers, of philosophers. People that she thought that I would not know. *Sorry babe, I knew 'em all.*

She spoke of the sixties, of drugs. *Sorry babe, I lived in Hollywood and took all the drugs there are.* She spoke of her church. Invited me. *Sorry babe, church is not my style.*

Speaking of, (or not), and my main reason for my attendance at this particular location this evening; my Chinese/Vietnamese or Vietnamese/Chinese, whichever way the blood chooses to flow—be of Asian desire; where was she? The whole reason I had made the journey this evening...

I looked up. She was there/she showed up. She sat by the *j-cuzz-a* on a bench for a second, two, or three. I could see her eyes filled with pure jealousy, casting their glance my direction. Pissed, she got up and left. I smiled to myself, *No rap'n tonight.* Oh well, keep 'em guessing. I'll hit it next time around.

29

Finally, I had enough of the talkative *white-trash* bitch. I just couldn't take it anymore. I mean, it was *fuckin'* obvious I wasn't going to get to hit that pussy—at least not tonight. Not that I even really wanted to. But...

So, what good was she? Me, I bailed. Rap to nowhere, ends up in nowhere.

I got dressed. Hit to the upstairs. Had my traditional, on the way home, high protein, coconut/pineapple shake. In the car, I listened to the *Sisters of Mercy* on my tape player as I drove north on the *405*. I motored home and here it be/here I be.

All in a fog. This fog of literary Zen nothingness. Zero of the relationships that make up my life. Maybe tomorrow will prove more interesting. Be less AM traumatic. I mean she, the bitch isn't here. I'm sleeping solo. So, at least I will be able to wake up at my time— eleven, twelve or so. Not her time. Not 7:30 in the AM.

It was surreal—this day...

*   *   *

may the nighttime close in with me
in with me in its mercy
may the fog describe another life
another time
and hand me another dance
another chance

30

deep in the night
exists the fog

deep in this life
exists the illusion

so dreamy
so lost
so surreal
abstraction/attraction

kiss me
for all the words
mean nothing
all the experience(s)
even less
all the enlightenment
only an illusion
and the thinking man is only a fool

The wind is blowing about a million miles an hour outside. The waves they are *a-kickin'* big time. The sand, well let's just say that the wind is *blowin'* the sands of time together. And, the world moves on and on and on and on and on...

Thing(s) change...

Creation/destruction; all in its divine form and format.

It's late autumn now. And, already in the, *what may be termed,* early afternoon; it's dark outside. Dark like the outside of midnight.

Usually, I love the winter here in California. But, the time change, *Spring Forward/Fall Back,* it has thrown me off at bit this year—left me wondering where has the day gone?

November, it's generally my favorite month. Generally, in format and form. For then/now, I am generally lost within the bounds of Asia. Somewhere out there on the extremities; out on *The Hard Road.*

This year, it's different. Money and life and state of mind...

Money, I have none. Life; high and dry. State of mind, on the positive upswing. Yet, the curse of the evils of society and culture, programming, and childhood—all of the devil's vices, hold be bound from continual peak experience.

I still believe in miracles though and/or however... And November, it's only about halfway done. So maybe I'll make China before this sweet little thing's birthday party that I was invited to it. Or maybe, I'll make Japan, for this young dancer's love. Make it, before the setting of the rising sun. And yes, maybe I'll even make Singapore, before my airline stewardess flies away. Or maybe, Bangkok, before my hotel lady gets too much older.

God, I feel so bad... I popped her thirty-year-old cherry and just left. I really need to get back to her to tell her it actually meant something.

Maybe I'll even make Kuala Lumpur (KL) while my advertising agent, of a sweet little few night stand, still has my photo in a picture frame upon her bedside table. I don't know, maybe...

And, as the wind blows these chances, I can see the past go and the new dreams come. The wind blows, the sands moves, I move. The wind blows us into *never-never-never-land.*

*   *   *

Five o'clock. Yes, I was on my bicycle doing the miles to keep this body in shape. In a passing glance/in a passing chance, there she was; this woman who I had once lived with/once loved—such as my love is/and or is not.

Yeah, I tried to love her. But, that was many-many-many moons ago. Yeah, I tried to live with her. But, I don't want to think about that...

Yeah, I did what I did. The main thing I learned from all of that was—you can never make a person what they were never meant to be. I know, because I have tried.

The lies... They were on. A rap in. A rap out. I wrapped myself in way too tight. She didn't want to let me go.

But then, there came too many others... Too many times, I fooled around. And, I still remember her once saying to me, *"What a mistake,"* while we were having dinner.

You know... Maybe that's the picture. The picture that should best be kept in mind. For there we were. There I was—she invited me. I didn't invite her. I paid the tab—as I always paid the tab; and all she could do was complain.

I don't know... We all have our faults. Well, I maybe have more than most. But, settling down—settling with someone who never touched that spot—never held the perfection... Settling... It was never a dream of mine.

Now, the fact of the matter is, most people do it. They take whatever/whomever they can get. Anyone that will take them... They accept second best. Not me. I have too many dreams to live—too many chances to take—too many rules to break.

                    *   *   *

The wind blows hard tonight—night in the terms of the darkness; outside and all around. Dark in the night. Dark in the light. Her hair was so dark that it blended into the darkness. It kissed the realms of the abyss.

The abyss, my home. My only friend. My friend—the ultimate stranger.

                    *   *   *

Out in the elements, I was moving northward—moving by... Northward on *The Strand,* next to the ocean. In a flash, there she was; that girl from long ago that I spoke of...

She wore her very long hair down: loose, free—something that she would never do with/for me.

I remember a discussion that we had many years ago. I said that she must learn to be free. The wind in the/her hair: the essence of poetry; the foundation for the formation of art and the dream. But, she forever wore her long wavy locks, tied back—locked up tight.

I remember desiring that freedom that freedom of the wind. The wind, my friend. The wind, my confidant. The wind... Yes, the wind, it drove me away from that woman. How I ran and ran and ran and ran and ran away from her. But, she never took, *"Away,"* for an answer. I would do her wrong, again and again and again and again. And/but, she would continually drag me back, *"In."*

I ran into the alone/the abyss. I ran to the kisses of some other fool/many other fools. Fool(s) like me. I ran to the tears and to the contraction of the lost/lonely Asian nights.

*   *   *

For when it is there, it is all there; when is not, (like now), here I sit all alone—coming and going; thoughts equal no-thing. Just lost moments to a lost fantasy. I glance across the room as I write this. I see myself—my face, my body, my picture on the cover of a French magazine. I smile. My brain laughs, *'That's me!'* Or, is it?

Lost; I sit, I write, I remember the night that photograph was taken and the momentary love of infatuation. (The best kind of love). The love I loved with that French maiden that night. That night, after the photo session.

But, back to the woman at hand...

I played the field. I played around. Though she prayed that I would stay with her; literally prayed, I did not. So much for the praying...

Once, I remember... Once, before it had all gone so bad. Once, I remember her asking me; begging,

"Just stay with me one more week. I know you will fall in love with me again. I know you will... I will make you!"

36

One more week I gave her. But, her plan, it did not work.

*   *   *

But, she was always there when I came back—back to *The States*. Back stateside. Last time out, I sent her a *Rolex*. They are a bit cheaper in Asia. It was the least I could do. I mean, all the love she had poured upon me. And, all the shit I gave her.

If she got it, I never really knew. For upon return from that journey, there was a postcard in my P.O. Box. A postcard saying she was off—out and about. She got a new job in a new city. She sent me this, (after again), I had gotten caught with my hand; well, actually my dick, in another cookie jar. She thought it was better that we never communicated again. She said, *"I had just hurt her too many times..."* I smiled when I read her words. My first thought was, *'Finally!'* Then, a moment of sadness came over me—all those years... All that time... It meant nothing.

My fault, I know.

*   *   *

You know, it's funny... I laugh now, as I did then. I laugh because it's so easy to say, *"No more communications,"* when you owe someone as much I-O-U money as she does/did to me.

Funnier still, I think; in the judgment of

37

all forms and terms, she even owes me a surfboard—a *long board*—agreed upon, if I put dollars in her hand; which I did.

She needed furniture for her new apartment up West Hollywood way. Up, just below Melrose. Furnishings that I paid for. For that, she was going to give me this surfboard. She did not.

I sent her around Europe once. Once, back when I had many more dollars to spend. I bought her a sports car once—money gone, never to be seen again.

Though I couldn't give her love; though I couldn't give her forever; I could give her money. She took a lot of mine—all with the promise of the payback. Every time she took it. *"I WILL pay you back!"*

The payback, which never-ever came... Or, maybe it did. The other kind of payback; karmick payback. I don't know? I just do not know!

Actually, it was very typical of her/this girl. I gave her so much. Some people just are the givers—some are just the takers. And, karma it is just chucked out the window and who really knows *the name of the game?*

So, I didn't hold her to it... Hold her to all the I-O-U's. She wanted. I gave. I gave her everything but what she really wanted—me.

Release and relax. Laugh in the fluctuation of the intense wind. Release and relax, then you are free as you can be. Free from me. We all pay a price for our freedom.

38

*   *   *

As the night air, it was *a-comin'* on. A ride into the wind on my bike. A pass of a person who said that she had left the city. I heard the news on a postcard sent to my P.O. Box.

A pass in the night. A pass it is alright. Gone are the glory days.

She had a smirk on her face as she saw me approaching on my $3,000.00 *Colnago Equilateral* Italian racing bike. She was walking arm-in-arm with some other guy. A guy, with long blonde hair, who looked an amazing amount like me.

You know they say pay-back it is a *mutha fucka*. But, sometimes pay-back comes too late for one, someone, (me), to even care.

I rode. I didn't stop. I smiled as I rode. I was happy for her. My ride and the road ahead held far more illusion for me than looking back to a past that I did not want to relive.

But, as I drove forward, in my northward pattern, *ridin'* on my bike, my mind did go back to when we, (her and I), had met. *FLASHBACK.* A million years ago... Back when punk was young—we were young. She met me. I met her at a punk nightclub; listening to, (or should I say, *slam dancing* to), punk music. *"Punk rock music,"* as they term it now.

Back then, we met—two maybe three weeks just after I had been released from the hospitable. My head/my face introduced to payment. I already spoke about that/this in the

39

previous chapter. Me, post being hit while in motion on my motorcycle. Hit, by a brand/nearly new *Mercedes Benz.* A young girl at the helm.

They, the medical professionals, thought I wouldn't live. I did but my face, my body, certainly my mind, never really the same. Skull fractured/face fractured in a thousand places. Forehead shoved against brain. They did save me. But me—no, I was never quite the same; broken, shattered, tattered—far more volatile; for sure. Punk was good for me.

The young girl who hit me in the *Mercedes,* went on with her life. My life was forever altered.

Some say, (the professionals that is), state in exacting scientific terms that it/my temper grew in that moment/those moment(s) of my life—face to payment and all. It/me is all due to my motorcycle accident; frontal lobe trauma, (or something). I don't know... I was turned into *Street Pizza* once upon a time. All that be as it may. This is what I am left with. This is all I have left. Who I am.

And, that's perhaps the saddest thing about life—how people have the power: the right, the possibility, to change your entire existence forever; do it without a thought. And then, they get to live the rest of their life as if nothing happened—as nothing did happen to them. But, it did happen to someone else. And, then life is left forever different. Different is not always better.

So again, punk was good for me. A lot of expression of misplaced violence.

I met her, this girl; the one I'm talking about—the one this story is about. Yeah, I met her, just after that. Met her at a punk nightclub. She had these big beautiful Spanish eyes.

Yeah, she was stunning. But, she was a major *Space Case.* One of those people that you ask them a question and they give you some *spaced-out* answer five or ten minutes later. An answer that has/had nothing to do with the actually question—at least not with the reality of the question.

Yeah, she was like that then. Back then, when I first knew her.

She told me that one time; during her lunch break from work, she had gone to a restaurant to eat. There was a guy awaiting his date. They sat her down at his table; thinking she must be the date. So *spaced-out,* she said *nada.* He, the dude had to ask her, the girl, to leave.

Weird, very weird...

But, I got her out of that. Told her, *"STOP IT!"* Told her more than once. Finally, she did. Did eventually... My gift to her, I guess. Making her one with *the here and the now.*

Yeah, I thought back to the flashback; if only for a second. To those early days—our meeting; as I continued on my northward journey.

My journey has continued, continuing... I never looked back. Not even on all the money she owned me.

Life... I smile.

But, back to the point at hand...

Yeah, I guess she owes/owed me one. Well, actually more than one. I remember her waiting at my crib—on the doorstep of my crib, (on the stoop), of my by the beach apartment, in Hermosa Beach—way back in the day.

One of those deep in the relationship nights. Yeah, she was there. I was out—another bush to grab. I pull up with this *nine-out'a ten* fine, sweet young thing, of a Japanese babe that I had hooked up with. We, her and I, the Japanese babe, we were seriously ready to go at it, if you catch my meaning and I think that you do.

She, my main and central, (in waiting), babe sees me as I pull up front and center. The new babe, drunk, ready to party hard on the body side of the picture. Me too. I was way ready to dive down deep into her being.

I pull up. See her, the other babe... I look. She looks. Our eyes meet. Not wanting to embrace the *melo-drama,* I jam out with my new babe in my bad little *'64 Porsche 356 SC.* She and me, we were *out-a-there.*

And, for the record, I never did get a chance to hit that new snatch...

Yeah, and etcetera, there were a lot of other times... Times that she found out. Once I saw her driving—coming over my way. I was *ridin'* shotgun, a babe driving me *out-to-the-night*. She was on the wheel.

Her and that night belong in the annals of the sexual history books. But, and in any case, I won't cover that here.

Me, I drove by *ridin'* shotgun. I saw her, the other babe. I ducked down just a bit, so I would not be seen. But, I was seen. Didn't know it until day next, however. When her, the babe I be discussing, smashes through my front door screaming, *"Why?"* She then took one of my guitar; one of my way loved guitars: a *Guild D40* and smashed it.

Too many times. Too many rhythms. As I say, she owed me an ego shot or two. A shot or two, in addition to all that money. She should never have killed that guitar though. I loved that guitar.

Anyway... She, (the main babe of the discussion at hand), she said she would fix her eyes, die her hair black, just so she could be like the women I like. She, a full-on beauty in her own right: Spanish blood via Cuba. But, my tastes had shifted. They went another *dirección*.

But, that was all a long, long, long, long time ago...

*   *   *

So, the wind it blows the sands of change. Chance and change, everything gets rearranged.

"I can't imagine making love with anyone but you."

She said that once to me. I think we were in Paris. But, words/feelings, they change. They mean nothing...

As for the incident. My riding past them on *The Strand*... No doubt, she thought that I would rearrange his face—the guy she was walking with. Hell, knowing my schedule the way she did, maybe she set the whole thing up so I would. Some sort of test, don't you know?

At least, (no doubt), she thought that I would try to contact her after the incident. But me, I have way better ways to spend my time.

I laughed as I rode on. I laugh now.

In actually, I wish her: her and him, all the best. I hope that they both have found what they are looking for.

A man in the hand is worth me in someone else's bush. And, as we all well know, it would not be hard to find a far better man than I.

So, whatever was; was. It can never be that way again. Personally, I would not want it to be. Prices paid—prices are high. We only see them in our rear-view mirrors.

*   *   *

A rap in. A rap out. In/out... For years, I searched for a way out. But, attachment holds the mind. It becomes bound. And, the games, they are for the losers. The winning is for the

44

dancers in the night.

Me, I would just prefer to chill on over and back to Asia. I have many dreams there waiting to be lived.

*   *   *

The wind blows with its full-on intensity. The wind, it changes everything. It goes round—life goes round—the earth moves around, and we dance for so short a time.

Kiss me night. Kiss me wind. Kiss me love that I have not yet seen. Kiss me, *"Hello,"* for I have kissed the past, *"Goodbye."* Like a gentleman, I never even looked back.

The wind is blowing tonight at a million miles an hour. The waves are kicking big time. And, the sands of change, they get rearranged. And life, well it does have the tendency to move on.

OM TAT SAT OM

Have you ever seen the people walking down the street, or maybe in a mall, or maybe in a restaurant eating alone and their head just looks like it has a brick in it—their aura just exudes the pain.

Me, I look no farther. I look in the mirror. I cannot run away from it, though I have tried. Here/Now it is me.

It began yesterday. Yesterday, it started out...

Yesterday began in the so okay-ness. But, okay must be kept in context. For okay to me; well... It may not be okay to you. As okay to me is a far stretch into the far side of the realms of dark suchness. My okay is lost into the abyss of time, space, and illusion.

Anyway, as the story goes... I had plans to go to this punk store. Yeah, a few still exist here in the late 1980s. That is, I had plans to go until the world blew up in my face— *Armageddon.* But, I'll get to that in a moment or three.

Yeah, you know, I had first gone into this aforementioned store about four months ago. In there, with this babe. The babe in question. The babe this story is about. But, I'll tell you her story in a few...

As stated, I went in there, with this babe in question. Her, and two of her friends of a similar bloodline—Asian.

Asian girls lost in the realms of fashion/passion—seeking out a sale to adorn their bodies.

The store... Me, I didn't even know that it existed. One up in SF, (San Francisco for the uninitiated); yes... But, not the one here in L.A.

Anyway, back to the backstory of the story at hand...

Now, the babe in question; a serious babe in all shapes and forms. The other two, not so much. That's not to say that they each didn't have their own unique qualities. But, it was a comparison *thAng.* Compared to the central babe in question.

But, let's be real; for on any night in a club/at the bar/on a long and lonely walk on *The Strand,* that runs along the beach here in the South Bay of L.A., had I seen either of them, I would have been more than happy to say, *"Yes."* But, I don't want to get too distracted with that point...

So, that day/not this day—we drove. The girls and I.

It was a warm summer's day. We were in my Jeep. Jeep, with the top down. Her two friends *ridin'* backside. Me, I rode shotgun. I passed the keys to the, soon to be discussed, babe. She was at the helm. She knew where we were going. I did not.

The music blared as the wind blew through our hairs.

There I was, in my perfect environment: three, highly doable Asian babes, the wind in our hair, and the music playing. I should have been in heaven. I was not. But, we drove on, *none-the-less*. On and in the direction of the store; the aforementioned store, a store central to the context of this story.

*   *   *

Should I say it now or save it for later?

Well, here seems to be as good as place as any to tell the backstory to this situation.

The girl/the babe, (her and I), there was always this lie going on between us. Not so much between them, (her friends), and I, but between her, (the babe), and me.

"The lie..." She thought I was a somebody/somebody else. She always projected this reality onto me, that I was something more/something bigger/something other/something that she wanted me to be. Yes, I played along with the lie. I admit it. I guess I shouldn't have.

Her and I—I thought it would never last. I thought it would be just one night. One night of passion/One night of cold hard sex. Something for the books/Something for the poetry. The kind of books/poetry I write about such said situations. The kind of situations that last only for one night.

But, a night turned out to be ten months. She dug me deeper into it, (the lie), that is. I would try to cover my head/cover my back. But, the more I tried to lie my way back to the truth/to something—the more it made me feel like nothing.

48

Nothing... Here in status conscious L.A. Here, L.A... It's all about the car you drive, the clothing you wear, the credit cards you pull out of your wallet, and where you eat. I got wrapped up/trapped up in it—the lie that she pulled me into. It blew me away.

*   *   *

So, we went into the store/the aforementioned store—the three of them, (the Asian girls), and I.

I looked around. I was instantly board. I mean, I lived this Punk World back in the late 70s, early 80s.

They looked around—nothing too important/nothing found/nothing purchased.

But... Just as we were about to leave, I see this stunning Asian goddess of the night; perfect poetry. She must have worked there, for she was walking upstairs to the office. I mean; kill looks and style: long black hair/long black skirt, and a face that was sent to me by the gods. Obviously, I stared.

The one babe/my babe/the babe in question, she saw me looking with that glazed look of lust in my eyes. She, she looked at me. She looked at the goddess dancing her way up the stairs. She looked at her friends. They looked at me, looking at the girl, going up the stairs. The girl, the one walking up the stairs, turns. She catches my eye. Our eyes meet. It is/was one of those magnetic glances where your eyes are drawn deeply into one-another's soul. You feel the perfection. You know that she/you are the perfect match—the one you have both been waiting for. You glance, but what can a glance equal if physical contact is not made?

She, the babe in questions; my babe, grabs me by the arm and literally pulls me out the door with a crazed look in her eyes. She whispered in my ear as I was being pulled through the door/as my eyes remained locked on the vision of passion—her's locked onto me. She said, my babe said, *"How could you embarrass me like that!"* My thought was, *'How could I not?'* But, I said nothing.

The moment(s) of that day ticked on. Chill came to shove; I took the three of them out to a fifty dollar a plate, AMEX platinum card lunch. Forgive and forget...

*   *   *

I had almost forgotten about that vision, a sight worth seeing once again; that girl dancing up the stairs. My *Porsche* long in the shop, transmission problems; two months plus. Thus, and so forth, my contention to drive up into *status-symbol-land* and make an impressionable impression was not at hand. My journey there had been on hold. Plus, I had gone to Asia for a few. But, I'll discuss that in a moment...

Then, the other night at this restaurant, (by my crib), the night before the day last; this dude comes up to me and comments as to the fact that I am/was the only person, *"With style,"* as he put it, that he has ever seen in the South Bay.

In any case, he inquired, did I get my shoes at that store? That store! I was reminded. The one previously discussed.

With that question, the almost forgotten vision of that Asian goddess came to mind.

I realized he probably was a fagot, but I replied to his statement/question. *"No,"* I answered...

He then clamored on, he was surprised as, *"West Hollywood style, look'd to be my scene."* I told him, *"I grew up in Hollywood and, to me, it was just another fucking ghetto, now filled with all the tourists who find it oh so fucking fashionable and cool to live there."*

And oh, by the way—the directly to be additionally discussed babe, the babe this story is actually about, she is one of them. She lives, West Hollywood.

But, to conclude the discussion of the fag dude, there is one of the paradoxes of my life—my style and my standing out. I get it all the time... Questions, like the one above. The looks/the comments/the nothing but nothing. What do they really mean? Style—such a temporal *thAng*. So transient... For style to one is heresy to another.

I mean, I wear baggy clothing: baggy suits, big sport coats, untucked shirts, a vest, big shoes; so what? I have worn them for so long—long before they ever became fashionable. Hell, I am the one that made them

51

fashionable. Are they fashionable? Even as a yogi, I wore lose clothing—wore baggy drawstring pants and *kurta* shirts.

Style—my style... To whatever curse that leads me.

But, enough with the jibber jabber. Now, to the main segment of this tale...

Day last, at these typing keys, a bit of writing needed to be done. As I typed, I thought/I remembered the journey, (just detailed), into the journeying chance(s) of that daylight vision of that perfect poetry—Asian princess, now a few months the previous. My *Porsche* finally out of the shop, I was set to go.

But, as I sat at these typing keys, my telephone rings. It is the telephone company—an operator. I am told that this woman/the woman who was the central focus of the previously detailed hair blowin' in the wind/go to the store/go to lunch situation, had called and screamed, *"Emergency!"*

She couldn't call me. I had changed my telephone number. (Something I do quite frequently). So, she called the telephone company. Asked them to call me. Asked them to tell me to call her. *"Emergency!"*

*   *   *

But now, let me step back just a bit, in order to set the set-up of this story with a bit denser foundation...

After the day/after the store/after the lunch with her and her friends, after the ten months of the nothing, I just had enough. It just wasn't working: her and I. So, I said, *"Bye-bye."* I hit the trail to Asia. I had been gone about two months. I had returned just a couple of days ago.

Now, you may ask... The question may obviously come... Why did I stay with the woman; the one we are *a-talkin'* about, if it wasn't working for so long? Why exist in her space for ten months when I wanted out every second of every minute? Why did I stay with her if she was such a fucking cunt?

"Why?" You inquire... Because bitch could fuck! I mean she could fuck long and hard! We would hit the sheets, the couch, the floor, the table, the bathroom sink, the bathtub, the front or back seat of a car, the limo, wherever—and then we would fuck for three or four hours at a session. Sometimes more...

Now, understandably—this is common-place when a relationship is new/fresh/just a few days or weeks into the ON. But, we were deep—months deep. And, she still kept me long/strong/gone. She would suck/fuck, then fuck/suck again. I mean it was ALL that the ALL could be. And, she was always happy to please her man as he drove off to *never-never-land* behind the wheel of the car. If you catch my meaning...

But, I digress...

Here/there/then is the operator calling. Telling me that this woman MUST speak with me.

As I heard her, the operator's words, I wished that I were still in Asia. I wish I had not returned. Not yet, anyway.

Later, I also wished that I had not/did not returned this/the, *"Emergency,"* telephone call. But, I did. I am a fool. I care about people. I worry about people. I have compassion when I should not.

*   *   *

"So, what's going on?"
"What do you think?"

*   *   *

We had a met set for downtown L.A., Little Tokyo. She was working there. Worked at some art studio/magazine design house. She wanted to talk—discuss and sort out the details. She, someone that I had hoped that I would never see again. But, see her I did.

*   *   *

Fashionably late—ten minutes. I arrive, a dozen long-steamed roses in my hand. That's just the kind of *player* that I be.

I pulled up. She's sitting at a table in front of this little restaurant of a place. Coffee in her hand. Coffee in her hand, like always... She was/is so superficial to the max.

I studied her as I walked in her direction. I thought of the road that had brought me here/to her. Her, the one sitting over there.

A beautiful babe. Yeah, she is beautiful.

I studied her as I got closer. *'Did I love her?'* I wondered... *'No.'* Never really loved her. Infatuation, yes—at times... Attachment, for sure—it did build up. But, love—no; not love. It wasn't in the picture—not in the black and white photograph.

*   *   *

The aforementioned lies—the lies of a doomed relationship. Doomed, before it ever began. Yes, lies that had begun this walk down this road/this walk towards her. Towards her—with roses in my hand. I thought to turn around and leave. Just leave!

I really did. I was about to turn and walk away. I continued on...

*   *   *

But, back to the lying...

She, on the same and/or other hand, depending on how you lay/play the cards; she lied to me a lot. Lied about everything... Lied about talking to old boyfriends. Even lied about smoking cigarettes.

How fucking stupid is that? Smoking cigarettes!

She was a way far gold-digger. Loved to be in the pants of the rich and the famous. Well,

small-time rich and very small-time famous—
as her hands in the pants of, seemed to be.

Me, here I am. I guess she had some
vision of certainty for me. Music, art, poetry,
literature, spirituality, something...

But, there I was: alone/lost. As I am
now. Nowhere to go. No one to run to. And,
this is L.A., the city where I was born.

So, one thing leads to another—as one
thing always seems to do. All for the sake of
not being alone. The price it was so high—so
high for her chance to love me.

Love... The perpetual nothing.

I just played the game too well. It cost
me too much. But, anyway...

*　　*　　*

We sat there in the cool of the shade on
a balmy downtown L.A. afternoon. It almost
felt quite nice.

There were the traditional tears in her
eyes. The basic throw shots at me. The typical
questions of, *"Why didn't I love her?"* How
*could I have ever left her like I did? How could
I have just run off to Asia without even a phone
call?"*

"I tracked you," she exclaimed. *"I called all
the hotels in Tokyo, Hong Kong, Bangkok, until
I found you! I knew where you were!"*

56

Great! A fucking psycho stalker from the far side of the pond. She was pure *Psycho Bitch!*

"I hope you had fun getting in other women's pussies! I guess mine wasn't enough!"

Guess not...

But, most imperatively or importantly, depending on how you look at it—when she finally ended her rant, she spewed out the staggering news,

"I am pregnant. Pregnant by two months!"

Two months, just the amount of time I had been dancing around Asia.

My fucking heart fell out of my body. My *Being* totally disintegrated.

But, what could I do? What could I say?

It's like the reason my bro, Saturday Jim, named my part, *"Dirty Harry."* It takes no prisoners. It has gotten so many women knocked up.

We; the girl and me, talked as talking goes. Our talking it says nothing; means nothing; leads to nothing.

Then, out of nowhere, she blurts out; as if to catch me off guard,

"Aren't you surprised that I'm not on a factory line? I'm Chinese, you know."

My answer, *"No."*

I mean, come on... She, she has a big family behind her. A large family home to run away to if she decided to leave her apartment just off the Sunset Strip. A house, a family house—up in the hills of Orange County.

She rambled on and on and on and on and on; claimed that she was alone. Alone and with a million friends. I do not think that she has any idea of what ALONE really is.

*   *   *

Words said/words complete, she walked back to her job—didn't want the fifty dollar's worth of roses which I had purchased to chill the scene.

She walked away, saying that she was thinking about keeping the baby. *"Like saving a lost and stray puppy dog,"* she smilingly states, *"I think it will be like that."*

You know, it's almost funny, some people they want a child so much... Me, it's the last thing that I ever wanted. I mean there are enough children and problems in this world. Why bring another life into it?

Now, just for the record... It's not like she has not been down this road before: unwanted children/unwanted time. Two, that I know of—disposed of, prior to/previous to me.

In any case, I went to my car. A parking ticket had found its way under my windshield wiper. Fifty dollar's worth of unwanted roses and a parking ticket. An ex-girlfriend who claims that she can't stop loving me—pregnant

58

and thinking about keeping the baby. And me, after my last trip to Asia—the one from which I had just returned; broke. No money in the bank.

I took the roses. I threw them in the nearby city trashcan.

I got in my car. I drove off in a cloud of despair.

Any mystical positivity I may have possessed walking into this day or that meeting had vanished. I was empty: numb/dumb. A pain stabbed through the wall of my being—ripping my soul into ten zillion pieces. I was smashed hard into the wall of destiny/reality. Pulverized by the hands of fate. Demolished like only a true *player* or a true absolute fool can be.

I got home. I prayed for all this to not be happening to me—not be happening to her.

My mind in shambles from spending the better part of this last two months lost completely to the oblivion of the nights of Asia—where all dreams are just so fucking havable. Haveable, until the grim reaper of life/destiny/and sexual karma comes knocking upon the door.

I punched a wall. Drove my fist deeply into it. I lay down.

The sound of the ocean waves caressed my ears. Normally, the perfect pitch. Always, the perfect sound. Passive perfection in the ever-evolving patterns of life.

Normally/always—but not today/not this day/not then.

Lost in all my fear/my anguish I continued lying on my bed. The ocean roaring to my side.

Lying down, it comes to me—*speak with her again*. If I am in the picture, then I can reshuffle the cards. Play the hand I am dealt, my way. If I don't, I have no say if it is *Hold* or *Draw*.

So, I call her. Call her at her place of employment. She talks for the ears of other people—the people around her. Instantly, I understand that there is/was nothing left to say.

*   *   *

The pain/the confusion, they begin to come on strong. No one to blame but me. It was I who had fucked up. I danced where I shouldn't have dance—with whom I shouldn't have danced with.

That's the problem with lust. That's the problem with alone. You do all these things that you should/would never do if life were different. But, it was not. So, I did what I did. Did what got me to here/there/this/that/now.

*   *   *

But children, they are not like the aforementioned *lost and stray puppy dogs*. She is one of those women who wants one—a husband doesn't even matter to her. I have heard her say that many times. But, raising a kid like that; no father, no family, just a crazed high priestess of *glam slam*, fashion passion, who incessantly drinks coffee and smokes cigarettes—the kid will be just another basket-case. Another basket-case/fuck-up just like her/just like me.

*   *   *

Then, the evening comes on. The sky has changed from the overcast normality of the California beach marine layer to the hallowed, dark blue/black shadows of the night. This happens far too early in this change of time zone.

Usually, I love the winters. But, the days are just too short this time around.

A call comes in over the telephone lines. It's the lady who keeps my books. She tells me, this last trip wiped me out. I was forty thousand in the credit card hole.

I didn't know it. I knew I had been *live'n* large over Asia way; hoping from country-to-country, *First Class*. But, I thought I'd come back maybe twenty in. Which I could easily pay off if I sold a couple of my vintage guitars. Do that if the money didn't readily and quickly come my direction via other ethereal sources. But, forty... I never dreamed...

Her words came on like, *"Kill me."*

*   *   *

So, here's the story. Let me lay it out for you.

Stage One:

A woman, who I do not love, is pregnant and may want to keep my child. My child, so she says... But, she has been known to lie.

But, more than that, the life of a child; the ultimate creation. The only art form that I want no part of.

Stage Two:

So deep of debt...

Money can buy you freedom. Money can buy you escape. Money can buy you absolution. Money can buy you a lot of things. But, no money buys you nothing.

*   *   *

As I drove home from the previously discussed afternoon meet, I realized I did not even have any friends to go and talk to about this situation.

L.A.—superficial L.A.

I wished I had never gained any depth.

I mean, the friends I have, they are hard. I mean hard! Like, if I were to tell them this story, they would tell me, *"Just go slap that bitch up and tell her to fuck off!"*

Hard—the friends I choose. But, I have a bit too much humanity left in me to follow that path.

Hell, I can even think back a year or two. I had been out with my bud, Venchinzo and saw this fine little element of a babe of a fallen

62

angel in a nightclub. We hooked up for a time; the babe and I.

Prior to my knowing her she had been one of those felines that had passed her pussy around a little too easily. A little too easily, in my book. I mean, she was pretty—really pretty: Japanese.

Anyway, just prior to my knowing her, she had been raped by some asshole breaking into her apartment when she was living down San Diego way and going to college. I told the story to my bro, Saturday Jim. Having heard of her past, his response was, *"Sound like she just got lucky."* Cold man, that is cold!

But, that just lets you know the breed of hard guys that I hang with. No prisoners sought—none taken. So, telling this heart wrenching/life-perplexing story; well... It would have been to deaf ears...

*   *   *

So, the anxiety hits me hard. I was spaced. I was feeling like I was going to go insane. I knew this feeling/that feeling. I had gone through it before—age twenty—mega breakdown; based in anxiety—based in not knowing what anxiety was and letting it take control over me. But, I fought my way back from the surface of the abyss; alone—all alone. No help. It wasn't till years later that I even found out what it was/what was happening to me. My fate, I guess: my karma, my destiny—alone...

Pay the price for my actions and the actions of others—and I pay them alone.

* * *

Alone, always sounds like poetry. But, it is poetry only to the mind's of those who have not truly lived it—have not truly known it.

Those/them; they want it. They believe it is somehow holy/sacred. Trust me, it is not.

Alone is just as it sounds: zero/nothing/no-thing.

Not no-thing, in the spiritual sense. Not no-thing, it the abstract sense. But, no-thing in the purest sense of definition and reality. A reality that slaps you hard/drags you down/and leaves you with the understanding that alone is the only true demon-inspired enemy to kill life and rob enlightenment.

* * *

But here/there/now, the walls closed in on me. In, as they tend to do. In, in my small beach apartment.

Me, I knew, I had to get out. I had to... But, where? There was nowhere to go. Nowhere... No, not really.

With no other choice, I drove down to the Huntington Beach Health Spa. Much nicer, on the whole, than the one in Torrance, which is actually much closer to me.

En route/on the way, I thought to cry— as there seemed to be no other release for the

64

frustration of this situation that I could think of. But, *"Crying is for sissies,"* I remember my father telling me that when I was little boy. Then, he would hit me and if I cried, he would tell me, *"If you cry, I'll give you something to cry about."* The whole father thought almost brought me to tears, as well. And here/there I was, almost/possibly a father myself.

I arrived at the gym. Ran my daily-dose of four miles. Though I thought to look around for those fine young Vietnamese ladies that inhabit this/that location. A habit I am fond of—because you never know what new illusion may be encountered. But... But me, I just couldn't get my head around it. So, the only place my dick got wet was in the *jacuzzi,* as I attempted to chill back and relax. It didn't work.

Finished, I left—still alone.

*   *   *

Home, I opened the door. The door/this door, the door over there, behind me. I walked in. The door closed. It was like a cage. I was like I was an animal—trapped no way in/no way out.

I remember I had recently spoken with this lady I know,

"I cannot go on living like this," I told her. *"My whole life has been nothing but one bad hell after another. One carrot dangled in front*

of my nose after another. It all sucks me in and there is nowhere left to run."

As always, she heard but she did not listen. She had other things to think about.

"How's your new book coming?" she inquired.

* * *

The feeling of the need for death permeates me. I wish I knew a way. Like I thought to myself on my drive to the gym, I said in my mind's eye, *"Time to die."*

* * *

I fell asleep on the couch last night—the couch with all the lights on. I slept for eleven hours. I woke to no further insight on anyway in or out.

* * *

Today, I went and sold a watch. Three hundred and fifty dollars is what they/he, the watch guy, paid me for it. ...A vintage gold *Schaffhausen* watch that she, the aforementioned, previously discussed girl, had given to me with a price tag, nine hundred and fifty. But, I need the money...

No problema, me selling the gift—at least in the *karma* department. I gave her three or four watches in our short time together: a

Tag Hauer, a *Rolex*, a *Gucci* are the ones that come to mind...

Then, I went to *Farmer's Market*. A hang out, I like to hang out at. Still, all my chances seemed to be lost.

I ate my traditional waffle with fresh strawberries topped with whipped crème and a double *latte*. I had to force-feed myself. I had no appetite.

Then, I called my doctor. I needed some meds. Something to take the anxiety away.

I got an appointment. I went in. She psychoanalyses me.

I mean, let's face facts, this is not the 1970s anymore; they don't just give you *Valium* because you ask for it.

Deep into her psychoanalyze, she asks me of my childhood. Post, she told me I was/am still living the pain from twenty-five years ago. She said I had never really gotten over it—my dysfunctional childhood and all.

Tell me something I don't know...

Told me, I needed deep psychoanalysis.

She told me nothing I don't/didn't already understand. She gave me some pills. Not *Valium* like I asked for, but *Xanax.*

I heard the shrink of a radio doctor last week taking about them, *Xanax.* He said they were highly addictive—had a lot of side-effects. I'm almost scared to take 'em.

So, here I am... The story vaguely told. 1:08 in the AM. Cosmic, yes? I had to turn around and look at my other digital clock, (one minute faster than the one here on my desk).

*   *   *

Thirty years old... It's just that I always thought that life was going to turn out differently. And, I do not know what to do now that it has not. I just don't know what to do.

I want to go back to Asia—run away from this situation. But, I don't have any money. I didn't know my bills were so high. And, I always thought that if you really took life to the limit, and were spiritual about the process, that all of your needs were supposed to be/would be answered. But, it seems like the gods have turned away from me.

A girl off in the distance: cigarette smoking and pregnant—desire in her hand. The sad joke is; she always tried to make me get her pregnant. I thought I had made it out with no child. Now, I do not know.

And, my anxiety, it is full-on *pumpin.'* As I complete these words, I have been breaking down in my silence—hidden from the world.

As far back as I can remember, I would say, *"Don't have children. Even loving parents, fuck their kid's up."*

And mostly I say, *"Don't be an artist. In reality, creating art—it doesn't mean a goddamned thing. Maybe when you're dead. But then, it doesn't matter to you. And, especially, don't be a believer. Believe in what? Believe, and you end up like me. End up selling what you own just to pull your head*

above water. And, a job, what a waste of life...
Fuck that!"

*   *   *

Enough with the philosophy...

I feel like I'm dead. I feel like I have died. I'm just being ripped apart from the outside in.

Life it hurts too much to go on living. And death, what does it hold?

If I had the energy to write a poem, I probably would. But, I do not. What I do know is—it's all-different. For now, I have died. The living/this life has killed me. Now, time is just waiting for that moment until this physical body finds a way to leave its human form.

*   *   *

And, as for traveling back to find that perfect poetry of a long black haired Asian beauty who inhabited/inhabits that punk rock store, I guess that trip will only be cast to the realms of the words on these pages. She will be left to the never-known forever.

She is just one of those passing glances that you know could have equaled life-perfection, but it never had the opportunity to be planted and grow.

See you in my dreams, sweet lady. See you in my dreams...

L.A. 4

Now, for anyone who knows me; they know I have spent a lot of time in the P.R.C., (The People's Republic of China).

I commonly bounce around between Hong Kong and *The Mainland*. But, for whatever *karmic* reason(s), I kept ending up in Shanghai.

While there, I did have a love affair with this one woman; as has been well documented in my other writings. So, I'm not going to cover/mention her any further here. But, there was another... Yes, there was another one; a different lady that did rock my world for a second or three. This is her story.

If I were giving the chapters in this book titles, I guess I would call this chapter, *The Other Woman from Shanghai.* But, as I'm not, I won't.

She, the one this story is about, was vastly different from the other one—the one documented in other accounts. Oh yeah, I said I wouldn't mention her... But she; this one, was dark. The two were almost like *Yin and Yang.* Perhaps these two women were a good depiction of China—the positive and the negative, the good and the evil. The fact of the matter is I have known/I have seen both while I roamed through China's realms.

Also, as this book is about L.A., you may be wondering why I'm telling you a story based in Shanghai. Well, this story begins in Shanghai, but it ends in L.A. So, to add a little international flavor to this book, I guess this is as good a place as any to present it; the story, that is.

On to the tale...

As mentioned, I had been bouncing in and out of Shanghai.

Shanghai is a very curious city. Many say it is the most modern city on *The Mainland,* as it had been influenced by the international, *comings-and-goings:* both positive and negative, of and from a previous age. Maybe? I don't know if that's true. I don't know if that's the reason. What I do know is that Shanghai has a vibe. It has an essence: a dark and foreboding unearthly essence.

For those of us who travel in the realms of the ethereal. For those of us who understand that, *"Yes,"* there is another world. For those of us who dance in the mystical. We understand that the non-earthly realm(s) can be damning if one does not know how to maintain control over them.

But, for those of us who know how to turn the influence(s) off from that other realm. For those of us who can control what walks past the spectrum of the visible. Then Shanghai, which is a passageway/a portal to those other realms, can hold much illusion.

Now, for people, like myself, who dance between realities, the physical and the ethereal, the known and the unknown, Shanghai offers a lot of enticements; especially for those of us who know how to live the life of *The Fallen* and *The Damned*—in other words, those of us who know how to party.

I *gotta* tell you right here and right now, what I live; the way I live, is not for everyone. In fact, this path can only be consciously transversed by a very few. So, stay conscious here, as you ramble through these words. Because, believe me, what you're living right not is at least much safer than dancing out here/out there, on the dark-side, with all of us yogis who are hidden from view by a veil of an illuminated haze—those of us sentient beings who dance though the night.

In any case... I had hit back into town, post a session up in Beijing. I always seem to hit Shanghai after some-place else... But, anyway... The time, the travel, had only left me with a lot of lingering desire. Desire and a few thousand more photographs of the city and the outlying areas.

I hit my hotel. The one I always stay at in Shanghai, *The Sheraton.* From my window, I looked out across the city as the sky began to darken, as the evening was coming on.

There was a lot of noticeable high-rise construction taking place. I knew times, for Shanghai, were *a-changin.'*

"For better or for worse," was the only question. Only the ancient Chinese soothsayers, who roam the realms of the celestial, could say.

Me, I didn't know why I had returned. But, *none-the-less,* I had.

72

A pocket full of cash, a wallet full of credit cards, and no place better to be, I guess.

I closed the drapes. I lay down on my bed. It had been a long night the previous. I had been dancing with this white chick in a Beijing nightclub, the evening last. There are actually a lot of white chicks up in Beijing roaming the realms. Nothing jumped off from it. Just another *Exchange Student* looking for wisdom gained at the hands of the Chinese and relief from her realization that nothing means anything at all.

I poured down a few dozen glasses of the elixir, evening last, as well. They didn't really sit well come the AM. And, my having to get up to hit the airport, to hit a plane, to take a plane ride; well... It didn't make me feel too *fuckin'* special.

But, there I was/here I am. Hotel room; Shanghai. Me, laying on the bed.

I dozed off for a while; maybe thirty or so. When I awoke. Again, I pulled back the drapes. I looked outside. Shanghai was dark. The sun had set.

I went and grabbed a shower. Put on the hotel room robe. Opened up my suitcase. Hung up my clothing. Threw the duds from today into the hotel laundry bag. Hung it on the outside of my door for the concierge to pick up and dry clean. I grabbed a new outfit. Blue baggy, cuffed, pants. Grey print shirt. Grey double-breasted sport coat.

I checked my look in the mirror. My long blonde hair still wet from the shower and the shampooing. I smiled. *'Fuck... Another night. Guide me to the illusion!'* Yes, I exclaimed that to myself.

I hit out, down the hall. I get to the elevator. I push the button. The elevator arrives. I get in the elevator. It is filled with fucking white tourists. I fucking hate white people; especially when they're out here/out there on *The Hard Road*. They just don't get it. I'm embarrassed to be seen anywhere near them.

The elevator arrives at the lobby. I let all those before, exit first. Then/me, I strut out in all my abstract imperfect, perfection. Ready to rule the night.

I walk thought the hobby. A few of the staff they nod to me. They know me. They know me well.

I hit outside. The sky is dark. The night is illuminated by the radiance of the million watts of light expanding from the hotel. The temperature is warm. A bit warmer than I actually like.

The doorman hails me a cab. It pulls up. I get it. We drive off; pulling down and through the driveway were the millions of Shanghai's people line the hotel, staring up at it, like it is a god; an image of god. They stand there, praying to this false god.

I have long wondered why they do that/do this? What do they hope to find? The men, the women, the children.

That is the sad state of people with no hope. No way in/no way out. They are trapped.

74

But, as mentioned, Shanghai seems to be changing. New construction equals new possibilities. So, time will tell...

We: the taxi driver and I, we cruise through the dark streets of Shanghai. It is as it is—just another city in China.

We pull up at my destination of choice. A bar for lack of a better term.

For the record, Shanghai has very little nightlife. At least not nightlife in the sense of nightlife. No nightclubs in the large five-star hotels like Beijing or Guangzhou. No hidden secret-spots where only the locals know to party like in Shenzhen. It's kinda vacant of all that.

But, there is this one spot. As pre-described, a bar for lack of a better term. A place where all the Japanese businessmen hang out and sing karaoke.

Karaoke, that's one of god's curses on this earth; upon humanity.

But, in any case, without a babe latched up, it's a place to go—place to be.

I go in. Yes, the fucking Japanese businessmen are singing karaoke. Fuck me! But, I do know a spot over to one side; if no one is already sitting there; if I can squeeze in—it is drastically more quiet.

My spot was open. The bartender saw me/knew me. He hit me up with a greyhound: vodka and grapefruit juice. My drink of choice on the outskirts. He knew it/I knew it/We knew it.

He lays it in front of me. He smiles. I smile. I give him the number two with my fingers. I power-slam the first drink down. He smiles again. I smile again. The next round is placed in front of me. I power slam it, as well. Let's go for round three.

I sat there pounding a few drinks; listening to the shit singing in the background. Me, I was wondering why I was there. Me, I was thinking that there must be some better place to be. But, aside from walking along the river, with all the locals and dreaming about some dream happening, I was blank; I could not come up with any other place to exist in Shanghai in this/that moment.

Then, the savior of the evening arrives. A sullen dark image, dressed in black. Black, like all the whores that roam the realms of places like this: seeking, looking, longing to find someone just like me; a guy who doesn't give a fuck and wants to get his dick wet; wants to plant it deep in any appropriate female cavity.

She sits down around the corner from me. From there, she has clear eye contact with my plane of sight.

Now, to detail this bar situation a bit further. It is red. The walls, the seats, the top of the bar stools. And, as mentioned, if you want to be sheltered, (to whatever degree from the shit singing), you have to hit over to the far corner of this establishment. What it is, to describe it; the bar is kind of a long L-shaped thing. The main section of the bar spans out

76

across the room, skirting all the tables, and ending near the karaoke stage. If you walk further in, over at the far side, behind a bit of a wall and a pillar, where you can't really see the stage and, as such, not have to listen to all the shit singing quite as voluminously; that's me. That's where I sit. The cheap seats. Can't see the stage. But, still can see some of the bar.

There she was. Playing it all cool and stealth. Glancing at me as she ordered her drink.

The bartender took her order. As he turned, he looked at me. He looked at me, looking at her. He shook his head, in the negatory, and smiled at me.

'Good,' I thought. Disapproval... It must mean that she is/will be, all that I expect.

She was nothing to write home about, even if I had a home—just your average, round-faced, P.R.C. girl/woman. Early-to-mid-twenties; shoulder length hair.

Now, for all of you who think that whoring is something bad. That it's only for dudes who can't get pussy, let me set you straight. Whores are the perfect women. You don't have to love *'em*. You don't have to romance *'em*. You don't have to say you're sorry. All you have to do is to have the money to pay their price. From that, you get the perfect moment of life perfection.

Now, here also, I need to go into a little side note...

Getting a whore is not just about sex. It is not just about *cuming*. That's only for the

77

unenlightened. Getting a whore is about taking a moment to live in the perfection of that moment. It's perfect *Tantra Yoga*. I mean like, there you are; a women, often times beautiful, and she is offering herself to you in totality. Totality, for a moment. And, isn't that what the whole purpose of life is? Isn't that what *Nirvana* is? Living life in the moment; in totality. If I may answer myself, *"Yes it is."*

So, to this end; whores are the perfect vessels for a pathway to *Satori.*

She looked at me again as her drink arrived. I motioned to the bartender to put it on my tab. Again, he shook his head.

She, the whore/goddess in question, motioned for me to come and sit next to her. I shook my head, *"No."* I didn't want to explain that by sitting over there it would mean that I would be listening to that shit karaoke much more loudly. So, I just smiled and nodded for her to come over to me. She smiled and glanced at me with those perfect Asian eyes. Then, she looked away, as if to see if there was something better. But, she and I already knew there was not. Just a bunch of *small-dicked* Japanese businessmen singing shit karaoke; sprinkled in were a few Chinese locals who had climbed their way to the top of this repressive regime.

She came and sat next to me. My fate/her fate, it was sealed in blood.

Now that I had a bitch, I could not stay in that place any longer. Post another drink for her and a quick shot or three for me, I suggested we bail.

78

Just for the record here... She spoke very little English. My *Shanghai-wa,* (the local dialect), is marginal at best. But, I didn't want to have conversations with her anyway. Me, I had other plans. You know, the pathway to enlightenment via *Tantra Yoga* and all...

So, we walked. We got into my taxi. I had the guy/the driver waiting for me outside, just in case something like this situation jumped. We cruised on back to my hotel.

Now, whores in five-star hotels, at least in the PM, are no-go on *The Mainland.* There are a couple of ways you can handle this; pay the bellhop or sneak *'em* in. The reason for this is that a normal person/a respected citizen, if you will, has all the right papers to show all the right people. But, the whores are usually from the out-country. From some small village. So, *they ain't got none.* In this case, the chick asked my driver to cruise around the back of the hotel before he dropped me off. He checked if it was okay with me. AOK. I guess she had done this before.

We dropped her off. He cruises around the front, through the hordes of locals. I get out. Pay him his due. And, I walk on in.

I'm greeted by all the nighttime staff. I hop in the elevator and cruise on up to my floor.

I get to my room. But, no babe. I sat down. I waited. But, nothing...

I was thinking, *'Fuck! Did I buy her drinks for nothing?'*

About fifteen, twenty in, I get the knock-knock. It was her. My first thought was, *'I hope she didn't have to suck some guy's dick to get up here or take it one-time real quick before I got to it.'*

But, a whore is a whore is a whore. So, what could I say? I just let it live.

Inside, I gave her a drink from my hotel room refrigerator. She was *hittin'* the whiskey, as she had done in the bar. This and thus, I was not looking forward to kissing her, as I hate the taste of whiskey.

Now, just a couple of points here...

One: The reason I hate the taste of whiskey is that I hit a couple bottles, (literally a couple of bottles), of *The Jack,* in one sitting, a few years back. I had a hangover for a week. And, to this day, I still can't stand the smell of it.

Two: Whores do not kiss! So, forget about anything that you have seen on T.V. or in the movies. They do not do it! This being said, on *The Mainland,* if they are staying the night, and this one obviously was; then, they will kiss you.

Three: On *The Mainland,* and to a lesser degree in Bangkok, whores want to spend the night in your hotel room. Why? Because it's far better than where they live. So, for them, it's an upgrade. They always ask if they can stay.

80

AOK, I always figure, more pussy for me. You know, *"Pussy,"* the vehicle to enlightenment.

So, she sat there on my couch. She had a drink. I had a drink. In Mandarin, I ask her,

"You ready?"

She was.

I stand her up. I begin to take off her black dress. I tried the reach around for the zipper in the back, as I kissed her. That was no-go. So, I spun her around, unzipped her dress. I slowly pushed it from her shoulders, as I kissed the back of her neck.

Now, here's a little tip for you guys. If you want a hooker to dig you, to do you right; play it like you actually care about *'em.* I mean, if you just pull their clothing off, stick your dick in, and fuck *'em;* zero will equal zero. But, if you want them to get into the process. Then, do them right!

So, with her dress off, her back to me, I continue to kiss the back of her neck as I unfasten her bra.

She's digging what I'm *givin'* her. She reached around, holding the back of my head, with one hand, my butt with the other.

This is going to be fun...

With her bra off, I turn her around. She is much shorter than me; which make her smile, as she pivots. But, I lean down and kiss her lips.

Her lips... They were full; like many a Chinese woman. That's a good thing. Her kiss it was okay. Not the best; but certainly not the worst I have experienced.

I touched her small breasts for a few. Then, I put my hand down her underwear.

It's almost kind of funny, you know. In *The States,* and some of the other, more civilized realms of Asia, women always wear these lacy, nice underwear. But, on *The Mainland,* the underwear is always grandma style. Anyway...

As I start massaging her bush, and what is in between, she begins to take off my shirt. We are still standing, so I helped her.

Then, she goes for unbuckling my belt; unfasten my pants. They drop to the floor.

The *kissin'* continues.

Me, I'm massaging her zone of pleasure. She is obviously *digin'* it. She starts to put her hand down around my cock.

"Okay," she asks in English.
"Sure." I answer, also in English.

Now, to keep this from tuning into a porn novel, or something like that... Basically, we move to the bed, I stick it in. And, she is ready. She *cums* really fast.

Here's another point. You gotta get the hookers you link up with to *cum.* Now obviously, some are all fucked up on drugs or whatever... But, those aren't the kind you should be going after anyway. They're just too much of a mess. And, you don't know what kind of a nightmare they are going to bring your direction. So, you gotta get the ones that are whores just because life left them no other choice. They're the ones that can still feel. Still believe. Still *cum*.

So, we did it a couple of times. Then, we took a shower together.

I really like to take showers with a babe.

We did it in there, as well.

One more time. Then we went to sleep.

AM, one time.

I took her to breakfast in the hotel. All eyes, of course, on her and I.

Me, long blonde hair and a baggy Italian suit. Her, dressed in the black garb of a late night/midnight whore.

Oh wait! Sorry for the distraction/my indulgence here... Let me get onto the main story.

The hooker gone. I was again lost to the alone realms of Shanghai.

There's this street, *Dong Tai Road,* in Shanghai. It has a lot of shops on the street and on the streets around it. I guess it has been a center of selling, trading, and the like, since way back in the way back when. With nothing really better to do, I grabbed a taxi and hit over there.

Got there. Walked around for a bit. Shot a couple of photographs. Had some tea at one stall. Had a beer at another.

I was *killin'* time, soaking in the abstract nothingness of a city vibrating with the promise of tomorrow. And maybe, just a hint of the promise of illusion.

I decide to go over and have lunch at this one place I knew. It's over on the second floor of this old white concrete building by the river. And, it's clean. I'm always a little leery about eating at some of the shops off the streets in Asia. I mean, I do not want to get sick.

But, on the high side of the issue, I have spent so much time out here/there on the outskirts of *The Hard Road,* I rarely get sick. But, just to be on the safe side...

Anyway, I cruise in. They sit me down. Slap a pot of tea and a cup in front of me. They pore me some. I order up a *Tsing Tao.*

Just as they are pouring it, the beer, I see/my eyes encounter this beauty of a longhaired Chinese goddess; eating her lunch alone.

Now, me being a savvy traveler, I knew Shanghai chicks, at least not chicks on the up-and-up, ever eat lunch alone. While I pondered this situation for a second or three, the food cart came around. I pointed to an item or three and my *eat's* were *gettin'* on.

I check out the chick *eat'n* alone. Was she a daylight hooker? A day walker? Did she leave her black dress at home? Was it getting cleaned? Or, had it been torn to shreds the night before by some pimp of a low life *mutha fucker* or some local police dude who force(s) the hookers to fuck *'em* just because they can? I don't know... I didn't care! Hell, look at who I had spent the evening last with.

My mind was doing what my mind does; trying to figure out how in the hell I was going to hook this up. Hook up: her and I.

I watched for her looks. I studied her glances. Like all dudes on the prowl, I tried to time my completion of lunch with her completion of said same. I tried to give us a reason to meet.

She had gotten there before me, so she was done before me.

She called for the bill. I motioned for mine while slapping the last bits of preordered food in my face.

I was asked if I didn't like the food. It was very good, I told them in my broken, *Shanghai-wai.* I'm just not very hungry.

She paid. I paid. She stood up. I slammed the rest of beer. I stood up. She made her way for the stairs. I made my way, (quickly), for the stair. She walked down the stairs. Me, a few paces behind, trying to catch up, I walked down the stairs.

At the base, just before you go outside, I had nothing to lose. I ask her again, in by bad *Shanghai-wa, "Do you speak English?"*

She did, to a degree. And, that was the end of that.

*   *   *

Now, this was one of those romances... I don't want to say a romance of convenience; because it was not convenient at all. It was more of a romance of lust, desire, love... But, not the kind of love that romance novels are written about. It was more love in the animal sense of the word.

Was there love? Did we love each other? Yeah, we did. I did fall in love with her. She with me.

Was there passion? Yes, there was a lot of that. It was fucking intense.

But, in and/or of all that, there was this strange, misplaced essence of lost subject matter—lost somewhere between her poor English and my poor *Shanghai-wai*. As it was lost, as it was Shanghai, as Shanghai is a portal to the netherworld, a whole course of events were set in motion that would change her life and effect, (not affect), my life forever.

We: her and I, hung for a few days. She would come and pick me up at my hotel in the mornings. She would take me to places around Shanghai and the outlying countryside that she thought I had not seen. But, I'd been there/Shanghai a lot. Sadly, I had pretty much seen it all.

That's kind of the fate I hold with most/much of the world—I've seen it/lived it all before.

I guess that's what's sad about a life like mine. I've lived a lot. I've done a lot. I've experienced a lot. More than most, I think. But, in that, all the *naiveté'* is lost; it's gone forever. Everything that you can do, I've done. Yeah, pretty much... So, there's nothing really left to do, except the re-do.

Now, re-doing can be fun. It can spend some of your, *"Lifetime."* But also, re-doing is just that. It's re-doing.

Sorry for my divergence. Back to the story at hand...

Somewhere along the line: the line/our time, she made it up and into my hotel room. There, we drank a bunch of beer from the room's refrigerator and then we ordered up some more via room service.

She knew it. I know it. It was time to hit the sheets.

A kiss led to a touch. A touch to a caress. A caress to the removal of this and that.

Nude, she had a gorgeous body. Thin, like most Shanghai women. She didn't shave, her beaver, her legs, her underarms. Just the way I like it.

Mostly, in this world, it's just the women in *The States* who are all trimmed, all shaved up. But me, I came into my own in the sixties/the seventies. I dig all that natural shit.

We kissed for a while; her and I. Held each other's nude bodies. I stuck it in. We rolled around this way and that. And yeah, we were in love.

Now, I'm gonna tell you right now, don't fall in love with a chick in a place like Shanghai. If you've read another of my other works on the subject, you can see it can get mighty intense. I mean, the chicks have virtually no way out. So, it's just better to just, *hit it and quit it, just to say you did it.*

Her and I, it wasn't really like that, though. She wanted more. Me, I had been down this road and knew there really wasn't any more.

We hung. We fucked. I spent a lot of money. I bought her a couple diamond rings over at this one high-end jewelry shop. And, it was what it was.

But, I was running out of money. Living in the *Five Star Hotel World* is not cheap. I had to get back home; back to L.A., where I could generate some needed income.

So, I bailed. She promised she would follow me there, ASAP.

I told her I would be waiting for her, thinking/knowing, (all too well), it would never happen.

To shorten the story up... I would get calls from her, occasionally. A letter here or there.

Then, she told me that she had found a way to get into the U.K. I never really wanted to know why or how. But, we can all figure out/imagine how she made that happen...

I never thought the girl was a virgin. I never thought she was a saint. I never thought much about it at all. Because, in reality, I didn't want to know. I never asked what she did for a living. Or, how/why she had so much free time.

I don't know what it is... I guess I have been very blessed. For whatever karmic logic/whatever cosmic reasoning, there have been a lot of women who have been very-very devoted to me. This, when I have been nothing but a complete abusive asshole to most of them. I don't know why? I am thankful for all they have given my life. For example, stories like these. But, I still don't understand why...

In any case, she was going to go. I didn't know how. She asked if I could meet her there. I was kinda broke and latched up with this new specimen of love flavoring on the L.A. side of the picture. So, I told her, I could not. She went, *not-the-less*.

There, some-how/some-way, she got a job at a restaurant; a Chinese Restaurant, owned by a Chinese couple. I would hear from her from *time-to-time*. She would always tell me that she was on her way. She was coming. She was going to get to me. I didn't pay it a lot of mind.

Then, one day, she called. It must have been about a year deep. Thank god, my local babe wasn't around, when she did... She told me that she had purchased a passport from the Netherlands. She gave me her flight number. She gave me her arrival time. She wanted me to pick her up.

I mean, fuck me! What was I going to do with this?

Now actually, in actuality, it made me kind of paranoid. I mean like, I was the only person she knew in *The States*. She was obviously coming to see/be with me. And, I thought that there was no way in hell that she was going to get through U.S. Customs with a fake passport. I figured they would grab her

and she would be *a-throwin'* my name around.
I was very paranoid.

"Will you pick me up at LAX," she asked.
"Sure."

Of course, I had no intention of it.

The day the flight was to arrive, I get a
telephone call. Immediately, I could hear it was
on the international side of the picture and I
expected it would be her, my Shanghai Babe,
probably latched up in jail for trying to bail the
U.K. on a fake passport.

But, no. It was not. Who it was, was the
Chinese wife of the Chinese owner of the
Chinese Restaurant where my sweet little
Shanghai lady had been working. She/the lady
spoke complete with her very proper British
accent.

I tell you, man, Bitch just went on and
on and on and on and on and on about how she
just found out that my Shanghai lady had been
fucking her husband. He had given her all his
money. He sold his gold *Rolex* so she would
have some money to travel. But, with that, she
still didn't stop. It went from crying to
screaming to crying to screaming to crying
again.

*"Why does this girl love you so much that she
will do anything to get to you? You know she's
a whore. She's a very low woman. She took all
our money. She destroyed my marriage. She*

destroyed my husband. She broke his heart. Now, we have to sell the business!"

Like I say, it went on and on and on and on and on and on.

Now, in another situation, if we had been on the same continent, I may have proposed to her that we hook up and have some *Revenge Sex*. But, we were a million miles apart. So, all I kept hearing was that bitch was going to do this, that, and the other thing. She was going to call the authorities. And, the *etcetera*.

I listened. What could I do?

Did it surprise me? No, not really. I knew she, my Shanghai lady, was up to something. Something that I had closed my eyes to.

But again, all I, (personally), could think about... Think about while all this bullshit was rumbling in my ears was, *'Why? Why me? What do I have to offer anybody?'*

The *convo* it went on for almost an hour. Whatever... I couldn't feel her pain, nor could I correct it, nor did I even care about it. *Men will be men...*

Finally, I got bitch off the phone. I grabbed a *St. Pauli Girl Dark,* (my favorite beer), sat back, turned on the T.V., and chilled.

But, one thing was for certain... Now, with the alerting of the appropriate authorities, there was no way in hell I was going to show up at the airport.

Her plane, my Shanghai babe's plane, was supposed to arrive at 8:00 in the PM. At about 8:45 my phone rings. I let the machine grab it. I listened. The volume was up. It was her. She was in. She had skated right past U.S. Customs, *no problema.*

Now, this is all straight-up truth that I speak. So, if you wanta know how/why the U.S. got fucked up, here is a prime example. They let people in with shit-fake Netherland's passports.

You may think that I would have been happy to see her—to have her here. I was not. I was latched into this new babe. She was fine, nice, and had none of the baggage of this other girl. The fact of the matter is, there was probably a lot more baggage to that Shanghai lady than I will ever know about. And, not knowing—well, that is probably a good thing.

She, the Shanghai babe, kept calling. The machine kept picking up. Her messages were all the same,

"Where are you? Are you here looking for me at the airport? I am at terminal whatever. I'm waiting for you. I love you. I am here."

Finally, I guess that she got smart; realized I wasn't coming. She told me, via another message, she was going to go look for a hotel. The next message told me the name of the hotel, where it was; the room she was in.

Well, what's a guy like me supposed to do? I hit out in the direction of LAX and her hotel.

As I pulled into the parking lot of the relatively funky hotel/motel over on Hawthorne Boulevard—about a mile East from the airport, I was checking hard to make sure that this wasn't some sting operation; that I wasn't being set up. I looked hard/deep for INS and ICE agents. I mean, I'm a fairly paranoid guy as it is. It has just been life-proven to me that people can't be trusted. Then, with her/all of this. Well...

But, it all looked clear. I parked. I got out of my car. I slowly entered the facility with my eyes wide open.

I get to her door. I check for any signs of the faltering/the improper. It looked okay. I knock. She opens.

"Where were you?"

In her eyes, I could see that she had been granted every wish she had ever desired. She had fought the gauntlet and had emerged victorious. She had made it to the U.S. She had made it to me.

I went inside her room. It was a little funky: a gold bedspread, red carpet. I figured hookers probably brought their high-end Johns here.

I kissed her. I lay her on her hotel bed. I unbutton her shirt. I lifted her bra. I kiss her small, firm, perfect breasts. Her skin, the color

93

of Asian milk. I do this as I think of the words of the wife of the man who financed this journey. This journey from England to L.A. This journey for her to me.

My dick was hard though. I throw back the bedspread. I pull off her skirt. I take off all of my clothing. My body moves next to hers. It had been a long time...

I think to lie there; embrace/embellish this moment. I cannot. Not this time. Not here/not now.

I stick it in her. I make love to her, like I really loved her. I did/I do. Yeah, I love her. I make love to her for a long-long time.

She finishes, several times. She dried up, so I finish.

As we lay there, she slices me a compliment,

" I forgot how big you are."

I laughed. But, I could not help but think/realize, what she said was all based in comparison. Who knows the last time that Chinese guy hit that pussy? I'm thinking she had to have given him *one for the road.* So, it was probably only a dozen hours ago or so.

I made myself stop thinking.

I told her that I was glad that she was there/here. But, I had to go. Had things to do, people to meet.

I could see it in her eyes, her world was crushed. All she had fought for, desired, was

94

about to walk out of her semi-sleazy hotel/motel room door.

I couldn't stay. It was the wrong world/the wrong time. Too much life had passed. Too much *karma* created. And me, I had another babe. Another babe that I was seriously into.

I left. She cried, as I left.

I walked down the hallway. It had off-white, almost dirty walls, brown carpet. The rooms were quiet though. I heard nothing going on.

I walked out; outside. The night air was cold. It was dark in this semi-funky part of town. I got into my car. I drove off. Headed home, towards the ocean, to my babe, my real babe. That night, I made love to her, as well.

She, my Shanghai lady, she called me for a while. Called on the telephone lines. She left many messages on my telephone answering machine. Sometimes, if I wasn't careful, I would pick up. But, when I did, there was nothing to say.

When we spoke, she would tell me about where she was working, what she was doing. Mostly, it was at Chinese Restaurants. She wanted me to come by and visit. I never did.

Often, when she called me, she needed money. It was always subtle how she would ask. She would try to sell me something; Chinese stocks, foreign currency; stuff like that.

I saw her one more time, maybe a year or so later. She wanted to meet me at the beach in Redondo. I don't know why, but I went.

There she was, this once stunning beautiful-beautiful girl. Now, very-very-very thin. She had some sort of sore near her mouth. Not, a cold sore. It was something way far more obviously deadly than that. Her skin had lost all its color. Something was up—something not good.

It was happy to see her though. But, I knew, I could feel it, I would never see her again.

I don't know, maybe she had AIDS or cancer or something. Whatever it was, it was eating her alive.

She said she was thinking about going back to China. There was a lot of new opportunity happening there.

As she spoke, I couldn't help but wonder how she was going to do that. She had gotten into the U.S. with a fake passport and that wouldn't/couldn't work again. But then, she HAD gotten into the U.S. with a fake passport. If she could do that/do that for me, she could pretty much do anything, I guess.

In any case, her phone calls stopped.

That was that. This is this.

The last time I ever saw her, it was on a beach in California. Thus, this story is in this collection.

But, in my mind, I remember the dream. I remember what could have been if life would

96

have only let it. If she, her and I, would not have walked down such dark roads.

This is life. We live it. This is death. We all will die. In between is all we have. These few fleeting moments, where we are promised the lie of forever; promised that it will all mean something.

Sadly, just like her and I, it does not.

I hear a door close—movement in the hall outside. I never realized how much movement could be heard within the walls of this apartment complex. And, the melodrama of it is far too fucking real.

Movement, who is it? Movement, what does it mean?

A moving motion placed upon my door. What will it spell out?

And, I will be fucking goddamned honest with you; this piece of literature is not worth the confusion and the pain that I had to live through so it could be brought to type.

You see, there was this babe up San Francisco way—at an art opening. I met her. Eyes—her eyes were distant. It looked like she was *duped* up on, *"A,"* (LSD). But hey, it was San Francisco, you know. All those idiot, *Dead Heads,* up there who are still locked into the shit music that came out of there in the '60s are all still *tabin'* down on A.

Hell, I dropped it a few times more than I would care to mention myself. More times than I would like to remember. But, that was back then. Way, back-then. Not now.

Anyway, she looked *duped*. But, she starred deeply into my eyes, with the promise of unknown/untried passion. She wanted it/wanted me.

So, she waltzed me back to her

apartment.

I took it for a ride/took her for a ride. A nighttime folly. A fuck for no good reason at all. I wasn't even into her. Just your average white chick who stood close to six feet tall. Like they say, *"You can't keep your dick in your pants, can you?"* I guess I couldn't.

Well, be that as it may be/as it were... It didn't mean anything to me. Just a hit it/to quit it/just to say I did it.

The next AM rolls around—after having spent the night meaninglessly dicking her every-way I could think of. The morning—the look of glaze still in her eyes. I began to worry...

Bail time... Stroll time... Post that momentary second of realization that she wasn't *duped*—she was just fucking insane. Post that secondary second, that I thought that maybe I could help her. But, *"No,"* I realized; leave that to the shrinks. They get paid to deal with that type of energy, not me.

Speaking of me... Me, I was *out'a there.* Out, onto the extremities, barely holding on.

I tried to walk. She fucking freaked out on my ass: screaming, blocking the door— didn't want me to leave. Wanted me to stay there and lay my dicking on her throughout eternity. I mean, she unleashed a serious *skitzo attack.* I thought that I was going to have to blaze that bitch up. But, I mean then/there is all the ramifications of that and the thereof. You know, like a dude—dot his eyes, jam him up, *no problema.* But, a bitch... Now, that is a whole different ball game—psycho or not.

Finally, I got out of there—thinking never to see her again. I wish that were the case. But... The fact of the matter is; this whole scenario/story is better/more fully told elsewhere in another novel; *Ten to Thirty.*

Anyway... She had my P.O. Box number. She mailed and mailed and mailed and mailed letters of love every day. Telling me how I was the only man who ever really mattered. The only one for her. She piled my P.O. Box full for months. But, I thought, *"No Problem,"* she doesn't have my address. In fact, I got so bored with her ramblings that I just began to toss them/her letter(s) in the Post Office trash receptacle before they were ever read.

Then, somehow, she got my telephone number. Fuck me! How she did that, I didn't know—made me really paranoid.

Then, I realized I checked my message(s) on my telephone message machine from her crib... Stupid, stupid, stupid!!!

I changed it. My telephone number that is. No problem. I do that all the time.

But, then came the nail in the coffin—my coffin. She got my address. How the fuck she did that, I will never know. But, that was no-go. I mean, I am basically a very private/reclusive sort of guy.

1:00 AM, the evening last, I was romancing this sweet little, too-long lived, love affair of an Asian babe session. We were waltzing into my crib. Serious love to be made.

100

We both had one intention. It was on both of our minds.

The door across the hall opens. No thought came to my mind. The three hundred pounder of a tenant, who lives there, does it all the time—opens his door that is.

In my rear ear, I hear my name being called—called by a female voice. *"Oh fuck, what's next!"*

*   *   *

That is the foundation of/for the/this story—laid down as it be.

I told her I didn't remember her, as she made her way across the hall. Told her, I didn't even know her name.

But, as stated, this bitch is big, pushing six foot high. I tried to walk into my crib, get my *gettin'* on with my sweet little Asian *thAng*.

She, the other girl, put her hand on the door. Tried to not let me close it.

She said that she had some tapes that she wanted me to listen to. *"Sorry, I don't have the time."* I concluded, *"Let go of my door!"*

I looked at her with violence in my eyes. People tell me I can be scary. They say, push me and look-out, *"I have murder in my eyes."* I shoved the door hard. It was closed.

Why does the shit come down on me?

I mean, put yourself in my position. A fucking chick who goes *skitzo* on your ass, and somehow/someway she finds out where you live. I mean fuck me! This is no-go in the purest sense of the word, or two-words depending on how you look at it.

Fuck this/and fuck that. It did put a scare into me at how easily I could be found.

So, I had hours of explains to do to my *none-too-understanding* women who I love to hate. I understood her anger.

The game was in motion. In motion, all night. Not the kind of motion I had planned for in the bed, however.

In bed; up and dressed—back to the bed times three. She kept attempting to make the bail.

She was pissed. I didn't blame her.

I will tell you straight-up that there is one thing that I do not like and that is to be controlled by an outside influence that I have no control over. No matter how much of a fucking nut they may be—there is/was no excuse for this.

You try to control the control—refuse to let it happen/refuse to let it control you. But, it is not always all that easy.

And, when all the world comes crashing down on you; as it has seemed to do on me, and you can't even turn to the woman who claims so much love for you—then where is it that you can go?

So, and in other words, (and again), my main chick was pissed off. I understood. I mean, if it had been a dude at her door, I would have just knocked him out and then maybe/probably slapped her up.

This was a touchy situation though. The

bitch across the hall was fucking psycho.

I lay there in bed that night/last night, deeply in fear about what was to come next. I mean, now if this was just some normal person you can tell 'em to, *"Fuck off,"* and they'd be gone. But this is a fucking nut-job central, *cribbin'* up with some fat dude across the hall. I wanted out! But, with my babe lying next to me, and me trying to play it cool, there was nowhere to run.

*   *   *

Now, when you're in these situations there are a couple of way you can play it. I mean, how you play it for the mind of the babe is what defines all... You can be all hard, like you don't give a fuck about your babe-central. And, tell her to, *"Fuck off,"* if she doesn't like what's going down—tell her she can hit the streets. You can also do the nice-guy *thAng*. Play it all like, *"What? I have no idea what's going on... Who, me?"* But, by this point in time, my main and central babe knew me well enough to know that, *"Nice-guy,"* wasn't in my vocabulary. So, I concluded the best way to play it was to make her feel sorry for me. The troubled soul that I am and all...

So, I told my woman how, *"There was nowhere for me to run."* I asked, *"Where had my life gone so wrong?"* And, *"It is so unfair. I have no family to fall back on like you do. It is all just so unfair. My life is so unfair..."*

With a tear in her eyes, she chilled.

Make-up to no break-up. She understood that I had nowhere to turn—only her.

With that out of the way... She wanted to make love. What could say but, *"Yes."*

Though, due to the previous distraction, my mind was obviously elsewhere. But, I did give it to her right.

*   *   *

Morning... Set to hit the breakfast picture. I open the door/my door. There are three thousand fucking *Sticky Notes* placed all over the fucking door and the doorframe. They were orange, pink, blue. Obviously, the crazy bitch, she went through several pads of said.

The notes, they tell me how much she loves me. How much she misses me. How she wants me to fuck her long and hard the way I had done up in San Francisco. Tells me to get rid of my girl. *"Kill her if I have to."* If not, *"She will kill her for me."* She writes, *"I am prettier than her. I have a better body. I can fuck better."* The notes continue... *"If I don't want to leave my girlfriend then she will fuck both of us. Fuck us like we want to be fucked. She can do that, because she loves me."*

Obviously, my chick was pissed. For once, I didn't blame a bitch that is on the downside of my fucking around. I mean really, this was a fucking hardcore slap in/across her face.

I don't know? Maybe she deserved it? You know, how you never know how a person's

104

karma is going to be dished out.

But, in that moment, I was so mega pissed at the intrusion into my space—add in anger and embarrassment... I mean, what did the neighbors think? Not to mention the three hundred pounder, across the way neighbor, that she was cribbed up with.

Pissed/angered was the name of my game. But, my mind was on my babe and cooling her out. So, I didn't just walk across the hall and simply lay the pimp hand across the psycho bitch's face—give the cunt the bitch slap she deserved. In fact/in truth I was a little perplexed about what to actually do.

Angrily, I took down the *Sticky Notes.* Threw them away and tried to set out on to living the day—living the day the way, my babe and me, had planned to do.

Breakfast on the expensive, out of my pocket, side of the photograph. A *shi-shi* little restaurant in Beverly Hills.

Had to try to chill things down. You get my meaning?

While there, at the restaurant, she; the woman/my woman, said some mean things about my ruining her life. Just a way to get back at me, I supposed, due to all the chaos of the night the previous and this AM. She said I ruined things because I preferred to play. Because I didn't have to make a living the way she did. Play, rather than to let her run off to do her Saturday homework.

Oh, by the way, this was now Saturday. She, the girl, had a little patterning-making thing she had to do for a clothing line she is trying to launch. Whatever...

I looked at her. I played the game. I told her she was being cruel. But, she already knew that she was.

Her words they were/are like poison. And, it is/was only my addiction or perhaps god's diabolical plan that keep(s) me hanging on to her for no good reason. In reality, I could really give a fuck about her either!

But, with that dose of negativity, and breakfast finished, I took her to her car parked at my place. She drove back to make *fashion-passion* at her crib over Westwood way. Me, I was stuck with going home. A place where I had no idea of what was to come next/a place I did not want to be.

*　　*　　*

I didn't want to be here. Did not want the confrontation. But, I was inside-alright, no one saw me *a-comin.'*

A bit of a nap from no sleep the night before. You know, the sex and the attack of the intruder. A nap... But, I was awoken by the neighbors upstairs.

Up, up there.

Nowhere for me to be. Creativity dominantly held down/held back by the furthering bullshit of this fool's world. So me, I am on my way out.

About to leave the door, I hear her voice, that *Psycho Bitch,* from the fat man's open door—the apartment; the other side of the hall. Fuck! I'm trapped. I look out the peephole. I see nothing.

Trapped! No fucking way! Not me! I will not be trapped! I will not be controlled by this situation! I walk out of my door, and I move down the hall, towards the outer door to the outer world.

Out. I hear my name being called as I walk down the outward stairs that lead to the outward parking lot. I walk on. She chases me. I re-act/re-spond,

"Look, I got nothing to say to you. Just let the past be the past. I'm married now." (A useable lie, I thought). *"Married, and I don't want you to fuck it up!"*

I was nice but I was firm.

"Do not contact me!"

*   *   *

Just like in the *Tao Te Ching*, where it says to meet any adversity with kindness... So, I spoke.

She told me that she was surprised that I had picked such a, *"Tough looking chick."* I told her, *"I am from the gutter. I am a street kid. I like 'em that way."*

Actually, to me, she is really beautiful; my babe—my Asian babe. Though, even my mother laughed when I showed her a picture—

saying so many of my other girlfriends were so much prettier...

But me, I think she is stunning. I fall into her/fall for her, all the time. I don't know, maybe it is that she looks tough/hard/used/and abused?

But, back to the storyline...

I went out for a while. Hit over to my friend's guitar shop. The guy who makes and customized guitars for me. Hung out with all of those of us who hang out there. Spoke about the nothing that life is made up of. Just the usual... Told them the ongoing-ness of this story. Nothing new. They expected nothing less. They all laughed at me.

Then, I went back to my apartment on the beach.

There/here, I continued to hear the movement(s) in the halls. I feel my safe-space has been invaded, you know.

I mean, there is all this talk of the fucking obsessive nuts running around in the world now. You see it in the movies—you see it on T.V.—you see it on the news. Now, you see it here, in my apartment building. And me, this *happy-go-lucky* bohemian, I fucking do not need this kind of bullshit.

You know, it is like one of those things that looks to be a gift from Heaven, (sex and San Francisco), and then turns out to be a ticket straight to Hell.

And, how she ever found out my address? Fuck! Maybe a P.I.? Perhaps a door-to-door, knock on every door, down *The*

108

Strand. I don't know. Shit happens, I guess...

*   *   *

I'm felling a bit rushed right now. I got a bullshit Christmas party, via my main babe, to go to tonight.

Sorry, I'm just not a social guy.

Go get dressed; 6:46 PM. Out the door, post seven. A few changes of clothing in my hand. I do not think that I want to be around. Think I'll go crib up at my bitch's apartment for a few days.

*   *   *

Now, we *gotta* face facts here about a few things. A few things that need to be said...

I am not one who gets pushed well. I mean; if you push me, I will push back. And, this whole little stalking/haunting thing did begin to work on my nerves and seriously pissed me off. And really... Pissing me off is a bad thing to do. Trust me. It is... You don't want to meet that person.

I close the door, my door. I double lock it. I check it to make sure it is locked/tight. I walk down the hall, out to the out-door of the apartment complex. I hear a secondary door close behind me. In-coming... Fuck!

Out, the out-door, I walk down the stairs towards the parking lot. I turn/I look. Peeking through the door, like a thief waiting to steal the souls from the unconscious in the night—

yes, it was she—nut-case central.

I had tried the nice treatment already—nice in and of the previous time. I guess it didn't work...

I turned. I looked her straight in the eyes...

"Look," I tell her. *"I do not go for this shit! I do not know how the fuck you found out where I live. But, you can take this fucking fatal attraction bullshit and go and park it on the couch of some shrink!"*
"But, I'm not sick anymore," she exclaims.
"I don't give a fuck! You stay the fuck away from me! You stay away from my lady! You write these stupid fucking notes that you want to make love to me and my chick and then you put them all over my door. You are a fucking nut-job! If you ever come around me again, or if you ever put another note on my door, or send one of those stupid fucking letters to my P.O. Box, I am going straight to the police department and get a fucking restraining order issued again you! Do you understand me?"
"I just wanted to see you one more time."
"Just stay the fuck away from me! I mean it!"

I walked away...

*   *   *

So, story told... End of subject, *ectera-a-mundo.* The fat dude that she was *cribbin'* up with, hopefully he dipped his cookie. Hey, I

110

don't even care... It would be fine with me if the porker got some nookie. Normally, if I had any feelings for a bitch, that wouldn't be the case. But, I don't. So...

As for the bitches, take my advice, choose them better than I have and don't let your *ole' one eyed jack,* rule your life. Because believe me, a lot of times, it is more trouble than it is worth. Case in point, just discussed...

"I will be in L.A. on SQ 2, 27 February at about 1:00 PM. Will you be free?"

So came the letter from this more than semi-fine, sweet thing, twenty-three-year-old, of a Singapore Airline Stewardess that I had met while out there on the dark side of Asia; screaming for dream, several months the previous.

L.A. and her. Yeah well, it could be interesting...

*　　*　　*

I guess I should tell you the backstory here before I get/go too deeply into the *why-for* and the *what-not*.

I was out on the outskirts—deep in the outback. Bailing from this one chick—my main L.A. squeeze.

I had—had enough of the, *"Here,"* in L.A. I was tired of answering the, *"Whys?"* of the local woman. I was leaving her. I was on the bail...

Therefore and thereof, splitting to the deep realms of Asia seemed the quickest and most efficient way to do the said.

Thus, without a word, I was out. Hopped on the plane and flew, thirty-five thousand miles high, in the First-Class Cabin, to Japan,

112

to Hong Kong, and then...

Well me, I was *en route:* Jakarta to Kuala Lumpur, (K.L.), via Singapore. I headed out to the airport from my Five Star Hotel— *The Hilton,* in Jakarta. Headed out—out and into the heat.

Me, I transversed, post the night the previous spent with this ugly Indonesian hooker who charged me two hundred bills for a bum fuck. I mean, I'm more than happy to pay for it. Hell, I've paid a hell of a lot more for a hell of a lot less. And, paying... Well, it alleviates all the pains and postulations of all the nonsense of getting it for free. And, believe me, it is never-never-ever free. But/and, none-the-less, it was a bum fuck.

Anyway, at the airport, I check in my bag. Hit the *First Class Lounge.* I had a couple of cups of the simi-uck *First Class Lounge* java.

'Java on Java,' how poetic I thought.

Coffee down, flight time approaching, I bail towards the gate.

As I walked through the airport, I wore my very-very long and baggy blue suit of an Italian piece, draping across my bones. I had these big saw-tooth soled shoes upon my feet. The kind the cops of the 1960s and 1970s used to wear. My traditional round sunglasses hid my eyes from the/this world. My long blonde hair down, *a blowin' in the wind.* I walked, *hittin'* the direction of my plane's disembarkment.

I moved towards the gate. I see a crew of stewardess waiting to board a plane. My plane as it turns out. They stood there in all of their uniformed glory. Should I salute? They wore long, almost sarong style S'pore Airline's flowered dressed. They all had short—very short, black hair.

They stared at me—hard stares, as I approached. Like *devis,* (goddesses), desiring to be stolen from the realm of the ethereal and taken down here to earth; the domain of the anti-gods where they could live, if only for a moment—exist in; live out all for the momentary suchness of love, lust, passion, desire, and death. All the elements that can never be felt in the heavens. The heavens, they are far too pure for that; up there.

But, in truth and in fact, it is not all that unusual for an Asian babe, (Asia-side), to be warm for my form.

It is a funny... Well, not that funny— fact of life, however, and etcetera. Though it is true that it is oftentimes the case, there is a lot of times on the opposite side of the photograph; (Asia side), where I have been left waxing the *ole'* banana, solo. But, anyway...

As it has been proven, for whatever stupid reason(s), my clothing hanging baggy and long, my *do* falling upon my shoulders— the ladies of Asia, well, they do seem to dig my scene.

But, enough with the/my egotism...

I checked in at the gate. They got on. I too boarded the plane. Climbed into my *First*

114

Class Seat. I was the only homeboy riding *First Class.*

Almost immediately up dances one of them. The one this story is about. *"You look like a rock star,"* she exclaims with all forms of lost lust and desire in her eyes. Like she has/had finally found the man she has been/is looking for. The vision of life/love that promises to answer all of her desires throughout her lifetime. I have seen that look in the eyes of women before. But, believe me when I tell you—I am not that man. In any case, I smiled. I had never really thought about it. But here/there, in the far-off realms of deep Southeast Asia, I guess I did. Yes, I did look like a rock star.

I smiled. I said nothing.

Me being solo in *First Class,* I had three babes of Singapore Airline stewardess/flight attendants falling all over me. AOK. She, the babe this story is about, was just one of them.

Then came the point. She sat down. She had a word or three hundred to say to me. Singapore/Chinese. Told me of her life—working in a hotel, then as a stewardess. She took the job because she wanted to travel—wanted to see the world. Told me, she really wanted to go to Tibet. *"I'll go with you,"* I said. *"I've been there before."*

So, it was your basic *love in the making, lust for the taking* session.

Unfortunately, I was on my way to K.L. I was just transferring in S'pore. And, though the thought did cross my mind to chill it on back and crib up S'pore side. I had actually put in a week or two there, just a week or two the previous. So, I decided to keep my plans as they were as I had been out so long, (out there on the hard road), that my *danero* was getting tight and my plastic was finding its way to the limit level.

I elected another dream/another time, and I kept the motion moving forward. Plus, Bangkok was on the horizon after K.L. And, I really needed a session in B'kok. If you know what I mean...

K.L. and B'kok and all that. Other stories to tell... Stories for later, not now. As this is a book about L.A. And, there are more than a few untold stories to tell about, *"The Out There."*

*   *   *

Now, you know, I have LIVED my life. Or, should I say, I have LIVED my life within a space of totality. I mean, it is like, if you are not willing to live your life one hundred percent, be willing to throw everything you have away for nothing, then what is the point? Though few ever live, (can ever live), in that space of totality. But me, that is who I am!

But, back to the storyline...

When I received the letter—the aforementioned letter—the letter from the girl this story is about, I was cribbed up, (for the most part), with this local babe—here in L.A.

116

Like a fool, I had fallen back into the arms of my *Main and Current, L.A., Central Squeeze.*

I had come back. She had been awaiting my arrival. She apparently had been tracing my movements across the globe; knowing the hotel(s) I stayed at—she would call to see if I was there. If I was there, she knew I was there. There, not here. Not L.A.

Stalking? Yes, I was/had been stalked. Internationally Stalked. She stalked me. She figured out when I was back. Called until I answered. I didn't. Phone number changed, (again). Got the operator, to get to me. *"I'm pregnant. Pregnant with your child."* Well, maybe... (Story pre-told...) I spoke all of that in another story in the pages within this manuscript.

Within/with-out... *None-the-less,* post the pregnancy, the fool I am and I guess I will always be, I got sucked back in. Sucked back into her illusion; her lust; her beauty. Yeah, she was a sight. Yeah, she could fuck. But, yeah, we destroyed each other's lives. Her and I—it was the road to pure demise.

Now, it was not that she wasn't beyond fine in her own way. And, it wasn't that I didn't dig her—to whatever degree. It was just that she was... Well, she was, who she was... I had been there/done that, and in the, *"There,"* there was no promise of anything more. At least nothing more that I wanted to want from her. All that was left for us: (her and I), was *suicide slowly.* So me, being who I am—hating to be alone, I kept her on the line. But, I hated myself

117

for doing so—was constantly leaving: any chance/any reason that I got. This, the girl from S'pore was certainly one of them. A reason to leave...

So... The AM of the day where I am/was supposed to meet this fine little *thAng* from S'pore rolls around. The babe, my babe, still locked in, crib central. I had tried to get her out for the past day or three, but her sex promised too much illusion. Holding her in my arm's allowed me to pretend that life/that her/that us, could mean something more. But, it does not/did not/could not.

But hey, I got to stay in practice. I mean a new/untried babe on the way, you got to be in prime form in the sexual *departmento*, if you catch my meaning and I think that you do. So me, I had a practice partner...

The babe, my babe, my main and current L.A. babe, I tried to get her out the door that AM. But, there was just no way that she was going to go—not with-out a fight that is. But, instead of fighting, I played it a whole new direction—one I'd never tried before; at least not with her. I played it like I was *losing-it* due to all the relationship pressure she was putting me under. In truth, she was asking too much— too much from a *playa'* like me. So, I put on my best James Dean: confused, damaged, deranged. I did have to throw a lap down on the ground to sell my point. But, other than that, it went pretty well. She left feeling sorry for all that she had put me through.

118

I smiled as she walked out the door. After she turned her back, of course.

Now, if I could have watched it/watched this/that performance from a far, it was probably pretty amusing. I mean there I was, *throwin'* down all my best acting chops, and she bought it. I'm sure I appeared all *dazed and confused.* But then, the moment she walked out the door, I'm back! I got dressed, checked my look in the mirror, and headed for my *rendezvous.* Yeah, if I could have watched it— it probably would have been pretty funny.

I hit my car, The Jeep.

I took the top off. As it was her first trip to L.A., (the chick from Singapore), I thought I would let her bask in the L.A. sun. Me, I put on my Jeep *ridin'* safari hat. I hate the sun!

I hit off and over to her hotel. I looked at my watch. Man, I just pulled this one off. I got the babe *out-a-there* and I hit the streets just in time to arrive on time.

The babe, the new babe, the babe this story is about; via S'pore, she was staying at her stewardess hotel over by LAX. Actually, it wasn't too many miles, as the crow flies, from my crib to hers.

Got there. Called her from the hotel lobby phone. She came *a-runnin.'* Literally running.

Outside,

"Where do you want to go; breakfast?"
"No. I want to go to Mexico. I hear Ensenada is very nice."

Well, fuck me! Mexico... I do not want to go to Mexico! Not only have I been there way too many times. But, it is fucked up! You can't trust the cops. They pull you over and extort all kinds of money from you! I have even known a few of my *hombres* who have ended up in Mexican jails because they didn't have enough money—at least not enough of what the local *federales* thought was enough. Fuck me!

But me, being the nice guy that I am; I drove her to Mexico.

The fact of the matter is, the Mexican border is only a couple of hours from L.A. But, that didn't make my paranoia or anticipation of crossing said border any more hopeful.

The reality of this day/this trip was it faded to the fade. We drove. We spoke. Me, with all my charisma made her fall in love with me—like I do to all the willing babes.

We hit the boarder, drove across. We looked for the signs and continued southward. We drove through the squalor of Tijuana: cardboard shacks and destitution beyond belief. We drove along the Baja coast. AOK if you like that kind of thing. We arrived in Ensenada a few hours post the beginning of our journey.

She wanted to eat. Eating in Mexico makes me nervous. I never eat in Mexico! But, there I was; there I did—anticipating the results, the *Montezuma's Revenge.*

We grabbed a beachside restaurant, and we ate. She wanted to drink. We grabbed the waiter and drank Margarita after Margarita after Margarita.

Bitch could pound! We got fucked up.

She took a few pictures. Had the waiter take a few pictures of us.

I hate it when people do that!

Then, she was ready to leave. That was it/that was that. She wanted to head back.

I drove up the coast: toasted; fucked up. Lost in all kinds of forms of paranoia about getting pulled over by the *policia*. Not only for the fake speed limit(s) of Baja California, but for being fucked up. Fuck me! I was nervous.

But, up the coast, to the boarder we went. My *Guardian Angel* must have been looking over me/protecting me. I did not get pulled over.

We got to the border crossing; where, like always, there were a million cars waiting to cross. It was dark now. We waited. We drove up to the U.S. crossing guard. He knew, could see, I was a local. He knew she was not. I thought we were going to be fucked as she didn't bring her passport—Singaporean and all. She told me this later, of course. But, she with her smiley face, she told him, (the crossing guard), the story of being a *Singapore Airlines Stewardess*—he kind gave me the, *"Yeah, dude, you scored,"* eyeball. And, we crossed the border gate, *no problema.*

By now, I was sober. We made the couple hour drive up to her hotel. She was flying out tomorrow. I expected... Well... You know.

We got to her hotel. I parked the car. I walked her to the front door of the hotel. She hugged me. She told me, *"I love you."* She walked inside. I walked back to the car with my dick in hand. Thinking, *'Fuck me...'* Unexpected; very unexpected...

The only thing worth a mention was that back in the car I realized she had kept my bad, leather motorcycle jacket. In the PM of the Jeep ride, it had cooled down. I had loaned it to her.

Now me, I dug that jacket. Fuck! Should I go back, call her up and get it? Or not? Should I just play it cool and let her keep the memento. No, I dig that jacket!

I walked back towards the doors of her hotel. As I did, she had apparently realized her folly and she was running out the door to catch me to give it back,

"It wouldn't have fit in my suitcase. I love you,"

"I love you," again. But again, like again, I was left with my dick in my hand.

So, this all being stated, *'What's a guy like me supposed to do?'* Me, I hit over to my main L.A. babe's crib and hit her pussy. Spent the night and hit it a few more times... She loved me too!

Okay, that's that. That's the first part of the story. The first chapter if you will.

Then, a few weeks goes by. She had hit me up with several *postcards from paradise*—locations she had been. Whatever... Then comes,

*"I'm going to be in San Francisco on March
31. Can you meet me there?"*

What's a guy like me supposed to do?
I make the plane res's.

*   *   *

The flight up there was kind of
interesting, and worth a note, I guess? Next to
me sat this wonder white bread of a chick.
Talkative; wanted me—somebody, anybody...
A train engineer by trade. Liked to smoke
weed. Was upset that, (now), they *piss tested
'em;* (the engineers)... Kinda seemed like an
obvious to me. But...

Overall, she was a nice chick. Okay in
the okay department. I had my thoughts... I had
my fantasies... In fact, as I was set to pick a car
up at the SFO car rental, I offered to give her a
ride to her hotel in the city. She accepted. She
obviously wanted more than a ride. At least
more than a ride in my rental car.

I drove her to her door; all the way
wondering if what happened to me down in
L.A. was about to happen to me again with my
sweet little Singapore Airline Stewardess. I
wondered. But... I got to the door, the front
door of the train engineer's boutique hotel, and
I let her off. *"Call me,"* was the last words I
ever heard her speak.

The fact of the matter is/was, as you may well know, white bread just isn't my flavor of choice.

I hopped over to the next hotel on the agenda—wondering; questioning, had I done the right thing? I parked in the hotel gay—rage. Went up to the lobby. Called her room. *"Come up,"* she said.

Promising. Very promising...

As I rode the elevator; ascending to the San Francisco skyline, my mind; well, it was obviously in question. My determination was, however, very focused.

Knock, knock. She opened the door; still in her thin white cotton nightgown.

"I'm so tired..." She exclaimed.

Well, this was not the first time this line has been used on me. Whenever you arrive and a babe is still in bed or she tells you that she is tired and needs to take a nap; that is, *"The Go."* That means sex is in the works.

"Lay back down," were my words.

She lies down. I pull off my sport coat, vest, shoes, socks. (I hate being in bed with socks on). I lay down. We speak—small talk and it goes from there.

I'm checking her out. She has the mildly hairy underarms that most Asian chicks possess—unshaven. AOK with me. I study her face as she opens and closes her tired eyes.

124

Pretty, yeah, she is pretty. In a subtle—not stunning sort of way. Her skin is the caramel color of the Southeast Asian Chinese. Her hair, as previously stated, very short. But, she has pretty eyes...

She leans over and extends her lips to me. I do what I do. Which means, I go forward towards the kiss but then pull back at the last second. She tries to kiss me again. Again, I go forward and then pull back. This drives the bitches nuts. I jokingly do this a few times until our lips finally meet. We kiss. We kiss for a long time. Her tongue caresses the inside of my mouth.

Her kiss; nice. Nice, but not impaling— not devastating—not stunning. Not like some of the girls I have known. But, the push leads to the shove; such as the push leading to the shove tends to do.

She unbuttons my shirt. I lift her nightgown; exposing her small, perfectly formed, Chinese/Singaporean, Asian breasts. I kiss them. I lick them. She unfastens my belt, unbuttons my pants. She reaches in for the kill.

One thing leads to another. We get naked pretty easily. Not hard and awkward like it is sometimes.

In my mind, (for a moment at least), I had the thought, *'Maybe she's a virgin.'* At twenty-three, there are still a lot of them left, over Asia way. I thought maybe that was why, last time, she had traveled up the stairs to her hotel room solo. But then/now, those ideologies were long gone. Her lips, her tongue, embraced my cock.

After that, I roller her over; I lay her down on her back. I planted it deep, hard; rock solid, inside of her. I could tell she had only been playin' Asia side when she met *Dirty Harry*. You know, comparing size and all. I knew/could fell; she expressed without words, her surprise and tantalization.

We fucked as we fucked. Nothing to write home about. Nothing to write here about. Just, we fucked...

She *came*. One of those chicks that once they *cum,* they dry up fast. Okay, that's fine. Makes it easier on me. I *came*.

We went out to dinner. Hit over to this little Cambodian place I dig, up SF way, over on Geary Street. Went back to the crib, I did her a few more times.

"I am going to be so sore tomorrow..." So, she said.

AM, she had a plane to catch, as she was a waitress in the skies. Me, I had a plane to catch too. Back to L.A. I offered to drive her to SFO. But, she had to go on the bus with her crew.

A shower with her. A fuck in the shower—gotta do it, man... And, I was gone.

It was what it was what it was...

I mean, how many times do we have fantasies about the, *what could be?* Then, there

126

they are. And, that is all they are. Just what they are.

* * *

Back in L.A.; (what this book is all about), a month or so post, I saw her again. She flew in on a flight with her crew.

This time, what we were going to do was set in stone. No more Mexico!

I hit her hotel. A different one than the one; two months the previous. We did what we did, (if you catch my meaning), and then we were out. She wanted to see my L.A.

I took her to *Farmer's Market* over on 3rd and Fairfax for AM brunch. Showed her some of the dark dives I inhabit in daytime L.A.

She wanted to buy her brother a Rap cassette, as Rap is banned in Singapore. Yes, it is. A lot of things are banned in Singapore. Hell, the first time I went there I had to hide my long hair under a hat. But, as a flight attendant she gets to pass through *Customs* no-checky. So, her bro wanted some L.A. Rap.

She asked, *"Who?"* I suggested NWA. She bought it, *Straight Outta Compton*.

PM, we did the similar. Fucked, then out to the dark spots of my dark L.A. Back at her hotel I hit the pussy again and again and again.

"Do you know how sore I was last time?" She exclaimed to me.

Then, she was gone. Back to the skies.

127

She wasn't due back to *The States* for the next three months. She asked me to join her elsewhere, on the international side. But, in that interim a poetry chapbook deal that I had scored was published. I sent her a copy. In it, I had written a little ditty about our trip to Mexico; describing her as, *"So-so."* I think that worked on her a bit. Whatever...

She *post carded* me/she called me; but I had finally gotten rid of the previous and hooked up with a new, *Main L.A Squeeze*, on the very-young side of the photograph. A fine little Asian number that when/while I was in Bangkok, the last time around, (a month ago), while writing a book there—there at *The Oriental Hotel,* I actually dedicating it to her; saying, *"... The woman who all other women should be judge by."* Yeah, she is fine. Yeah, I am into her.

So me, I was onto something new.

Something new; that is the name of the game.

The name of the game and the end of this story.

But, back to the back to... The interlude between the beginning of and the conclusion to the previous said story.

It involves, you know, my main chick; Asian, on the far side of L.A., (she is originally via Taiwan), and is currently riding shotgun on the *in-progress* bus to hell.

Well, she gives me this call; evening last. A call asking, *"Did I want to go and see this magic/performance art piece—hanging on the wall of this theatre central Wilshire, L.A. way?"*

My first thought was, *'I used to go to that theatre as a youngster, The Wiltern.'* It was only a couple of blocks from where I lived for a year or three. Now, the area is called *Koreatown.* They even have a big sign, stating as such.

Sometimes, back then, sometimes with friends, sometimes alone; I would go and see movies. I saw *The Wild Bunch* there, Bruce Lee's, *The Chinese Connection.* I saw, *2001 A Space Odyssey* at that theatre. *Butch Cassidy and the Sundance Kid, Che, Two Lane Blacktop.* Hell, I even saw, *Superfly* there. Fuck, the late '60s and '70s were cool! Way cooler than now.

I even remember once I had this kill sore throat that went into deadly tonsillitis. I never had it before—didn't know what it was. What I

129

did know is that it went into a repertory infection that literally felt like it was killing me. In actuality, it was/would have. I lay in bed the night the previous gasping for air. Anyway, my mother was way pissed that she had to take a few hours off of her, *oh so precious,* work to take me to the doctor. He gave me a shot— gave me some meds. My mother grabbed the bus to head-on downtown to her job. Me, *en route* waking home, I walked past the theater in question. I checked in. I watched the first, *"Made in Hong Kong,"* Kung Fu movie to be widely released in the U.S., *Five Fingers of Death.* Good movie!

I mean hey, due to my illness, I was going to miss my martial art training for a few sessions/a few days. So, may as well make the best of my off time... But, all that was many-many-many moons ago...

Anyway... The chick wanted to go to this *thAng.* You know the one, the *Main and Current L.A. Babe.* She had gotten tickets from the film production office she part-time/some-time(s) worked at. She called me from the same.

"All the people who work here are going," she exclaims. *"It's Penn and Teller!"*
"Like, who the fuck cares?" I replied.

I don't know, they call me antisocial... But, the fact of the matter is, I just don't relate to all the bullshit, small-talk, of the people who go to see something just because it is free

130

and/or because it is such a fucking hip environment to be *hangin'* out in.

I mean, check it—me lost in all my multi-levels of neuroses; I just didn't want to go. I told her so.

So... Post the basic hang-up on me upon the telephone line(s) from her work: one, two, no three times; all with instantaneous callbacks, on her end, not mine.

I mean like, this chick is twenty-six years old. Give me a fucking break!

So, again... Post all the callbacks, all the, *"I'm pissed off at you,"* stuff; all the, *"I will speak to you once I get home,"* sternly said. Whatever... Fuck you!

You know, all this is just a world I don't relate to—attempted domination by someone's something else's—their space and their time. You know, like, *A glitch in the space-time-continuum,* and all.

I mean, *"Come the fuck on!"* The egotistical/egocentric/egomaniacal person that I am, I want the world to revolve around me. And, not to sound prejudice or judgmental or ethnocentric here, but I mean like, the Chinese babes are just not the subservient type. The Japanese and the Thai babes are way better in that department.

So anyway, and etcetera... As stated, many times the previous, a relationship I have been trying to get out of since the dawning of man—the dawning of it; the relationship that is. Trying to exit, (stage left), since our first date—a little cruise up to a penthouse suite;

131

unappreciated $500.00 dollars a night, up S.F. way. Another story, told elsewhere.

So, a call comes from the babe once she has slide in home-side. It hits my answering machine. I was out, dealing with the modern realities of this bullshit modern world. Which, universally, has a dollar sign attached to it.

I mean, I had used a check to add to my checking account to pay for a thing or two. The thing was/is, it was one of those checks sent by the credit card companies. They send it. I had deposited it in my real-life checking account. But, fuck me! It fucking bounced.

A credit card check from a major bank. And, it bounced!

That was two days in the past. I did call upon the main 800 number on the telephone line. When/where I was informed that their issuing bank was no—go *mojo* anymore. And, though they loved me, and my credit rating was excellent, and all that bullshit; there was nothing they could do. They would, however, be happy to send letter(s) of explanations to all of the unknowing people(s) which I had given and/or sent checks to and tell them that it really wasn't my fault... But, there was not a fucking thing else that they could do to get those checks to cleared.

Once again, here; it was me/I was FUCKED!

You know, during our conversation, on the telephone line that day, they claimed they sent me a letter a month ago—telling me to not use the said check. But, I guess I just trashed it; the letter, that is. I trash everything. I never read anything.

They tell me, they sent me a new and full-on, fully useable set of checks weeks ago. There/where? I guess it/they are/were tossed somewhere in this mess I call an apartment.

So me, I live or die, they don't care. That be that; what it is—is what it ain't.

Me, I was forced to go out and try to chase down some of the said checks, written from my checking account, based upon a bad check, before they were attempted to be cashed and then bounce. Out—me, like a broken, beaten little pup, with his tail between his legs. I do not like this/that feeling.

*   *   *

The chick called—called my machine. The basic, *"Where are you? You live a secret life, don't you?"*

You're goddammed right I do.

So, I get back. I call. She cries. An obvious ploy to get her own way. She does it all the time. I guess up until me she was way far out in front in the, *get her own way departmento.*

I mean, come on... As previously detailed, she came up, way rich, on the other side of those far off Taiwan tracks—limousines to grammar school; anything that she ever wanted. Moved L.A. way; a step down from a mansion but not much: own lake, own pool, own etcetera...

133

Now certainly, I wish all people the best; no jealously down on this end. And, if I ever had kid, (but thirty and counting I doubt I ever will), I would want them to have that same level of STUFF that she had. But, her mind: be it Chinese, formerly rich, or just smashed hard against some distant wall of reality, (you know, it isn't too clear), but, she plays the guilt game; all-the-time... She plays the rebellion game to her parents, (to get her own way), all-the-time... She slaps their/her tradition in the face—goes and lives with some loser of a punk rock musician who beats her, fucks around, and then leaves her. So then, she goes and fucks every guy that she meets and says, *"They're not using me, I'm using them!"* Yeah right... Then, she goes to further extremes, post the intersection of her slut—dom, to trap me into her web of deceit, and do all she can to hold me manipulated with her screams.

Man, has she embarrassed me—even last night! But, I'll tell you about that in a minute or two...

And, mostly her tears... I mean, she just wants things her way!

I don't know, maybe some kids get it all handed to her; like she did. But, as per said example, the kids who do, *"Have it all,"* are not going to come up as the people that you would want to take home to meet mom. Do you feel me?

So, it goes back and forth on the *telephono*. I did not want to go.

134

"You ruined it! Forget it! We're not going!"

Now, in actuality, I was more than happy about that because as you see there was this more than sweet little Japanese object who gave me the corner smile, the evening before, at the old health spa down Long Beach way. My in—tent—ions were to hit down that way again and see where *karma* and/or destiny may lead. I mean like, anything has got to be better than where I am/where we, (she and I), my *Main and Central L.A. Babe,* are.

But now, here it all comes into a funny play of the cards of destiny; with this chick of/in question. It's like, whenever I try to bail her, I later run into her. I mean, it is fucking uncanny. Like, I bail her, hit over Asia way. *I Scream for the Dream.* Then, I am walking at the *Rose Bowl Swap Meet*, a bit post my return, and there she turns; face-to-face-to-me. Bizarre in the bazaar. And, like our last big spat, a few weeks back, Sunday morning, I hit over to FM, *Farmer's Market,* for a little morning java, read the *Sunday Times* session, and to dream of... Well... Whatever else may come. Driving back on the 10 West to the 405 South, on the crossover, I see in the distance two traveling java mugs upon the dash of this gigantic '70s pimp blue Lincoln Conti. Her pimp-a-nentinel. Fuck! It was her. Her, *en route* to find me. Bizarre, man! I just don't know...

And, for a chick that you do not even want to be with... But then, there is all the alone... Well, actually, I should use it to catch up on some of the creativity that I am way-way behind on—years behind. But... What do I do? I do the old run back to nothing: her—her and I. ...A fool's passion, huh?

So anyway, to reiterate, sorry to get off the point of the story in question and at hand... The yelling, the crying, the etcetera, the back and the forth on the telephone lines. I mean, if I could turn all of the hours of time that we have spent doing that over the last year plus into gold, I would be out of debt and be a way far rich dude.

A call here. A hang-up there. Another call here,

"I'm giving the tickets away. You ruined it!"
"To who?"
"Anyone, I don't want them to go to waste."

I intercede...

"Do you want me to come over?"
"No, I will go over there!"

Stupid fucking fool that I am; feeling guilty, and all that stupid shit...

So, all that, as it may be—be, being nothing. I await her stated arrival.

I am at my computer here, a poem had just been excepted by a publication up Oregon way. I was printing out a copy, off the disk, to place it in my, *"Published File."*

Oh, just another/secondary subtopic; slide to the right here—poetry doesn't pay

much. It's almost like no pay at all. You hear about all the poets this/all the poets that... But, I mean, man; it/poetry is zero in the cash *departamento*. They give you a copy or two of the mag. Sometimes you even have to buy them if you wish to see your name in the lights of print, as it were. And then, (maybe), they send you a check that is worth less than the cost of the paper it was printed upon; sometimes...
...Sometimes not. All this, after you send out hundreds/thousands of submission(s). But, most of *'em,* (the editors), just don't dig your style or don't dig where you are *comin'* from; geographically speaking, or some other fucking stupid thing such as that.

Now, there are a few, (poets that is), that their written ramblings have somehow become massively accepted. But, I mean, that number is very-very-very few. One in fifty billion. A job is way easier than being an artist/poet/writer/what—the—fuck—ever.

So me, I was at these keys; doing what I do. Another call comes. I knew it was her,

"What time are you coming over?"
"I thought you said you were coming over here?"
"No, I changed my mind. I want you to come over. What are you doing? Can you come over now?"

Post an explanation as to what I be—a—doing, when I am done; I will come.

"Why not now?"

And, it goes back and forth. I won't bore you, but she couldn't give the tickets away. *"Let's go, please!"* So...

"I'll come now."
"There isn't enough time!"
"I'll be there in an hour."

She, living up Westwood way, it takes an hour to get there.

She likes the city. Fuck that! I had to grow up in that shit hole of L.A. I don't want to live there, central city, now. Live next to all the, *"Move here tourists,"* and all the way too far rich kids/the rebellious from the suburbs, who still believe the fucking wet dream that it is cool to be in—side the inner city. Stupid; fucking stupid...

So, I don't want to live with her, as she wants me to. I want a way out. And, I am certainly not going to live in the city; too fucking hot and smoggy, if nothing else. And, my current crib, way too small for love on the *dos* side. Thus, we are separate my many miles. Redondo Beach and Westwood. Miles traveled up the 405.

Anyway, got dressed; bail out in the 6:00 PM department. Then me, I got to sit in all the *try to get nowhere so fast to no place* traffic jam; North up the 405.

En route, one of the weirdest experiences of my life happened. I am listening

138

to KNAC. *Motorhead's, Killed By Death,* is playing. I look over to the side of the freeway, a vintage 60s pickup truck has apparently flipped on its side on the shoulder of the road. Its frame is facing the freeway. I see the driver's side door open, as someone is obviously still inside. It must have just happened. That's why it, the crash, the flip over, hadn't created a major traffic jam as of yet. I could see the guy's arm lifting the door up. Just then, BAM! The truck blew. It caught on fire. I continued to drive. There was nothing that I could do.

Going nowhere syndrome of the city drive. Rush, power thrust and all the bullshit. So much for the think positive/feel good about myself—help tapes. I turned off, the turn on.

I get there; her crib. I go inside. She is way full of attitude.

Realization, big NUMERO UNO, you can go way far out of your way for a person, do everything for them, and in their mind, it doesn't mean a goddamned thing—especially when it is in the direction of the formerly rich. No prejudice intended, just stereotypical observation.

So, we drive off—off in my bad little *356.* In actuality, I am thinking about selling it. Just finished up the final re-read, proof-read of *The Passionate Kiss of Illusion,* a few weeks back to send off to the publisher. Final proofing... Man, it does take a lot of time... And, it does take it out of you. Happy to be writing new stuff again...

But anyway... Just the feeling, kinda like with the end of that, (the book), was the end of an era. And, the dude/this dude needs some bucks. So... Maybe... Maybe sell it. A classic car—a classic sports car; a *Porsche*—it costs a lot of money to keep it running. We'll see...

Anyway, I go to get some fuel and some brit—bro wants to know the way to Melrose, I tell him. He exclaims, *"Cheers mate."* *"Yeah, whatever..."* Gas in. We go.

"On Friday I am going to have dinner with Mary," states my *Main and Current L.A. Babe.*

Mary, being her twenty-two and still a virgin, cousin; who is warm for my form. She, Mary, not so rich, not so rebellious, not such a fool; as my little love muffin; here discussed— who has put her body on the line far too many times just to find acceptance in an unaccepting world.

Now this, her statement, pissed me off just a bit. She didn't even consult me as to whether I had made plans for us or not. Which I didn't, but I told her that I did.

In fact, and in actuality, it's no problem, in my mind's eye; out with her cousin for she is nice—way nicer than her; my *Main, (via Taiwan), L.A. Central Squeeze.* In fact, if I weren't a good eight years older than her, (Mary that is), I would probably marry, Mary. She is fine. But...

In any case, there I was driving; going to a place that I did not want to be going—dancing down under the star lights and the full moon that pierced out from behind the skyscrapers on Wilshire Boulevard. But here, now, in all the magic of the central city; the fight, it got serious.

"I don't want to go to this thing!"
"I just thought it would be nice for us to do this."
"For us! This is not for us! I have no interest in being there."

At this point, we pass the theatre. *The Wiltern,* remember? Though pissed, I find a place, pull up, and park.

"We can never go to any of the places I want to go to! We never go to night clubs, parties or plays!"
"You know me, I am not a social person, and I do not like to sit around and make stupid idle conversation with people that either have no opinion or are so fucking full of themselves but do nothing to act on their opinions."

As you may know, your opinion means virtually nothing. Your actions are the only thing that counts.

"And, I am just tired of getting my ears blown out in the night clubs you like to go to; full of bad music and bullshit plastic fashion-passion

141

*people that care nothing about enlightenment.
And, I hate fucking plays!"*

Oh, by the way, as previously stated,
karaoke is one of god's curse upon humanity,
theatre and plays is the second.

But, back to the point, as you may or
may not see, we, (her and I), are very different
people—temperamentally speaking.

It went back and forth. On her end,
major tears. She cries a lot. She says she wears
her emotions on her sleeve.

Then, she takes my portable binoculars;
the ones which she had asked me to bring, and
smashes them on the ground out the window,
on the sidewalk. She jumps out of the car and
walks off.

Now generally, I don't go the route of
chasing after people, but I have been trying to
be a nicer person of late, so out I go. She starts
to run like a child.

Our run continues. We pass a bus stop
with some on-looking *wet backs*. *'Fuck you,'* I
thought. Finally, I catch up to her, which leads
to more confrontation.

We sit down on a Wilshire building
embankment. As I child, I remember a session
of riding my bike with my friends on the
property and being thrown off. Awh, years
ago...

But, her and I, so it went; onward and
upward: the tears, the etcetera. She sat there
screaming at me. I mean, literally screaming.

142

Again, attempting to get her own way. The passing cars looked out their windows at us. As mentioned, I was going to detail how she embarrassed me. Well, there it is.

"Would you please keep the melodrama down, people are looking."
"What do you care? You don't care about me! And, you'll never see them again!"

You know, as true as that may be, I just don't dig the scene of announcing my problem(s) to the world.

Again, the difference(s): her and I.

She screams, makes scenes anywhere to get her own way. I would hate to see her when she gets old. She will probably still be doing this kind of bullshit from a wheelchair.

Finally, she gets up and walks back to my car,

"Just take me home."

Yeah, fuck me! Fuck my night! Fuck my energy! Nothing matters to a person who is self-involved. And, she fucked up my go to the Long Beach health club in an attempt to hook up with that new chick.

So, back in the car, we sat there for a while.

"There is still time to go," I say.

We get out of the car. We walk to *The Wiltern*.

We go. She won. What can you do, huh?

But/and, to keep the melodrama flying, she was sure to bring her big batch of keys in hand. *'Real bullshit,'* I thought. She brought them, so she told me, just in case I decided to bail. But, that big batch of keys looked really tacky. I mean, it is a BIG batch of keys—like thirty or something. I don't even know what they all are for. Does she?

Inside the theatre, it brought back memories... We had balcony seats. We walked up the stairs, past all the B-level T.V. stars and minor movie personality who inhabit such events. Sent there by their publicists, to get their face(s) scene/seen.

We went upstairs... There were all the *part-time* people from a *part-time* production firm. PART TIME...

All the basic, *"Hi's,"* and the etceteras were exchanged.

Not my scene. Not my type of people.

One fag dude, with his West Hollywood greased back *do* in a ponytail, had his booty boy *ridin'* shotgun—a bro who sells me suits at this store I like to get some of my baggy Italian clothing at in Westwood; *Politix*. But, no acknowledgement. Even though I am sure he has earned a lot of commission from my purchases. *'Fuck him,'* I though. He was probably embarrassed.

You know, the whole scene, just as I expected; everybody dressed up to go out for

144

free—take in the, *oh so fucking hip,* magical art; when all they were/are, were a bunch of non local(s), move to L.A., production paste-up workers.

Me, I got nothing to say to the people who don't live the art. In fact, I have little to say to most people; whether they live the art or not.

The fact of the matter is, bullshit, people are bullshit. They are all full of their book/newspaper knowledge. It doesn't mean shit. My people are the ones who know what they know, from living it—whatever it is; their knowledge is deep. I respect them. Fuck these kinds of people who, at best are, businessman artist, who come out to *The Coast* to stir-fry their eggs and kiss ass to get to the, all so revered, artistic top of the heap.

Some say I'm messed up. So what! Some say I'm insecure. Believe me, I'm not! I like what I like. I don't like what I don't like. And, what is mine, is mine. Any name, any culture, it is all the same. If you want to be self-actualized, just don't care about anything. It is as simple as that.

So, the show went on. She played the basic, sit there and pout, and don't touch me session. Her actions began to piss me off. But then, most of the things that she does/does...

The show went on: magic and comedy; vaguely funny and/or interesting. There is a lot of other comedy I way prefer.

Intermission, everybody bails. We sit. Time passes.

She decides that she wants a drink of water as the lights flash to come back in. We go and get her one.

Part Two. The basic, so what...

The show is over. She wants to leave before the rush.

"Don't you want to talk to your friends?"
"No."

We leave. We walk to my car, no hand-in-hand. She is not happy with me. Fuck her, and fuck that! The cool night air breathes down my throat like a warm female with a frigid body in heat.

We drive off. It starts up. The basic, the usual—we fight all the time. I was told/told by her, it was all my fault. Maybe it is? I don't know. I really don't care.

So, leave it to the philosophers to decide, the psychologists to analyze, who is right; who was wrong. I chucked my health spa evening desire to take her where she wanted to go. Vaguely selfless, I thought...

But then, we all want some return from something, even if that return is nothing. Nothing is a better hope.

Driving, it blew up. It finally got to the point when I put the vocal cords in gear and screamed back at her. It takes a lot to get me there. But, I can eventually get there. You can only take so much of the, *"Not enough of this. You don't do enough of that."* *"Then just leave*

146

me the fuck alone!" I scream. But, I doubt there is much hope of that.

Back at her crib I park. Just to give the one-step over the line statement,

"By the way... Since you aren't going to use it anymore, and it is in your car, and as you are very irresponsible; can I have the book back that I loaned you before you lose it."

The book: a very expensive hardcover art book with a picture of the painting, *American Gothic,* in it which she had borrowed to copy to do one of her, on the side job, cartoon shits, which she considers fine art, for a magazine illustration job which she had.

"Can you never say anything nice to me?"

I walked over to her car,

"Hey, your rear window is half down."

In the backseat of her car: my book, a very expensive tennis racquet I purchased her, and a bunch of other valuable shit. This, and her window is half down. Need I say more about the/her irresponsibility... She is a mega pro at it.

I reclaim the book. She walks over to make sure everything she left in her backseat is still there. We walk back across the street.

"Thanks for nothing," I say.

She flinches as I complete my sentence.

"Come on," I laugh.

All that old boyfriend slap her up bullshit: past-programming: garbage in/ garbage out. I hate it! I have never tapped her up; though she, more than any and all of the others, has deserved it.

Stupid... She/I; so stupid...

So me, I drive off into the night. Stopped, picked up a, *"Daily Fresh,"* pizza at the local supermarket. At home, tossed it in the oven and sat back to pizza and a glass, (well maybe ten) of the grape.

So, post all that, to sleep. Early for me; maybe 1:30 AM.

This morning; I get up, tap a word or three upon these keys. 10:30 AM I get a call from the babe; work side. Wanted to know why I didn't call her. Something I never do. Something she always complains about. It is always her calling; asking why I never call. *"Take the hint,"* as I tell her. But, a call, it did come in,

"What are you doing?"
"Writing a story."
"About what?"
"About last night."
"Oh, how it was all your fault?" she questions.

Typical...

148

"So, what time are you getting off tonight?" I ask, being the nice guy that I am.
"I don't know, but I have to go to jewelry class after work."

Again, there she plays it, the world not revolving around me.

"Oh well..." I hang up.

My day continued... I had to try to take care of a few of the aforementioned check problems. Then, over to see my friends at the music store. After that, I picked up some paint for canvases waiting to be painted. Had a bit of brunch at this restaurant I dig over in Manhattan Beach, *The Kettle.* Then, back here at the keys, 2:04 PM. Very-very early day for me...

My machine has been catching the phone calls. The babe, my *Main and Current One,* via Taiwan in question, she has called at last count on the digital call counter, seven times. I just don't want to deal with it/her. I plan to hit the old health spa down Long Beach way for whatever dream that may hold this PM.

You know, that's the problem, being an artist, your time is your own, but you are expected to be home; creating. She makes us plans. She probably has cancelled going to her class. She makes plans. I dodge them as best as I can. Leave her guessing...

149

And please—please, never let them tell you that psychological indulgence or attachment is the same as love...

L.A. **8**

Life, it is a bit funny, don't you know?
Well, anyway...

It's about 9:26 AM here, L.A. way. A bit
early for me to be on the upside—actually my
eyes they opened 7:30 AM. That is complete,
of course, post going to the sack-side Valium
induced last PM. My life...

Well, as the story goes—me; somehow,
I just play/pay for the melodrama/play into the
melodrama—live for the dance. But, when the
fire comes down on you and there is nowhere
to turn, and you become the patsy, the fall-guy.
Well... It feels pretty fucked up.

As you may or may not know, I have this
one chick on the mainline. My L.A. babe via
Taiwan. One of those that you, (I), know you
should have never been with—never really
wanted to be with, but their pursuit of you so
ongoing and the stones of loneliness pounding
down upon you; well, you stay *hangin'* on; for
whatever foolish reason(s) and logic.

So anyway... Here I am in the middle of
nowhere with this chick. It is not that I do not
upon occasion look into her Asian eyes and fall
deeply into infatuation. And, it is not that I do
not, at times, wish it/wish I, could all be
different—wish that I was not so tainted and
she was not such a former slut complete with
herpes—which I have to way protect myself

from contracting from her. But, out is an in; and the cool is solo.

So, enough autobiography. To the story in and/or of question.

I try to be a nice guy... Morning last, well the day before that, actually; my main homeboy of a bike racing step-nephew, via Saturday Jim, had himself a race up Valencia way. So, cruise I did; give the guy support and all. The night before that, the main L.A., via Taiwan, chick in question and I have a little bit of a set-to. Well, we have those all the time. Her personality is just not like my So. Cal. kind. Pushy, yeah, she is way pushy. Maybe I am making a value judgment, a stereotype, or whatever... Maybe I am just seeing things through ethnocentric American eyes, but the Chinese are fucking forward people. Anyway... Enough set-up...

So, we: (her and I), are discussing the fact that I am always a nice guy and go hit all of her friend and family gigs, but she will never go to any of mine. She claims it is because all of my friends are losers and rednecks. She tells me that I am just a redneck with expensive clothing.

I laugh. Though I do not particularly like the title, nor do I agree with her definition; what I can say is, *'You can take a boy out of the jungle, but you can't take the jungle out of the boy.'*

And, as for redneck... I guess she means growing up non-privileged. Well, I am sorry, I was not driven to school in limousines like she

152

was. Given a choice, I probably would have been.

There is a lesson in all of this, however. That lesson is, don't hang with the rich chicks, they don't appreciate *nada*. There is nothing that you can give them that could not be supplied by their family. So, and because of which, anything that you do means *nada*.

Which brings me to another point here; Asian and all. The other day I was over at the old Post Office, when I had to ask a question; get some P.O. Box info. and the etcetera... The, in the back, P.O. Box babe, comes out to give me the said rap.

I was more than taken back. She was this beautiful, no doubt, via Vietnam, babe of a postal employee.

But, that is not really the story... The story is; she wore this very-very small, very thin, gold wedding band. It all just set me to thinking...

You know, this chick, my chick, so fucking spoiled into the finer things of life, (though she claims just the opposite), is always trying to get me hitched up with her. Now, for her, she has to have this one caret diamond engagement ring in platinum and this multi-diamond wedding ring to impress her family, friends, and all. Claims she will take nothing less. I mean what bullshit! First of all, marriage, no thank you. Secondarily, I mean like, there are these babes, they are out there, they are beautiful, and they way far appreciate the simpler things in life; like small wedding bands. So anyway; story told...

Maybe I am a redneck. But hey, this is my country. I was born here, and the majority of her family cannot even speak English. And, it really ticks me off when foreigners put down the locals.

But, back to the confrontation.

Now, to think about it—it had been going on for two days. Two days, the before, we had actually gotten into to it. Gotten into it about what? Who knows? Her selfishness or mine?

As for the race, the bike race, the one ridden by my step-nephew, via Saturday Jim, she gave me a ringy on the tele, 2:00 in the AM and said if it was important to me, she would go. *"No, that's okay..."* I mean let's be truthful here; actually the point being, I didn't want her to go. I mean, at times, there are some serious babes out at those contests, and I mean hey, if a new illusion presents itself to me, I am more than the one to take it on. Like last week, Monday. Today is what, Tuesday? So no, Tuesday—Tuesday, a week has past. Anyway, this stewardess chick I know flew her way into town. Not the Singaporean; this is another one; she flies Northwest. Actually, my favorite airlines.

Me, I had to dump the main L.A. via Taiwan babe. Made up the excuses; broke up with her and I was out—a—there and free.

The stewardess and me, it was our first time in the love grip and, actually, the joke is, she tried to give me the, *"I have never done this before,"* rap. *'Yeah right! Whatever,'* was my thought. I've heard it all before... But, then comes round *dos*. We are in her hotel room sack jack and we are getting close to going for the second round. She has to go hit the head. AOK, *no problema*. Back out, we get down to business, I pull out and the blood is all over *Dirty Harry*.

"You're bleeding."
"Yes, I told you it was my first time."

Well, be all that as it may... I am sorry there was a little aroma going along with that blood. A scent which I have, (unfortunately), smelled before. You see, Asian chick they use the old *Kotex* and the scent it does leak out. So anyway, *"Tell it to some-one who will believe it. Tell it to some-one who cares. Tell it to some-one who hasn't heard it six-million times before."* But, the proof, my friends, it is in the preverbal pudding. And, come on, *"You are so big,"* does not come out of the mouth of someone who has not been powered thumped by a few on the Japanese side of the picture before. I mean, if she knows it's big; then she knows what's small. Right? And oh, by the way, she; this babe, was Japanese by breed and texture.

So anyway, she had a flight the next day; wanted me to stay on through the night but I just wasn't into it. Especially after her last comment. I had done what I had come there to do. Then, just to let her know the way I really felt about her, I did it one more time and *came* really fast.

You know, with *Tantra Yoga* you learn how to control yourself. You can fuck for hours upon hours. *Tantra Yoga,* something I am a master of/at. But, there is a point when you want a woman to just feel like a slut. Let *'em* know what you really think of *'em*. In those cases, you don't want to give it to *'em* good. You just want to stick it in there and *cum* really fast. *"You're a hoe. I fucked you. I'm gone. You're gone…"* You know what I mean? *Tantra Yoga* lets you master that, as well. I did that, (did that to her), and I left.

So me, I bailed; hit back crib side. Love message(s) on my telephone answering machine.

What can a guy like me do? I went on over to my main L.A., via Taiwan, babe's and latched up at her love shack.

We got in a fight, day next. To set the stage, we were naked. I poured some water, from a glass I was drinking, on her head to chill her back. She freaked! Grabbed my pants, which were laying on her bedroom floor, walked to the bathroom, threw them in the shower; turned on the water. I grabbed her dress, walked into the bathroom, threw it in the toilet; flushed it.

I am sure you can get the picture of how our relationship runs.

156

She grabbed her dress out of the toilet; tried to beat me with it—all wet and ucky. I told her to stop that violent shit.

I never understand why it is AOK and cool for chicks to hit their dudes, but it is NOW so taboo for a dude to slap a bitch up. I mean, violence is violence, and it is no-go between couples in general. But, chicks somehow think that is alright if they smack up their dude.

You know, it's funny... I watched myself the night before—via the *Internal Witness* and all. You know, where you stand back and watch yourself from afar. Like you are someone else/someplace else, seeing what you are see, like you are on T.V.

Yeah, we got into it then too. But, that night/the last night, I saw that feeling rise; the one where when it came, I would previously grab and throw something, put my fist through the wall, or would tap the bitch up, so forth and so on. But instead, I just watched it; via the old *Internal Witness*.

Maybe I am getting old, I don't know... They say with age you chill. But, the joke is, I have been with women who far less deserved to be slapped up than this one. And, due to my volatile temper and all, they were.

Anyway, and in any case; this one, my woman, has for a year and a half basically stayed clean from my smack downs, even though, if I may go on here, she has kicked me in the shin, kicked me in the balls, slapped me in the face, punched me in the arm/in the jaw, etcetera, and so on. Yet, she has never met Mr. Hand. Who's the fool? Her or I? I don't know?

But anyway... I live the melodrama with her. Though it is definitely a love/hate type of thing.

So, post the water treatment—previous story just told, I hit on over to Saturday Jim's on Saturday. The usual session... Hang out, watch T.V., and drink a lot of beer. Me, again, thinking/planning I will never see her again.

This day, she calls up, with tears in her voice; saying that she is sorry. So, post the Jimmy Jam session, I hit back over her direction; another fight ensues. I go home. Thus, the calls. Thus, I already told you that. Thus, I go to the bike race. Nothing on the babe action front, I go home.

In heading in that direction, I stop at her Westwood crib. She was not there. I, being the lay the guilt player, that I am, and the one who desire the entire world to revolve around me, left a little note, to the effect/affect, *"I thought that we had plans."*

I head home via traffic on the freeway South. Too much so. I hit the surface streets, and cruise on in. There I was and here I am.

Actually, here I sit, on a whole big feeling of ickyness. It has been building. The life with someone you don't really dig, or the attributes thereof and a life in general, pounding hard below the belt with artistic frustration. I should write about it. But, who reads poetry anymore anyway? And, they sure don't pay you for writing it. And, the

158

publishers all want you to subsidize them—
want you to pay to play.

Or, I should paint it. Tell the story with
visuals. You know, abstract style. But, and/or,
art/painting(s)—who the fuck knows what to
do with those.

And, for that matter, I am so broke I
have been out of canvas for six days and no
danero to buy any. And, in truth, I have no real
creative artistic space at all, except for here at
these semi silent keys as the ocean waves
moves and groves outside.

Yeah, I know... All the books I should
have written in all of this never-employed time.
But, the frustration pounds hard. I seek excuses
to run away; anywhere, to anything—to the
arms of people I do not wish to be with; only
to be slam-dunked hard against the far side of
life.

So anyway, I guess that brings us to
yesterday. No, no, no... Still the day before.

The main L.A., via Taiwan, babe gives
me a ringy on the tele and apologies. She went
with her roomy to the *Brentwood Art Fair;*
didn't realize that we had made plans.

We actually hadn't. I just lead her to
believe that we did. You know, all for the sake
of the melodrama...

So, she is to come over *pronto.* I had
only caught about three hours of a Z-session
the night before, so I was tired after having to
get up at 7:00 AM to be to the race.

Funny, 7:00 AM... I once named a band
that. It was to be a beatnik kind of cool sound

poetry, etcetera. Had the whole concept. Saturday Jim sat in for sessions on the bass but he had a new family and other things on this mind, so after a few gigs, he was out—A— there. Never did find anyone else to do it with. So much for the memories...

Back in the present... I caught a few Z's, got up, made some pasta, and then she showed. Showed in one of her way bitchy, really bad moods that she continually gets in—blames them on everyone but herself; mostly blames them on me.

Her car had gone down at the gas station. Her bad blue '70s conti pimp mobil had blown its auto—trany bushings and the shifter was a-moving around. The gas hop fixed it on the temporary side but didn't do a thing about *fixin'* her.

She came way down on me for a time: complained, criticizing, eceter—a—mundo.

Finally, we bailed heading down *Corona Del Mar* way for a little dip that I had desired to do. I was to buy her a wetsuit *en route*. Me, buy her... Me, with no *danero*. Her, with a twenty dollar an hour paste-up job. Again, who's the fool?

All done to keep the savages calm.

Anyway, the good news, I guess, was, we couldn't find one that fit her. So, she was destined to borrow one of mine.

We get there, *Corona Del Mar,* in the late spring afternoon. The wind is blowing. It is cold. None-the-less, I was up for it. I gave her my long winter wetsuit. I took my summer gear; all *Body Glove,* of course.

Into the head she goes to change. Into, well over, the rocks we go. Into the water. Cold and murky as all hell. Me, with a short suit on. I couldn't see a fucking thing.

Well, so much for me complaining for several weeks that we only do what she wants to do, (which is/was true), but her now, I got stiffed by the *Divine Mother Ocean.*

So dinner, sex that she wasn't really into. Being in a bitchy mood and all. The old adage holds true. I mean like, chicks, once they are with a dude for a time, let their body go to shit and their sex get way boring. They do *nada,* just lay there and let you make *'em cum—* not like in the beginning(s) when there is something to prove.

We go to sleep.

Morning rolls around. A bit of a fight here or there. She is always a bitch anymore. We take her ride into the local gas station of a mechanic which I know and I am to drive her to downtown to work. A donut and a cup of the mud for her *en route.* Nice fucking guy that I am. I got up early, to drop her off.

Now/then, it was my job to go and hunt down the part that was needed for her ride. Here and there; did that—slid it over in the direction of the homeboy mechanic. Hit the P.O. Box. Then, came home side.

Now/there/here I was, way drained, tense, burned out, and generally in a really shitty space. I had planned to finish up this

161

book of aphorisms I am transferring paper to disk. But, energy = O. So, I decided to head on over to FM, *Farmer's Market,* up L.A. way for a little lunch. Well, actually, my breakfast.

I drive. The traffic sucks. I get up in that lo-cal and go to hit a bank. An ATM machine on Fairfax and Beverly to get a few extra bills for the chow. The *mutha fucking* ATM machine eats my card. Fuck me!

I go into the bank. Fucking long lines. I try to get someone; finally I do. I figure, *'No problem,'* just go inside the machine, pull my card out, and slice the card my dir—e~c—tion. But no! This asshole West H'wood faggot bank worker had to go through this whole fucking thing. First, he says I have to show him my driver's license and sign a form. *'Okay, let's do it so I can get the fuck out of here.'* Then, he decides that he has to call his main bank office to find out why the machine ate my card. *'Maybe your machine is fucked up, asshole.'* They say, his bank's main office says, to shred my card. Well fuck that! Then, he calls my bank's 800 number and they dick around for twenty minutes. Finally, post asking my social security number, they say it is cool to give me back my card. Fucking life sometime, man...

So, post all that, fuck the ATM. I just go FM with the cash I'm *ridin'* on. Get there and the place I had planned to chow down at is way crowded. I said, *"Fuck it,"* and I started to bail but then decide, *'This is fucked up! I dove all the way here. I cannot let this day be ruined!'*

So, I stayed; changed my menu plans and went and had a little pasta.

Came home, definitely worse for the wear.

Then, I began to work on my cars, which were both breaking down. My Jeep, which was the one I took up L.A. way, was way far bad. I mean something was up. The bad pup had no acceleration and so on. Finally, post a lot of bullshit and going to get parts, I get it back up to par.

My *356,* on the other hand, getting old. I go to fix it, but it wouldn't start. So, fuck me...

And/Plus I hate to fucking get my hands dirty!

About then, the chick calls. She got a ride over to Manhattan Beach and I was to pick her up there; which I did.

Funny, this little crib, the one where I was supposed to pick her up at... I pull up. I had seen it before. It was up on 28th Street. I actually looked into moving into that same place/space a few years back. But, it was way too small. And, as it was right off the street, you could hear way too much car noise for me to be able to get any sleep. Strange world...

Her ride; this thirty-five year old wonder white bread, who drives a *Corvette* and complains, (the first words out of her mouth), that she can't afford to pay for it. Complains about it, the moment I meet her. L.A. huh...

Post, we go for her, my main L.A. babe via Taiwan's ride—not finished. She is pissed and all into the bitchies again. I take her to an expensive dinner on the plastic passion. So-so in a so-so world. The chick wants to bail home now.

I could not fucking believe this. I mean she was not even going in to work tomorrow/today and she wants to go home. Tells me that she feels grimy, and that she has got to pick up a check tomorrow from one of the art departments that she works for or all the checks she sent out will bounce. And, if I would like, I could come spend the night her direction. But, she needs to go home!

Now. I mean come on... Am I a fucking fool or what? I do all her dirty work for her, today; add in dinner and the etcetera—all because she owes her credit cards maybe $500.00. As such as so, she has me to pay for everything. Me, when I got my own financial issues.

I mean take the dude for the ride and don't even chill back and crib down. I could not fucking believe it.

"Here, just take my car."

And, she did. She took my Jeep.

Here again, she being pushy, selfish, and the like... She was out-a-here, out-a-there; knowing that my *356* wasn't running and that I wanted to do a health spa session, ectera—a—mundo. I mean, that is way fucking selfish.

Now, my *Singapore Airlines Stewardess* babe calls me about this point as I walk back

164

in, crib central. Funny, I was just turning the phones back on, when she called.

When the babe stays over, like she did the previous evening, I have to shut them all down—down in fear of some other of my babe(s) contacting me on the telephone lines. Like said, which just occurred...

She, the stewardess, gave me the basic love rap; equally zero in a zero world, as far as I was concerned. Wanted me to head up Seattle way on Friday. She would be there. *"Thanks, but I think not."* So much for that.

The main and central babe; she calls me when she gets home. I tell her off. She turns it around on me as she always does, stating, *"I am this. I am that..."* But hey, selfish is selfish and fucked is fucked. But, I guess without all this—this minor piece of meaningless literature would have not been created.

So, the melodrama begins to thicken in my mind. I go down, try to start the *356*. No-go. The battery; yes. It must be that. I charge it up.

Midnight, a bit past, I am on the road: the soft road; not the hard road. I hit over to *Denny's* on Sunset. Down, sitting next to me, is a girl, Black; African-American. A dancer, so she tells me. She was very talkative. Talkative, interested, and available. Though I knew/know, that this could equal something more. Me, I am/was just not there—not really willing and/or in the space to put in the play on a stripper. They just have too many problems.

She was pretty; yes. But, I just did not have the energy.

Post, I make it to the newsstand off of Hollywood and Cahuenga. I look, I seek, I was handed a dream, but I choose to go home solo. No second dream being placed upon my plate.

AM, the phone, it once again rings. It wakes me from my sleep. I think not to answer it; for I know who it will be. I do. She tells me,

"I know I didn't leave your car unlocked..."

Fuck! I knew what was coming next...

My radio, in the *compartment de glove,* they took it out. I kept it in there, as it was a Jeep, and it needed to be hidden/locked down. I mean, this is L.A.—stealers/junkies/thieves; they steal everything. But they—they found their way to it. They took it out. They left the glove compartment opened. My tapes, my car cover; they took it/them too. Even my very special, go to Tibet, safari hat, (that I took and wore in Tibet), which rides shotgun central with me; keeps the sun off of my face; they grabbed it too. Even stole my spare tire cover, covering my spare tire; hanging/bolted to the back of my ride. Took my stuff. Left the car unlocked as she had left it unlocked. She denied it, but I knew she left it unlocked. She always leaves her cars unlocked. They left it open. Left it for her to find—emptied.

I wake up, AM—a phone call; as pre-described. With nothing left to do—post the call, I go outside. I go onto my patio. A cup of ginseng tea in hand. The wave(s) were pumping. The sun was out and warm. I thought/wanted to go catch a few waves, maybe even some rays.

Me, catch some rays, the one who avoids the rays to the maximum. I smiled as I thought that thought.

The rays? Me, I have a fashion show coming up in one month; first of June. Funny, huh?

Like I say, *"Life it is funny... Funny, if you see it as a joke."*

Bohemian me; thirty years old and walking a high-fashion runway show. Me, a high-fashion-passion model.

They called me. They want to pay me big dollars. Big money, like before. I laugh at myself. I smile as I type this.

It is not like it was—no not anymore. Not like it was, (way back when), in Tokyo. Back when they used to pay me big money to do that kind of shit.

They had me walk. They took photographs of me—wearing whatever clothing line that they, the fashion designers, thought was cutting edge—clothing that they wanted to hock.

They took pictures of me. They had me walk. They paid me for my services during the day. Me, I would dance, party, and drink all the money I got paid down at night.

I guess I should have kept those photographs. Funny, I never even really wanted *'em.* Didn't even see most of them. But, they're out there somewhere...

I thought it was all a joke; to be paid big bucks to do that meaningless nonsense. But, here I am again. Thirty and walking a runway... Doing it for the money. I am a whore.

But, it is like the games and the dance, go on and on and I got no more time. So, play like a *playa.'* Dance like a dreamer. And, I guess, do whatever is presented to me.

But, back to the story—back to the tale; for you see it has been going on as I write. A telephone call here. A telephone call there. She calls me this morning. I make the cardinal manipulation mistake. I told her what she did hurt.

"You are just weird and messed up," she responds. *"You are too sensitive and care about stuff too much. Plus, you always leave me. But, when you come back, I'm still here."*

She does have a point... But, what does that have to do with all my stuff getting ripped off?

Passion and the promise, all dished out by the girlfriend from hell. My fault, I know... Don't stick so tight. Don't get attached. Don't lay it on so thick. Like soul boy, Saturday Jim, my homeboy, always tells me,

"That's why you can't get rid of them. You lay it on too thick..."

168

You know, like I spell it out,

"I'm the man of your dreams. The one you've been waiting for all your life. Let's hit Vega and get married..."

In any case, that was convo one. Convo two, convos three, convos four equaled more of the same... She says,

"Calm down. It's no big deal."
"Yeah," I say, *"It's never a big deal when it's not your stuff."*

Sadly, she is so selfish that it doesn't even faze/phase her, getting all my stuff ripped off.

So right, that all else is wrong.

About 11:50 AM now. I still hear the waves crashing calling me out. I have looked, but as the AM has faded, they are not, any longer, *like so tubular dude.* They are flat shore-pounders. I guess I will just wait. She will be here in a relative few. Will wait and watch as this melodrama plays out.

Who is the fool? I don't know?

But life, where we end up, it is funny sometimes. Funny if you look at it that way...

I was cruising down the elevator of this old brick apartment building over on Wilshire Boulevard. It was about 9:30 in the PM. I was leaving a friend of mine's place.

Now, back in the day, this building was probably all the shit. You know, in the 1930s or '40s. It still had all the lavish and intricate decor from way back then flyin' high on its walls and upon its ceilings. Hell, Raymond Chandler probably set up some of his characters living in it; the apartment building that is. Or, maybe he lived in it. I do not know?

But, that was back then, not now... Now, it was just an old brick apartment building skirting Wilshire Boulevard on, what I would consider, the funky side of the photograph.

The elevator stops. In gets this young chick. Her eyes saw me. They glued hard onto my form. My imagination was set in motion, if you know what I mean and I think that you do.

The main thing that struck me about her was that she was young. My age-ish... I took note of this because, I mean, the majority of the people that inhabited this space were old. Old, decrepit, dying and lost in living in an age of another era. You know, like the 1930s or '40s; back when this building was probably all the shit.

I don't know, maybe they couldn't afford it back then. Back, when wages were

170

lower. But now, here, the *late-en-ing* 1980s; well, with their social security checks in hand and the building falling into disarray, the price; it was probably right. They could live where they always dreamed of living. Dreamed of being, back in the day...

Good for them! A dreamed lived is always a good thing.

Anyway, back to the chick...

She was average in the *so-so* department. Longish brown, wavy hair. Had on one of those average tops with average jeans on the low end. But, what she was—was a female. And, she had her eyes on me.

"Do you live her?" she asked.
"No."
"I didn't think so. I never saw you before."

But, there was more on her mind that that. It was so obvious.

Small talk leads to small nothings...

"You want to go see Johnny Thunders?" she exclaims.

Now, Johnny Thunders was the guitar player for *The New York Dolls,* way back when. When I was like thirteen, maybe fourteen, they were one of my favorite bands. The new breed of *Glam* rebellion verging into/onto *Punk.*

I knew he was playing. I am fairly connected, you know. But, I didn't really think about going.

171

He was going to be playing at the *Coconuts Teaser,* over on the edge of the *Sunset Strip.* It's a dumpy little shit club. More a club for the dreamers who wish they were on their way up, than a place for a one-time seminal rock star to be playing on his way down.

But, what was a guy like me supposed to do? A chick invited me. I had no plans on my plate. And, with that glimmer of lust she had in her eyes, directed my direction, all I could say was, *"Sure."*

Now, here is as good as place as any for, *"A something,"* I believe needs to be mentioned... Mentioned, for those of you who wish to embrace my world; *the realm(s) of the night.* The thing is, you've got to be ready to do what it is you got to do. Which means, you ALWAYS must be dressed for the occasion. Or, at least, have the appropriate *duds* with you in tow...

Me, I checked my look. I was clean.

To go back in time and space in order to place substance upon said statement, I first realized this *fact-of-night-life* reality when I had hit over to Saturday Jim's, on Saturday, a few years the previous. I mean, I just expected we were going to have one of our typical, do it every Saturday, sit around, watch T.V., and drink beer all day sessions. But, I get there...

"Were goin' to Vegas. I'm gettin' married!"

172

Turns out his lady was pregnant. And, though they had dropped the previous one. They decided they were settled in, and this one, they would keep. Their daughter, my godchild. The only baby I have ever held. Held her, at her baptism. Frankie Avalon was there. But, that's another story...

Me, I was the only one invited for the nuptials. But, I looked at what I was wearing: sweat pants and a polo shirt. All be it they were very cool sweatpants and a very nice polo shirt. But, I just could not go to their *nups* dress like that.

So me, I jumped back in my ride and headed on the return to Manhattan Beach where I was cribbed up at the time. They live(d) in *The Val*. So, it was one of those jam as fast as you can over a long and trafficked jammed distance: heart beating, blood pressure pumping.

I got down to my crib, grabbed a pair of 1940s vintage baggy cuffed pants, a 1960s vintage oversized sport coat, and a Gumby and Pokey tee-shirt, that I was into wearing back at that period of history. Then, I hit the local liquor store, bought S.J. a bottle of *The Jack* and fought my way back to *The Val* through traffic. From there, in two cars, we headed for Vegas. I mean hey, they needed their honeymoon space and all... Didn't want to ride with *'em* and be in their way, if you catch my meaning...

The point being, if you're not ready to do it/do anything at a moment's notice, you may miss out on life-changing opportunities. So, you *gots'* to be ready. This evening, I was.

There were a few problems with this situation from *the get,* however. She wanted to drive. Now, the *Coconut Teaser* was/is on the other side of town; northbound. And, I have long known that you always need an escape route. But, she was insistent that she drive. So me, I played along.

We got into her, verging on the junky, *Volkswagen Rabbit.* And, we were off.

She was nice enough, you know. No real obviously flaws. And, she was obviously really into me. So, I got sucked in...

By now; by this point in my live, I should have known better...

She was hungry, *en route,* so we hit McDonald's over on Vine just south of Sunset B.L.V.D. Did the drive-thru *thAng.* She ate. I did not. Not interested in that breed of food.

We get to the club. We park her car over off of Laurel Canyon and we head for the door. We get to the door. Me, being the gentleman that I am, pay for her and I to enter. Ten bucks per. Whatever...

As we walk through the door, she takes my hand. AOK in my book. I'm thinking things are getting more interesting.

The first band was finishing up. They sounded like shit. I was glad I had not had to listen to them.

"Johnny Thunders will be on next," comes the announcer blasting over the loudspeakers.

174

Now, just for the record, this place is dirty. At least it looks dirty—feels dirty. It has low ceilings. Its walls are painted like a fluorescent blue and orange. I never liked the place. I got sucked into going here/there more than a couple of times. You know, to see *uck* bands that my friends or *friends-of-friends* are in. But, I just don't dig it.

Anyway, with a few to kill, we hit the bar. I bought us a round.

We're *chillin'* at the bar as the elixir of the gods and/or the goddesses, (depending on how you want to view the equation), is *hittin'* my veins. Things were *goin'* as they were *goin.'* AOK, so I thought.

For some reason, she wanted to tilt her bar-lean, get up, and walk around. As mentioned, I didn't really dig the place, so I was content to kick back, standing parallel to the bar, and let the night of drink and impending sex, with a white-chick, live out its reality.

But, *none-the-less,* to keep the *goin' goin'* with her, I walked... She holds my hand.

Straight-away she sees a guy. He sees her. She goes up to him. He goes up to her. My hand is left dangling on its own—cast to the wind of aloneness.

I thought to look down and study its instantaneous isolation. But, I did not.

She walks over to the guy. She introduces me. She plays me up as *all-that.* A handshake of nothingness.

He was just a guy. A zero human being: short hair, a tee shirt, jeans, and a crap leather jacket. But, as if an instantaneous dance of illumination had just occurred—one that I had no knowledge of; she walks off with him. Him, that zero guy.

I look at myself. I study my drink in my hand. Me, I was standing there all alone. I had been duped. I was just a piece of meat brought into the mix to make the boyfriend jealous.

Now, all of this—this situation; the one I'm *speakin'* of, it probably lasted no more than a few seconds. But, it certainly felt like more than that as I stood there in all my alone emptiness wondering what the fuck to do. But, whatever the case may be; there I stood, alone in a nightclub that I didn't even want to be in, waiting to see a guy/his band that I didn't really care about seeing—great in his era, but those times, long gone past.

Here/him/this place; all it was—was lost; like all of the lost. Lost, just like me. Plus, and etcetera, I was surrounded by a bunch of losers. Those of my age group who remembered. Those of a younger age group who were trying to recapture a past that they could never truly live; never truly understand. But, all losers, just the same. It made me feel like a loser. I mean, FUCK! I had just gotten pretty seriously *bitch slapped*.

I walked around a bit; lost in my *lost-ness*. Trying to figure out, how the fuck I was going to get back to my ride which was parked

176

a good ten miles away, over there off of Wilshire.

And, as if to *bitch slap* me again, the chick, the one I came with, the one who invited me, she walked by me once, then one more time, *hand-in-hand,* in love with her man. Fuck me!!!

That was it! I was just going to fucking bail. I didn't care about seeing Johnny Thunders, anyway...

I put my empty drink glass down on the bar, headed for the door. Waved a, *"See ya,"* to the barkeep who I vaguely knew. Remember, I had unwantingly been here/there before.

I step outside. Just at that moment, walking up, comes this sweet little white-bread of a curly long blonde-haired vixen, wearing a purple miniskirt and a black, almost see-through, top. She had a friend in tow; a female. Her friend, well... She was extremely average—about all she could hope for was so-so on a good day.

"He's hot," she, the blonde vixen, says to her friend.

She says it, so I can hear it.

I mean now, come on... What's a guy like me supposed to do? Neck-in-neck with them, I'm back in.

It was like one of those moments, where the babe sees what she wants. And, in this case, what she wanted was me.

Alright... I am ready. Two can play this game.

There was like no discussion as to what was to come next. It was accepted. It was known. It was fact. In fact, it was almost like the same feeling as I had/as I experienced with the chick in the elevator; an hour or so the previous. So, understand me when I say, I was just a bit nervous. I mean, a man can only take so many *bitch slaps* in one night. But me; being who I be, all I could do was play the game.

Inside we go. She looks around studying the place like any new-be would do. She looks at her girlfriend. She looks at me.

"Where can we get a drink?"
"I have just the place..."

So, we stroll back over to the dirty, painted blue bar. Man, I just don't like that place! Nod to the barkeep. He smiles; seeing my new and improved situation. He comes over.

She wanted a gin and juice. Her friend a whiskey and coke. Me, I hit another vodka and cranberry.

I ordered. I was pulling out my cash. But she, the babe I'm *takin'* about, wouldn't let it happen—wouldn't let me pay. She pulls out a shit-load of ones and slaps *'em* down. AOK in my mind.

So, we leaned there, against the bar. You know, the dirt blue one, with a dirty brown top. And, we spoke; the girl(s) and I.

178

In a way, I felt sorry for her friend, (the so-so on a good day one). As she stood behind her; my babe. She stood behind the girl in question, (who was in-between), the friend and I. She/the other girl—the so-so girl, was looking around. I could tell she was feeling lost and alone; just like I had—just a few moments the previous. I kept trying to bring her into the conversation. You know, make her feel part of the team. That was until...

"You like her? I can move if you want, so you two can be closer."

I laughed it off. I mean, what can you say to that to not embarrass the friend but to keep my love-focus honed on the desire-full object front and center.

"I see what I'm lookin' at. And, I like what I see." I respond.

With that, all questions were answered. None remained.

We hung there for a bit longer; there at the bar. Then, the distraction(s) began... This dude, this young dude. I knew him from Redondo, (where I live), from the shop where they make and customize my guitars. I knew he was in a band. But... He was young. I wondered how he even got in. I don't think he was/is twenty-one. Maybe eighteen, nineteen; but not twenty-one. But then, I though back to my early teens. I had a friend whose father was the security guard at *The Whiskey A-Go-Go* and we used to get in and watch bands there all the time; way before we were supposed to. We saw a lot of bands. Some of the big ones that launched in the seventies. Saw them there/then when they were small; before they became big. So, I just pasted on this dude's presence with a thought to, *'Whatever...'*

Anyway, he was all dressed in black leather. Pants and a jacket. I though he looked kind of funny. But hey, he rocked the look. He was young and he was who he was.

He comes up, all excited to see me. Whatever... I tried to shew him away. But, he wasn't going anywhere.

Next came up the chick that had come with him. Also, all excited to see me.

Now, here is where things get/got a little complicated. She, the friend of this South Bay guy, was this very fine specimen of a chick on the Thai side of the equation. We had come close to *doin'* the dirty once. Once at this one rock stars house that lives over South Bay way. I guess you could him a rock star. I mean they did and/or do play his videos on MTV. Anyway, there/then; back then, at a house party, we got lip locked and all. But, it didn't jump off/didn't quite happen. I forget why. But/though I still held a cock-full of desire for her. And, from her glance, she held the same for me. Well, I hope she doesn't have a cock. But, you know what I mean...

In that moment, in that time-frame, in that club that I didn't even want to be in—it

180

was one of those weird situations that I realized I could have played it all kinds of different directions. But, I felt the longing lust of this new breed of, (just met), curly blonde-haired love standing right in front of me. So, my eyesight was fixed upon her.

That being said, as I still was remembering the *bitch slap* of a few minutes the previous, I was a little bit tentative. *'But fuck, how could I turn any of this down or turn away?'* The thought/realization ran through my mind.

I mean, she, (the blonde vixen), had appeared—a gift from the heavens, come to rescued me; save me from all the fate of *bitch slapped* zeroness. I mean like, how could I forgo her now?

"Let's get out of here," I said
"What? What about Johnny Thunders?"
"Do you really care?"
"No, it was my friend who wanted to see him."
"So, let's go."
"What about her?"
"Bring her along if she wants to come."

So, that was the first play in the play of motion. Leave this den of inequity. Bail on the people who knew me from where; over there. Leave the Thai chick for another time. Hopefully... Take the friend, (her friend), along for the ride, if you catch my meaning... If not, that's alright too. I had my vision set on my object of affection for the evening.

She spoke to her friend. I see nodding. I questioned what the nodding meant.

"Okay, let's go."

Her friend pushed forward. I knew what it meant. And hey, a little *manajatwa* never hurt anybody; right? We hit for the door.

"Where you going, man?"
"Were bailing."

The dude dressed in leather, speaks to the Thai chick. I see heads nodding, *"Yes."* They start to follow us. Fuck!

Outside, the basic discussion of what and where to go, went down.

As I didn't want to eat the shit McDonald's food with that other chick, previously described, I realized I hadn't eaten all day. And/so, in needing someplace to go... And/plus, I didn't want to get my drink on without something in my stomach; I suggested *Canter's,* over on Fairfax, as an interim to the interlude. I mean, it does have a bar in the back, and it does have a certain vibe, if you like that old-school Jewish deli sort of *thAng;* which I do. But, the friend didn't dig it there. She wanted to stay on Sunset. That meant there were two choices; at least in the department of the *departmento: Tiny Naylors* or *Rock n' Roll Denny's.* We choose the latter.

Though I didn't really want the other team in tow, you know: Leather and Lace, but

182

they were set on *hangin'* with me. Why? I do not know? But, they followed.

Just as we're starting to walk away, the situation even gets more complicated. This dude, also from the music shop, down the South Bay way, comes out. I hadn't seen him inside. Thankfully...

"Where you guys going?"

Now, just as in the case of Leather, this guy is not a bad guy. He does have this very nasty waist length hair, however. I mean, if it was thick and full it would be all-good. But, it is not. It is all stringy and shitty looking.

In any case, he decided... He was going too! I could tell my babe, the new one, was *a-wonderin'* what was *a-goin'* down and what had she gotten herself into. I wondered too...

I tried to bail us out and get us *ridin'* solo, but it did not work. So me, with my ride elsewhere, I pile into the back seat of her friends 1980 two-door sedan. It was what it was. The ride that is. I rode back seat bitch.

We drove a couple of blocks over to *Rock n' Roll Denny's*. My people and I... I, of course, use the term, *"My people,"* quite loosely. But, the people, they followed in their car.

Inside, the *peep's* from the South Bay wanted us to all sit together in one of those big booths. Thank god they were all full. We got two booths. Forcefully, I guided them to the booth behind us. I slide in with the two babes.

Now, getting to know talking goes as getting to know taking goes. The girl, my girl, told me she was a dance instructor.

Looking at her and thinking of all those one dollar bills she had paid the bar tab with back at *The Coconut Teaser,* I came right back at her.

"You're a dance; right?"

She played it off for a time, pretending that she was a dance instructor. You know, a real dancer: ballet and all that shit. But, I knew...

I mean, really... I don't know what it is; why do all the strippers try to lie about what they do? Like, they all say that they are bartenders, waitresses, dance instructors, and the like. I mean, are those jobs somehow better?

The truth being told, more times than I can count, I have smashed my head against midnight at places like *Jumbo's Clown Room, Cheetas,* and *The Star Gardens.* Now, in truth, I'm not really a big fan of strip clubs. To me, they're kind of for the dudes who got no other chance. And they, the dude with no chance, actually think that they are going to hook-up there. They're not! You're not! That does not happen there! The chicks, they all play you, to get you to throw down bucks for the private lap dances. And then, most dudes go home dick in hand.

184

I mean hell, fact be told, I am one of the few men that I have ever known to hook up at a strip club—which is something very few men can claim. Mostly, the fact of the matter being is, that the reason most of the dudes who go there can't hook up is because they're fucking losers. They ain't got *nothin'* going on. They walk in there with their dick in their hand and dream about what it could be like.

Mostly though, I kind of feel sorry for the babes in that profession. Though it is their choice to be there, and you have to be at least marginally fucked up to make that choice... But, they get so objectified. And, once in the/that lifestyle, it is hard to get out.

Anyway, it all is what it is...

So, we sat there in the booth, talking. The friend(s)/my friend(s), from the other side, kept trying to draw me into their other booth(s) conversation. I was not interested.

Me, I got my needed grub on. Remember, I hadn't eaten all day.

Next, I was set to go and get my party on. On with her and I and maybe her friend; who was actually a very quiet person. On with them, not including the ramblings and admirations from the booth behind.

Post, we hit the cash register. The two dudes from the South Bay were calculating who was to pay what on their bill. Acting/behaving like losers, I must add. Digging through their wallets to see who had how much money. The Thai chick, she had told the waitress to put her meal on my bill. I looked at the bill. I looked at her. I smiled. Yeah, she knows how to play it... I'll have to look her up on the flip side.

I paid. Quickly, I tried to get the two girls out of the picture before *The South Bay Three* could catch up. We're about to get in the car. They, *The South Bay Three,* however, come running up.

"Where you guys going?"

I look at her. Her, my new-found babe. She looks at me. But, she is good-natured. She smiles. I am not good-natured. I do not.

The plan set for the apartment of her friend. Down over off of Santa Monica and La Brea. We get in. This time my friend, my babe, exclaims,

"Let me climb in back with you."

I smiled. I don't know what I did, what I said, but whatever it was, I did it right.

We cruise on. I looked, and sadly, yes, we were still being followed.

The girl, the friend, the driver, up front, I felt sorry for her. You could see/feel she was lost in the alone. I could see it/could feel it, for I have known that feeling all too well.

Had my party bro, Venchinzo been there with me, he could have taken that feeling away from her. I thought to call him. But it, this evening, was so in motion, it was all so conceived/contrived by forces I had no control over, that I had no idea where it was going to

186

take me. Perhaps, someplace very bad. I knew it would not be fair to bring him into this web of deceit. So, I let that idea fade.

In the back seat, she; her and I, all smiles. It was going very well. Small talk. I even took her hand. I held it. She looked down at my action. She studied my hand holding hers. She smiled.

In front of the friend's place, she put the opening the garage door key into the open the garage door lock. It began to open.

"What about your friends?" She asked.
"Don't worry about 'em," I say.

Actually, once again, I had hoped to lose them. But, they apparently found a parking spot on the street, and they were there waiting at the locked front glass door of the building as we walked towards her apartment on the second floor.

All inside. The apartment was what it was: off white walls, a couch, a T.V., a chair or two... I was like all Hollywood apartments.

I hit the couch. The friends... I hate to keep using that term, but for lack of a better word... They hit the chairs and the floor. They, *The South Bay Three.* They were set to hang.

God, I hate hanging out. It is just not who I am. I hate parties: small or large. I hate small-talk.

The girls, mine and her friend, grabbed us a few beers. We drank them out of the bottle.

The mind altering/mind bending/ mind damning small-talk went on.

I was in hell. Hell, but next to me sat an angel. A stripper angel. Plus/and, there was that little Thai flower who kept giving me the eye of the almost remembrance, as well, from across the room.

Heaven and Hell, I had to do something. I could no longer sit/exist in purgatory. I look at her. My new babe. I say,

"I going to step outside for a minute, you want to come?"

Now, there it was; the magic set in motion—the moment where everything can either go one way or the other. Had she said, *"No,"* I was just going to fucking bail. Catch a taxi or something back to my car. Hell, maybe even walk the miles and the miles, through the night.

But, she said, *"Yes."*

We went outside. We leaned again the rail in front of her friend's apartment; stared out into the nighttime courtyard of a lost night in the lost/then found realms of Hollywood.

She stood close to me. I close to her. We both like what we were feeling.

Now, I knew something had to jump off or this night was going to be robbed from me/from us: her and I. I knew/had figured out this wasn't where she lived, so I asked,

"Where do you live?"

188

"Oh, I, live bout three blocks over."

I smile,

"Feel like taking a walk?"

She looks at me. She studies me. She smiles.

"We should tell 'em we're leaving."
"Why?"

Again, she smiles.

We: her and I, walked through the Hollywood night, *hand-in-hand.*

Now/here/there the small-talk, it was no so bad.

We kissed once or twice as we moved forward. Alone, we were alone/together; not being haunted by the ghosts that haunt the realms of my nights and those, like *The South Bay Three,* that haunted me.

We get to her apartment building; a bit funkier than her friends. We go inside. A small single apartment. A little bit messy. Not like her friend's place. That place was clear/clean. Well, at least clearer/cleaner.

As we walked into the apartment, the lights were out. But, lights did shine in from the street, through the window.

She reached. She turned on the lights. I reached. I turned them off. She smiled.

She leads me, *hand-in-hand,* to the couch. She had a couch, a chair, a mattress on

the floor, over there. We sat down. We kissed.
We kissed a lot. We kissed for a long time. She
kissed very well. It, her kisses, caressed my
lips like that needed drug, that sought after
elixir; which promises eternity—eternity in a
drop.

The clothing; well, it did begin coming
off as we sat there, lip-locked. Her top. My
sport coat. My shirt. Her bra.

She had fairly large, firm; very nice
boobs. I kissed them.

Then, the rest of our clothing began to
be removed. You know, the elements where
you have to stand up. Have to smile. Have to
make joking small-talk as it is being removed.

Naked/nude/bare; we held each other as
we stood. She was much shorter than me. But,
somehow our bodies fit together quite nicely.

We held each other for a moment. A
long-long moment. Then, she guides us to the
bed; the mattress on the floor.

We lay down. I could feel she was wet.
Very-very-very wet. We kissed. My cock slid
into her. I did nothing. She did nothing. It just
happened.

"Are you wearing a rubber?" She asked.
"No, are you?" I jokingly answer.

She giggled. We continue.

I guess in this day-and-age of herpes,
AIDS, and all the rest of the STDs, pasted down
for generation-after-generation, it is only a fair
question to ask.

190

She asked. I answered. But, in those moments of perfect perfection there never seems that there is a reason to question any further and/or to stop the perfect beauty of a perfect moment.

Saturday night; in the night air. Yeah, I had dumped *My Main and Current L.A. Babe,* I guess it was three days back now. So, I was *ridin'* solo.

The breakup was one of those big blowups where she came over and started to complain and yell, wanted to know why I wasn't serious about her, and all the bullshit that I have pre-described. She wouldn't leave or keep her voice down. I was sick of this shit. I told her that I was going to call the security guard, but when I went to do that, she grabbed the phone and set about to break a whole shitload of my stuff: telephone, java pot, telephone answering machine, T.V. remote control, and the etcetera.

Typical, if they are a nut job, I meet *'em.* And, they are always the ones I never really wanted to be with anyway. They just won't/wouldn't go away.

Finally, I ended up physically grabbing her, picking her up, and tossing her flailing body out the door.

Now, don't all you feminists come down on me. I am not trying to be *macho* here and I am not proud of it. But, I am sorry, sometimes there is just no other way to deal with the babes.

She finally left after crying for an hour or two, outside my door. She had sat down, leaned against it, and kept speaking to me though it; wanting to know how I could make her love me so much but not care about her; and all that dribble and bullshit.

Down at her car, I heard her do this little drive off/burn rubber session—try to re—gain some ego, I guess. I have heard it all before. May I never hear it again.

I laughed.

But, that is old news.

So, let's get onto the news of today; the now if you will. As the dreams keep pounding and the ocean keeps moving, the world it is spinning, and all of the time doesn't add up to anything at all.

Me, I hit my P.O. Box maybe 8:15 PM or so. A lot of bills came in and no *danero* to pay any of them. I went home. Tossed *'em* on the counter.

I was alone, you know. So, I kicked back at the crib. I had taken a bike ride down the strand to Venice earlier on in the day, so no need to go and get physical in that department again.

During the ride, I met a babe at a volleyball match I stopped to view for a minute or three. But, you know, like zero in a zero world. The ride, the time, the alone, and the etcetera—the day was just all too empty.

Like when you dump the babe and there's no one on tap to go and hit the sheets with. Life, it is lived like an addiction unfulfilled.

193

And creativity... I'm sorry, but I am just not full of it when I look around my place and there is still all this broken shit laying around that I have to clean up but just do not feel like doing it.

The other side of the issue... I didn't feel like sitting at home. So, post the P.O. Box, post the sitting and the staring at the destruction that my X had unleashed.. *"X,"* not, *"Ex."* X looks better. Anyway... Post all that. Me, I headed on down towards an empty little drive to Long Beach in the early summer, in my Jeep, with the top off.

I had a large cup the java *ridin'* shotgun. And certainly, no better place to be.

The night air felt good. The wind blowing though my hair felt even better. I looked around myself as I cruised down Pacific Coast Highway, (PCH). There were lovers in each other's arms, dates—a—going nowhere fast—marriages being proposed; everybody just casting themselves to a life of imprisonment where a promise only equals a dance in hell for eternity.

Fuck the marriages, man. All that leads to is someone to kill your time within a realm where there is no room for dreams.

I continued my cruise...

I drove past a *Harley* dealership and saw one of the new, more than *bitch'n,* Springer Front End jobs through the window. Definitely that is one of my current fantasies, a new *Harley*.

The java I drank was a large mug of the bad substance and I salted it down with *tres* sugars and had it *con letchy*. The caffeine did pump on an effect.

I was chilling somewhere in the middle of all of the said above. But wait! Excuse me, while I go set myself up with a java right now; 12:04 AM. The talk of the java got me *cravin'* the taste of said.

Okay... Coffee in hand, a quick and deep breath of the ocean air outside, and I'm back at it.

Now/then, I hit over to Santa Fe Avenue down Long Beach way. I thought that I would take a quick drive over on the industrial side of the picture to see if I could see any warehouse space that might be lease-able. You know, to use as creative space and all...

Didn't see much. Just a lot of Mexicans hanging tough outside the bars, eating at the roach coaches, getting in fights, and the usual things that people, with no place better to be, do on a Saturday night.

I hung a left onto Anaheim Avenue, drove over the little bridge, and was just hitting the main section of LB when walking to my left was this seriously intriguing babe of an apparent *Pavement Princess*. She looked me DEAD in the eyes.

You know, that is the way you always can tell if their love is for hire. The good girls, if they glance at you, then they look away. But, the children of the night; well, they stare you down.

Up just a half a block ahead, was *dos* of the roach coaches, full of Mexicans and a home bro or three on the side. So me, instantly, I became a little overwhelmed at the prospect of passion and/or having it taken from my hand if she successfully made her way to said locations full of a bunch of low-end guys with their dicks in their hand and I am sure a few dollars to spend in their pockets.

Being in the movement of motion, my ride drove onto the corner, next. Right turn, if you please.

Now, you know, life and especially its illusions—it is all a very funny dance. The, *"What ifs,"* and the, *"If onlys."*

More than assuredly, I was lost in *'em.* So me, I had to go around the block to check out this situation again; see what condition my condition was in. See if it/her was going to be lived my way.

The dark side streets of Long Beach, they are haunting. Lined with old houses, old apartments; filled inside with the less than affluent. It is a good place for someone like me. Someone who hasn't accomplished much; not much in the monetary picture. Its streets hold danger.

Danger, a place where you are safe. Well, at least safe from living too long.

Somehow the nowhere people, like myself, can find comfort/consolement in these realms/places where everything is easy—where no one has too much to lose, and the competition of the power hungry/money

196

flaunting L.A.ers—the successful sphere of influence/spaces of action, is not so much slapping one in the face.

But, back to the woman... Was she already there. There being bothered by the *may—hays* at the food trucks? Could this whole thing be real?

I mean, she obviously looked to be a Latina. One of those Latinas with an almost Asia vibe. They usually referee to them in local speak as, *"Chinas."*

She, she wore a red shirt. A black skirt. She had long stringy black hair. She, strutting her bad stuff down the boulevard.

I drove around the corner; the corner again and again and again. The thought of the whole picture made my cock get hard.

I pulled the pavement, turned the corner, and yes—yes indeed, there, in fact, she was still a—walking. Three quarters of a block up I see this car pulling up, he must have seen her too. The car, an old funky econo—box import.

It/he wanted her. I/me wanted her. But, then I realized; thinking to myself, I had the whole of about two dollars in my pocket. Mega—money, huh?

I drive past her. Our eyes meet: hers and mine. Meet deeply again, as I drove by. The car having pulled over, took his first dibs on the action.

I never saw inside of it, but my wheels turning and no bucks in my pocket to aid in the negotiations, I keep rolling.

I looked/I wondered, *'Where the fuck was a bank so I could get some cash and put my money on the table?'* I saw none.

Then... There... I remembered a few down by the new and renovating downtown. I, needless-to-say, hit on in that di—rec—t—ion.

I drove a little bit, over to where the elite of LB play at the large, new, international hotels. Hey, I play that game too Asia—side. But, here I am just a peasant, a peasant with big dreams, max—ed out credit cards, and style too serious for someone who is broke.

Me, I had to dick around the block(s) a bit to get to/find a branch that had an all-night teller ATM machine. But, I found one. I pulled out a hundred from my checking account and you know where I was a—head—ing.

Cash in my pocket, in a rush, I drove back down over to Pacific and on up to Anaheim. But, she wasn't hoofing. I saw her not. I was none too happy about that.

I drove the street(s). She was gone.

Fuck! I had lost my chance at casting a new dream to my life; maybe one that would have changed me/changed everything. Maybe one that would have killed me. Either way, I/it/this life, would have never been the same.

So, I cast it off to just another one of those foolish illusions that never quite happens. And hey, you never know what you're going to get anyway. Play it safe, right?

No fucking way! There is no art in safe!

The streets lights change in their patterns from yellow, to protect from the fog of the winter's night. The cars drove, the ethnic peoples, each frequenting their own desired establishment, lived.

I breathed fire/drove and drove some more—in search of/looking for. Finally, yes. There on the sidewalk. There she was. She again moved into the lost pagan realms of any man's arms who would pay for her attention.

I could not help myself, I needed a dose too. I drive up.

"Do you need a ride?"
"What?"
"Do you want to go for a ride?"

I stared at her. She was damn close to being the most perfectly formed and beautiful female person I had ever seen. Golden brown skin hiding the pumping blood which powered in her veins. Her long black hair fell almost to her waist. So greasy, it looked almost wet.

Age, yes. She was far too young to have worked this profession for far too long. But then, you never know... Some people are cast to darkest far too young in life.

But, what she was—was, a child to the streets. A child of the streets, just like me.

"Fifty dollars," she said. Those were her next word(s) after, *"What?"*

Now, that is not too bad of a price, considering inflation and the going rate. And, for sure, I had paid many times that rate in other time zones/other places. But, I had to ask.

"Fifty for what?"
"What?"

It was obvious she didn't understand English all that well. So, I re-stated...

"What do I get?"
"You get me."

I have to admit, I did like that answer. It was like perfectly Zen. So total. With that, I would have been happy to pay much-much more.

"Okay."

Damn, that was easy.

In the car she go. I drove off. She mentioned that she wanted to go to this motel up on PCH. *'No fucking way!'* I thought to myself. No way in the world am I going to go into one of those roach infested dives up there and maybe get stived by some lame pimp or something. And myself, not packing a piece or a blade. No way!

I told her that I wanted to do it in the car.

"In the car?"

She seemed to not quite understand. But, I knew where I stood in the situation and I knew where this interaction was going.

I asked her name, as I drove a block or three away; seeking a dark and desolated spot.

"Esperanza," she said.

Meaning, *"Hope."* I almost laughed.

As we moved onto the darker streets, where the passion plays for control over the heart center; *ajna charka.* I put my hand in-between her legs. I wanted to make sure what I was getting. For I don't play with no Oscar Meyer Wieners.

On her leg, slowly between her legs, I looked at her with a smile, as my hand made its way. No, no underwear; she was ready. And yes, in was insertions mode central, she was, in fact, a female.

I found this little spot. The houses of the area seemed to be shut down early for the evening. I pulled in. I pulled up. I was already stroking a mean *hard-on.* I mean, I had already had my hand in the soup.

"Here?" She inquired.
"Yeah, but wait a minute."

You see, with that large travel mug of the java I had drank; me, I had to hang one serious piss. And I did not want the moment in the motion to be lessened by one physical need out weighting the other. If you catch my meaning.

I got out of the car. As I did the interior light came on just for a second and I saw the contour of her cheekbones, the perfection of her jaw. Yeah, she could have been a model, an actress, a star, in any other world but the world of nothing in which we live. Chalk up another kill for the devil, another wasted life.

I went to the back of my Jeep and tried to get the bad boy down in order to piss. But, with action at hand, it is none too easy of a chore. Finally, I had to just deal with the uncomfortableness of the pain of pissing through/via a semi *hard-on,* and let the juices flow.

Zipper up. Why I don't know? Back in the ride, I re—unzipped.

The wild thing. She immediately said in broken english,

"I like your dick."

I laughed and took her hand, placed it upon my power pup. She started to stroke it till she choked it, then went down on it and gave me a little head.

I guess I didn't realize it then, I realize it now, that she must have thought that was all that I wanted, when I told her I didn't want to go to the motel. But, I let the moment live on.

Putting my hand on her hair, it was dirty, yet soft. It was like the perfect definition of life and not unlike myself; refined, yet plastered

202

hard, for whatever reasoning, against the slam-dunked wall of life.

I am sure neither of us ever asked for our fates. Yet, somehow, in the middle of it all—all you can do is live it.

I started to think of dis—ease as she was down there. But, as my eyes stared up to the heavens, my mind went to the fact, *'Damn, this was almost way romantic.'*

I thought if this/if she had not been a whore, and/or if I could travel though time and space and erase her past—all these feelings of perfection within the perfection of them/itself could have equaled something more. Hell, this could be love.

'Fuck it,' I exclaimed in my brain. *'This is romantic and way-way better that dealing with the mundane of some stale old pussy that has gotten boring and been fucked in the same position way too many times.'*

Yeah, I lived the night/that night.

While she was down there *doin'* what she do, I reached in my sport coat pocket, pulled out my wallet, grabbed a rubber. Lifted her head up.

"What?" she said.

I guess, *"What,"* is her favorite word.

I showed her my rubber, opened it, and slapped it on. She looked confused as to how we were going to do it in the front seat, but I leaned over and reclined my love abode for the evening.

She lifted up her shirt; exposed, in the dim light, her golden body. She lifted up her bra in a northerly directly, guiding my eyes to her large, full breast. She pulled up her skirt. As stated, I already knew, no underwear... She had a full bush down there. I hope it isn't/wasn't full of crabs, scabies, lice, or something.

I pulled down my pants farther/up-ed my shirt. With the seat reclined, I climbed over onto her. And, I nailed that bitch to the cross.

As I lay there pumping away, she held me tight almost like a lover—almost like a dream.

Whore(s)... I mean, you know. It is like they want you to get it in and get it off. That's what they get paid for. And, the more the merrier. But, she was like the perfect kind, like you know, the perfect whore, the kind where you feel like you are getting what you pay for, like she almost likes what you are *a-givin.'*

I was just about to lay a slob deeply down into her mouth. Maybe she would go for it? Maybe? But, just as I moved into the position for the kill, to do just that, the thought came to me of the econo—box that had taken her off less than an hour before. I don't know... I just don't/didn't dig the previously dunked cookie kind of action. It's not like I didn't know what she had been *doin'* but it is who she was *doin'* it to. Maybe that dude had blown his cookies in her mouth, like she had tried to do to me? Maybe? I didn't know. Anyway, you can get one too many dis—ease—s between those teeth. So, I chose to say, *"No."*

In any case, she held me tight as I pumped away. It was one of those times when the rubber straps itself on too tight and it is way hard to get your rocks off. I even thought to change the bad boy, (the rubber that is), as I had another one or two in my wallet. But, I pumped on as I listened to her soft breath vibrate to the rhythm in my left ear.

Something took me over though, this chick, she had passion. I mean, I can't even put it into words. Funny huh? Me not being able to put it into words... But, it was like love, you know, man. It was like I was there with a lover.

Finally, I got it off. I rolled off.

"Good?" she asked.
"Yeah, you are very good."

I don't know what it was. But, something just came over me... I said,

"Look, I'm not trying to save your soul or anything; for both of our souls are far too gone for that. But, would you like to maybe clean-up and a spend a few days with me."
"What? Fifty dollars. Okay?"

I guess she didn't understand. I gave her the money, tried to make small-talk as we drove back to the funky old commercial boulevard, still lined with drunken *may—hays* and the disciples of the dark. She got out.

205

So, here I sit typing away. I guess it is a few hours later. You know, like the feeling comes over me to go back and head on down that way/her way—find her, pick her up; see her again. You know, like one of those passing loves that you move by on the street; seen once and never seen again. And, you always wonder about the possibilities that could have been lived.

In reality, she is probably in someone's else's arms right now. Yes, four hours later. No doubt, several men's arms. Several more men have known her.

For a moment though, she was mine. And, if nothing else, her soul will forever be captured in the pages of literary eternity.

I guess maybe someday, if I ever get old, (which I doubt that I will), I too can look back and be reminded.

As for the babe, main and current L.A., which I discussed at the beginning of this tale, she called maybe an hour ago,

"Hello," I said.
"What are you doing," she asked.
"You must have the wrong number," I stated.

I hung up. I turned off my telephone.

I mean, you know, fuck all that matrimony shit. The dreams are out there in the wasteland. Even if sometimes you got to do your time alone. The poetry is born in the illusion and the mystic takes it all, judges nothing, placing everything into the realms of consciousness and living enlightenment.

I don't know? What do you think? 1:41 AM, should I take a drive back to LB?

For some reason, the idea/inspiration came to me to tie-dye a set of sheets and pillowcases that I had laying around. I hadn't tie-dyed anything since I had done a few tee-shirts way back when I was a teenager in the early 1970s. And this, being the tailing-end of the 1980s... Well, here/now there was/is no color(s) left—everything has pretty much gone black and white. Hell, even all my appliances are black: coffee pot, phone, espresso maker, toaster, blender, and the etcetera-a-mundo.

Anyway, they were/are a light blue set of sheets and pillowcases. I tapped 'em all up with the rubber bands—set in place to make the appropriate said tie-dye designed. Man, that took some time. I forgot how much work tie-dyeing was. I tossed them in the washer with the appropriate amount of purple dye. Blue and purple, I thought that made a nice color combination.

Out of the washer, rubber bands cut off. I was set. I had a new set of tie-dyed sheets. That's the beginning of the tale...

*   *   *

I think it is somewhat sad how people only care about themselves, about their own moment, their own space in time. That being said, I too fall prey to the selfishness of the selflessness. But anyway...

Venchinzo and I had been on a tear. We were parting very-very-very hard. We had a different club we would hit pretty much every night of the week. I would hit by his Venice Beach crib in the PM. We would throw back a few, maybe hit a bump or three, (you know, of the nose candy), and we would head out.

Now, Venchinzo has a *nine-to-five*. How the fuck he did what we did; what we do, was/is always a surprise to me. I mean, *yours truly*, I sleep till noon; sometimes later. Venchinzo, however, has to get up and hop the bus to work in the downtown *six AM-ish*. How he does it, I do not know. I mean it is rare, that I drop him off at his crib pre two in the AM. Anyway, and in any-case...

Tuesdays we usually hit this club up Hollywood way on Highland, *The Cathouse.* It blasts headbanger anthems and hosts its share of momentary rock stars. Neither of which are of any interest to me. What is of interest; there is a high percentage of babeage. More than a few to choose from each and every Tuesday night.

There, one evening, was this sweet young cutie of a via Japan; (Osaka to be exact), round-faced little doll. We meet, we talk, and that was that. It was on.

You know, she wasn't one of those women that take your breath away. But, she wasn't all that bad, either. She was what she was, what she was. Romance was in motion.

I did what I do... I play the game; promise 'em everything. *"I'm the man you been waiting for all of your life,"* and all that meaningless bullshit. My bud, Saturday Jim always tells me that is why I get into so much trouble with all the babes, and I can't get rid of *'em* when I'm done *doin'* what I do. I paste it on too thick. But, that is just who I am. Women, be warned...

Anyway, we went on a few dates. One night, I took her to this one club I hit on Mondays down here South Bay way, *The Raintree*. Monday is metal night. Again, not really my scene, but it is where a lot of my friends congregate and there too is a massive babe scene. So...

I pulled her in there. She likes all that headbanging shit. I really don't. We're sitting at the table with a couple of friends and up comes this one guy who, I guess, is considered a pretty big rock star. I'm not going to toss his name, as in a year or so his name will probably be long forgotten, as is the case with most, *"Rock Stars."* But... Her, my babe, was a big fan of his and her panties got all wet. Not all wet at him. He's kinda old. Wet that he was/is my friend.

Actually, it was kinda funny... We sat there that night, and he was all *talkin'* about all the anxiety attacks he had been having out on the road; equaling Xanax, Valium, and the like. Rock stars are human too.

Anyway, me knowing him, pretty much sealed the deal. But, I will get back to that in a moment.

210

She, (my babe on the line), had a roommate; also from Osaka. Not quite as cute, (not doll faced), as her, but okay in her own okayness. They lived in this very nice apartment building over on Franklin Avenue, skirting the Hollywood Hills. Her friend asked me to help her look at this car one day as she was in need of some guy to help her look at used cars. I had some free time. So, whatever...

We looked. It looked okay. She bought it. Turned out to be a piece of junk that some Middle Eastern guy had gotten as a wreck, did the basic bodywork to bring it up to sellable specs, and then dumped it on the unsuspecting; in this case: her.

Word; people only sell used cars for a reason!

Anyway, that is all what it is and another storyline. Post, the looking; as the car had been down Long Beach way, we hit back to my crib in Redondo, post. We hit the drink; pounded it out on my patio overlooking the ocean. We spoke only in Japanese. Then, we hit the sheets.

Did I think about her friend; the one I had originally met up with? No, not really.

She, the girl in the grasp, was what she was in bed. Okay. A place to dump a load.

I did. That was that. This is this.

My main intention(s), still on her friend.

Back to said friend... Her, my main doll faced girl, we went out a few times. She fell totally in love with me. Sorry, that's just what I do to the babes. The babes, who want to believe the lie...

Then came the time. The time to do what we do. It actually took awhile—awhile longer than most. But, that will be explained momentarily.

It was the early afternoon. Winter was in the air. I kissed her as I had kissed her before. Nothing great in the lips department. Like her roomy, she was what she was, what she was.

I removed her clothing. She had small boobs. AOK. She was a little chubby. Kinda funny, I thought.

Naked, I lay her down on my tie-dyed sheets. We kissed, licked; exchanged saliva. I tried to put it in. Didn't slide in on the easy side. In fact, it took quite a while, but I finally got it.

Not let me paraphrase here... It took quite a while to get it in. I mean quite a while! Ten, fifteen minutes; maybe more. I thought she was just pulling it together; you know, the pussy muscles. Holding it tight. Making it an adventure. Finally, I pierced the threshold. I'm in. I'm power thumping. We do it for a long time; missionary style. It's the only way she wanted it.

Then, in rolling over, one way or the next, I look down—look beneath her. *"What the fuck!"* blood all over my newly tie-dyed sheets.

"I told you I was a virgin," she exclaimed.

Yes, she had told me. Me, I had heard those words before. But, the so many before,

212

generally turned out to be liars. Generally, not always.

Me, when she told me, I didn't believe her. Her roomy certainly wasn't.

So, that was that. A cherry gone. Had I known, I probably wouldn't have hit it. I would have left it/her for someone far more worthy than I.

Also, my sheets were gone. My newly tie-dyed sheets. At least the bottom one. Fuck! I liked those sheets!

Post the present, into the future, I took her out to dinner and took her home. At her home; the nice two-bedroom apartment on Franklin, I hit it one more time just for good measure. I went home. I looked. I saw. My bottom tie-dyed sheet was destroyed. My mattress was also DOA. Blood Central. Day next, I had to trash it. Buy a new one. It wasn't cheap. We all pay the price for our actions— our decisions.

Okay, so that's the set up...

The girl in love. She called me all the time. I hit it when I hit it. Kept promising her the world. Sorry, (again), that's just who I am.

Venchinzo and I, as previously stated, we were on a tear. Out every night, a lot of *livin'* to be done. We did a lot, in a small amount of time. One night, we exited the clubs with our dicks in our hand. But me, I had an idea. We'll go and hit the babe's crib over on Franklin.

We pull up two in the AM or so. We ring the downstairs intercom. It buzzed. It is answered. We are provided entrance into the realms of the abyss. We get into the elevator. We ride it up. We walk through the hallways. We get to the door. We knock. It is answered by my babe. I immediately plant one on her lips. We enter. I precisely guide Venchinzo to the room of her roommate. She is in bed. I literally pull back the covers and put Venchinzo in bed next to her. She was fine with it. She was ready, willing, and able. I figure he was going to get his, so I went and got mine. I hit it for a few hours. She, my babe, went to sleep.

I get up. I go to get Venchinzo; thinking his sword had been polished. I open the door. There he lay. There the girl lay—next to one another. There they lay; clothing still on.

Though the girl was very willing; unlike I, Venchinzo has this moralistic side. He did *nada.*

Well, fuck that! As I had guided him into the bed, I guided him out. I planted him on the couch in the living room. I reentered the bedroom; closed the door. I hit the willing bitch good and hard. Fucked her for an hour or two. Like others have questioned, she asked me if I had a rubber. *"Sorry, I used it/used them on your friend."* I had broken a couple off with her roomy. They broke while doing my babe, the *Central Via Osaka Babe.* So, I went into her bareback.

During said love session, locked beneath the sheets, she exclaimed,

"I really love you. If you weren't with my friend, I could love you forever."

I smiled. I kissed her. I just kept *doin'* what I was *doin.'*

Done, we left. I drove Venchinzo home. It was almost daylight. He said he may call in sick. But, he didn't

That was that. He got up, went to work. How he does that, I don't know? Me, I went home and slept till two or so.

Skip forward a month; month and half, maybe. Though I had been *hittin'* the main and central doll face periodically, it had slacked off. Her friend called me one day. Asked me to come over. Told me she was pregnant. FUCK! Not another one...

You know, as stated, a few chapters back, that is why Saturday Jim titled my dick, *"Dirty Harry."* It takes no prisoners. I have gotten so many girls knocked up. Thankfully, they have all been willing to take the road less traveled and have them/the pregnancies dispensed with...

Speaking of thankfully, she, (the girl I was going to see), had told me what to expect— which allowed me to prepare.

I showed up at her crib in the eight or so of the PM. It was winter. It was dark. She met me downstairs. We sat on the stoop and spoke.

Now, a little backstory here. She, this girl, had a boyfriend. Obviously, she wasn't all that faithful to him. But, that is their business, not mine. This gave me ammunition. Here's how I played it...

"You're the only one who had sex with me without a rubber."
"Sometimes your boyfriend puts it in for a few minutes before he puts one on; right?"
"Yes."
"We'll there you go..."

I proceeded to tell her that it could not have been me because I had a vasectomy. Then, I pulled out a few photographs of my goddaughter—photos I had taking at different times of her young life. I told her these were my three children. That's why I had a vasectomy; didn't want any more...

"Your boyfriend must be the father, babe."

She bought it. What happened after that, I never knew. Never spoke with her again.

Her friend/roomy/my doll faced babe; soon after this, her visa was expiring, and she had to hit back to Osaka. I spent her last day Stateside with her. We drove around, ate, fucked, and did all that kind of shit. I promised that I would meet her at the airport; a ticket to Osaka in hand. Though I honestly thought about it, I really didn't have the money to make the trip. I heard via a letter, that I broke her heart. She waited. I never showed up. She got on the plane; solo.

I'm a coldhearted *mutha fucka,* I know.

216

Like I said in the introduction to this little ditty, *I think it is somewhat sad, how people only care about themselves, about their own moment, their own space in time.*

Me, I only cared about my newly tie-dyed sheets.

Those two other girls, they cared about me. Foolishly... I am no one worth caring about.

L.A. 12

One of those Saturday nights was approaching, you know... One of those solo; alone, zero equaling zero. Me, I have spent too many of those... But, no one wants to read about that.

I guess to look at things from an unbiased, clear/more enlightened perspective, I was in some way/some means, dancing into the hands of destiny by being alone with nothing to do/nothing on my plate on the evening of which I speak. Because, if I had been prepped to do something else... Well life, may have evolved totally differently. So, I guess we can just refer to this as a part/a segment of the dance of destiny. But, even as I sit here now, one week to the day, or should I say, one week to the night, later; I am not clear as to why or what, (if anything), it truly meant.

Anyway... I had been *hittin'* the local health spa almost exclusively of late. That is to say, that I have been *rapin'* to some of the local folk that hang there on a daily basis. You know, people like me: alone, no real family, no real life. I have met a babe or three there; of and in recent times. Thus, I have not chosen to make further and/or farther drives into the realms of the night to seek my illusion elsewhere at more distant; geographically speaking, health spas.

But, to get the point...

Saturday. It was Saturday, one week

ago. Today, being Sunday. Well, it is actually Monday. Monday, way early on in the AM, as I sit here having just cracked open the second bottle of the grape; after just having pounded down a double shot of espresso; direct from my espresso machine, which sits over on my kitchen counter. Having just sat down with a few words to spell put.

Anyway, I had spent the day, last Saturday, staring deeply into the abyss of alone nothingness. Not metaphysical or spiritual nothingness—just empty, life nothingness. Nothing, *no-thing* was on the horizon. The late afternoon was coming on, so me, I decided to hit on over to the HS, (Health Spa), and run my traditional four miles and then hang tough in the jacuzzi and see what/who I might meet. You know, in the babe *departmento*.

En route, I stopped on over at a little Chinese fast-food style joint on Torrance B.L.V.D. It's not far out of my way on the route from my crib on the beach in South Redondo to the aforementioned HS that I was *a-travelin'* to up on Hawthorne B.L.V.D.

Anyway, my plan was to pick up a bit on the nourishment side of the photograph. This one guy who works there, is someone I often speak to, during the week, in the late PMs at the gym I was motoring to. He's an all-right enough guy. Originating on the Taiwan side. Currently living in his van in the parking lot of said restaurant establishment. He always sets me up *por gratis* with the Chinese grub. Though I never expect it and/or ask for it to be delivered in that manner.

I had basically planned to just hit and run, at the Chinese establishment, and make it to the HS by six in the PM. As, the gym closes on the weekends at eight.

I was surprised though, that post my order, the dude came on out, lighted up a smoke, and sat back wanting to rap with me. Due to the talking, which I suppose was AOK, I was pushing my arrival at the gym to a bit later than my mind's eye had previously planned. This put me in the mode of time question as to the possible meeting of my visualized love attractions; if you know what I'm, *talkin'* about. But, what can a guy do when you are getting served up for free.

Done with dinner. The dude back to work. I drove. I hit the parking lot. Through the door, I flashed my HS ID to the attendant monitoring said activities, and in I went.

The minute I hit the locker room, I see one of the security guards for the apartment building where I occupy an apartment. He stood there in all his naked glory. He is standing there, totally naked, messing with the lock upon his *lock-her!*

A basically melon cat. He's a few pounds over, has a peace sign tatted upon his arm. He lives on his boat out in the harbor, which dwells, as I now sit, behind my back. He always laments about being an adopted child. *"My father always introduced his son as his son and me as his adopted son."* This when the dude is now deep in his thirties.

He's a bit of a friend, actually. He's a good dude. But, due to the *nose-up-in-the-air* attitude of most of the people who live in this/my apartment building, no one will ever even acknowledge him. That is unless they need something fixed or want to complain about someone.

Me, sometimes in the late night, when I'm getting home deep in the AM; and if I see him walking around, doing his rounds, I invite him over; cook us up a frozen pizza and we sit around and eat it while watching music videos or CNN and the like.

Anyway, into the locker room I go. I slap him on the shoulder as I walk by. We see each another there, at the HS, every now and then. He doesn't have a shower on his boat, so hits one up over this a-way.

To make a rather long story short, what came to pass was that he, the security guard, (maybe I should put that in capital letters). So, he, *The Security Guard,* had a crisis. He had left his stuff in an unlocked locker. And, some *ass-wipe,* I guess to be an asshole, had put a lock on the locker when he, *The Security Guard,* went to hit the showers. So, there he stood, naked; no clothes, and no way to get his gear.

I tried to loan him a pair of my workout shorts to wear but it really wouldn't do him any good, as he stated, for the keys to his motorcycle and his glasses, his wallet, and all the rest of his stuff was locked up tight.

So, I went to get the maintenance guy.

And, post the basic bullshit of prove this is/was his locker; call it out over the P.A. system, and the etcetera, the guy lock cut the lock off and, *The Security Guard,* was allowed to get his gear.

But now, *here-and-now,* on to the part of where destiny took hold, and all that... While we were waiting for all this; namely, his locker to be opened, *The Security Guard* told me of a party that was to take place in the building's Rec-Room that night. I explained to him that he was, in fact, the only person who I knew in the building, and though he invited me, I didn't really feel all that comfortable going. Well, whatever....

He got his stuff. Got dressed. Bailed. Me, I did my run, checked out the *j-cuz-zai;* nothing particular but ZERO.

Post and past, I went on home. I stared into my aloneness. I also starred at the computer that I knew I should be writing some words into for the, *whatever it is worth,* realms of literature. But, I did nothing but crack a bottle of the Chianti and slurp down my allotted serving. Namely, the whole bottle.

As I sat on Mr. Couch *sippin'* the grape, I decided that how I would handle this Saturday night was that I would wait until a *more-or-less* appreciate time and then I would brew me up a pot of the java—pour me, (some of it), into my very large travel mug, get into my Jeep, for all of its convertible-ness, head out, grab me some donuts over at this little spot on Artesia that I like, and take that drive on down to the LBC,

(Long Beach), and you never know what sweet young thing of a Cambodian babe and/or hooker I might find. (Just like the one I encountered a few weeks back. Remember)?

As I sat there, I laughingly remembered back when I was powdering my nose quite frequently; chalking up with the *caine,* and all that. I got way too high one night. So, I took a ride to the LBC as I talked into my portable tape recorder. No one else was around, I was *ridin'* solo, or *so-lo,* (depending on how you want to look at it). But, due to the amount of the dose I had ingested, I was high—very high. I talked a lot. Non-stop, in fact. I don't know, maybe I should find that tape some time. Transcribe it. You never know, it may make for some great poetry...

But anyway, and the point being, I remember how I rambled on-and-on, due to the drug. And well, life... It just felt like it was all going to be alright. Like things were going to come together and I was going to get my chance.

I guess that's how people get addicted. The promise; the lie of the perfection of the drug. It just makes everything feel all-right. Feel better; even if it is not.

Well, here I am, maybe a year and a half later, and though I try and try, I am still fucked: lost, alone, and in debt.

Tonight, (this night). Not the night I'm writing about with remembrance... I watched my traditional early evening Japanese television programming. You know, the little miniseries *thAngs* they, the Japanese, like to do.

I mean, let's face facts, I would prefer to be there; so much more than being here. But, no *danero*. Or, should I say, no *yen*.

My life, it's a tunnel with a way in but no way out.

Trust me, don't choose to be different. Don't choose to be an artist. Don't choose to be like me. Live the mainstream. It is one hell of a lot—way fucking easier.

Sorry to *dilly-dally* here...

Funny, I heard that expression in an old T.V. movie today. But anyway, back to the storyline...

Java in my hand. I've been getting into it, *con letch* style lately. I was on my way out.

Now, it is not that I was stroking all that tough. I mean I had grown a cold sore on my lip maybe Wednesday a week before. And, though I tried to hide it a bit, not a whole lot that you can do about *'em*. You know, I mean, it is like before—before herpes and all that; if you had one, you had one. Not cool, but no real big deal. Now, it is like everyone is way scared to even look at you if you got one *goin'* on; thinking, knowing... Luckily, mine was on its way out on this Saturday of which I write.

So anyway, I headed out to the central building courtyard where the Rec-Room dwells. I stop by, stuck my head in at the party, on my way out to the night, to the street, to the dark desolate nighttime of Long Beach. A very West Hollywood crowd inhabited said Rec-

224

Room. The dudes complete with their bullshit greased back ponytails, the chicks red lipstick to the max. My bro, *The Security Guard,* was hanging tight out in front. I said, *"Hi."* I said, *"Bye."* The party didn't really look like it had anything to offer; nothing my style. So me, I headed for the door to reenter my building in order to re-exit the rear and travel down to the underground garage. The door down to reach my ride—my passageway into the promises of the night.

But, as I opened the door: three, more than serious babes were coming in at the same time I was going out. One of them, being a kill Asian. They all smiled at me.

They were going in. I was going out. I realized then, my mistake. *"My-my-my-my-my-mistake."* Remember that song. No, you probably wouldn't. Early 80s local club band and all.

Anyway, in motion, I continued with my progress. I drove out and onto the night. I even talked to my Mr. Portable Tape Recorder for a bit—discussing illusion and confusion and how I never know what the fuck to do.

As I drove the LBC, I looked for my dollar sign babe, but nothing; *nada.* I decided to remedy my mistake, and I rapidly headed on back for the *par-tay, drivin'* down PCH. Nothing to lose.

Back at the building; into my parking spot; I parked. I walked up the stairs. I could hear the music blasting from the Rec-Room in the distance.

Though it took one of those emotional pushes—leap(s) of faith—full of question; I stroked it and I choked it and in I go. I thought I may stand out, as I knew no one. But, I entered to no one's apparent glances.

As the stories go... I'm not really a party going sort of guy. Never really dug *'em.* They always seem so fake/so contrived. But, with nothing left to lose; at least in this night, it seemed like the place to be.

That and this being said, it is kinda weird to walk into a party where you know absolutely no one. Though all the *peeps* were around my age, (maybe a little bit younger), but they were of and from a different crew. As it turns out, they were all friends from acting classes and the like. Me, I grew up in Hollywood and wanted nothing to do with all the bullshit that goes *hand-in-hand* with being an actor. So, as I studied the scene, it seemed like there was nothing to say and no one to say it to.

I checked the participations; the hot Asian chick, (previously mentioned), was over to my left, *chowin'* down on some of the grub over on a table that held such said supplies. Though she would have been my obviously choice, there were several other fine young specimens that caught my attention, if you know what I mean, and I think that you do.

But me, I was out of my element. Not really my scene. And, as I am not a very forward person by nature, I was thinking about the bail as I looked around. My Security Guard

226

friend was not there. He was probably out doing his once an hour rounds.

He actually has a pretty chill job. All he has to do all night is sit around and watch T.V.; listen to the radio, read a book, whatever... Then, once an hour, he has to walk the three floors of the two buildings and the parking lot. Virtually nothing ever goes down in this building; at least nothing in the bad way. So, he has a fairly laid-back job.

Just as I was about to walk, this one little Filipino dude who lives in the building stared a convo. with me. And, when I say, *"Little,"* I am being descriptively kind. The dude is maybe four foot nine on a good day. But, not a bad dude. I'd seen him around but never said much to him.

We got to *talkin'* and that was my in. He was one of those little hamster *rap-mysters.* He was going around *talkin'* to all the chicks, which gave me my intros.

So, the party went on. By bud, *The Security Guard,* came back from his rounds. I roamed the room with *The Hamster* and *The Security Guard.* Though, both nice guys, they were way un-cool; at least via the eyes of this West Hollywood crew. Man, I could just fucking feel it; the people checking them, then checking themselves, and thinking how much more cool they were then *The Hamster* and *The Security Guard.* I laughed to myself; thinking, *"Who the fuck are you? You're either livin' off of daddy's money or you're a fucking waiter during the day—waiting for that big break that will never come."* 'Fuck you,' I thought.

Now me, I'm not a *Hamster* or a *Security Guard.* My clothing was a hell of lot more stylish and expensive than what they, the people of the party, were wearing. And, I didn't see anybody else spouting a *Rolex,* like I was. So, that was that.

I mean exterior is always so exterior. Most of these *fucks* had no clue what the rest of their life was going to issue them. I mean, yeah, they're young now. And, when you're young, you always have the promise of tomorrow in your eyes. But, give it a few years and then we'll see how much ego you are spewing.

I always hate fuckers like that. I mean like, do what you're going to do, wear what you are going to wear. But, don't let it make you think that you are better than anybody else— because you're not!

Out, is always out. Out, can be gone in a heartbeat. People; real people; people with essence, that is who makes life worth living. And, it doesn't matter what they do, what they wear, or how tall they are.

Okay, okay, I know, I know... Enough of all that philosophy, let's get back to the babes and the story at hand...

The party, I didn't really dig it. It went on for a while until one of the dudes slammed massive amounts of the free whisky and ended up passed out in the jacuzzi. All the *peeps* speaking, *"Oh, he is such a drama queen.*

Always looking for attention..." I wondered had any of them looked in the mirror lately.

But, during the moments that passed, I met two girls that moved me. One was this sweet blonde *thAng.* Interesting. Just interesting... When the Neneh Cherry song, *"Buffalo Stance,"* started playing over the stereo, aside from me, she was the only one who knew it, liked it, and got all into singing along; complete with a dance all her own. I dug her moves/her actions. And, oh yeah, she was a waitress over in West Hollywood at this little *shi-shi,* high-end place close to the *Bodhi Tree Bookstore* on Melrose. I knew it very well. Their food was so-so. Atmosphere was worse. But, it was one of those places that when you needed to get some grub on, and there was no place else in mind; it was a place worth eating. Anyway, my desires were moved...

Then, there was this Iranian girl. Out of place/out of her element/out of her crowd, just like me. She was the date of this other dude. A dude, that was so wrapped up in speaking about *the-this-and-the-that* of acting technique that he didn't even notice that some other dude was moving in on his babe. Namely, me.

Eventually, the party in the Rec-Room ended. The drunken dude in the Jacuzzi had to be taken home. The dudes, most of them anyway, begin to bail. My sweet little Iranian girl, Samantha, left with her date. She turned, smiled at me, as she exited the door. I laughed to myself; her dude, so self-involved, didn't notice that either.

I was about to bail on into the night, back to my crib; solo. I had the numbers of the two girls of my desire, so I was looking forward onto the horizon of another day.

But, as I learned, the party was to be moved upstairs to the apartment of the girl who had thrown it. That chick, she was this little bottle blonde. Didn't really know her. But, I had seen her around the building once or three times. Anyway, she came up to me/over to me, *"You want to join us?"* Well, with an offer like that... How could I say, *"No?"*

Upstairs was as upstairs is. It was the same crowd; no one I had anything in common with. My bud, *The Security Guard,* had invited himself. He was *rappin'* hot and heavy on this one chick. *The Hamster,* I guess, he went home.

Me, I sat around and spoke with the blonde waitress of my said desires. Just one of those zero conversations.

Sadly, my security guard friend felt I threw the cock block on him. While we were all taking, I mention that he was the building's security guard.

Me, I thought it was kind of a compliment. I guess his chick did not.

Such is life and the words of a loudmouth, (me), and those of the younger persuasion who feel/believe that they have forever; that they are going to be star.

I guess that is the curse of youth. You always have tomorrow. You are going to get all you want/be all you want/do all you want to do. That is until one day you look in the mirror and

230

you realize that you have grown a few lines, maybe a grey hair or two; nothing happened the way you wanted, and you are latched up in a job/a relationship that you hate and there is no way out. Yes, that is life. At least, for most. But, youth—well, they never believe that to be the case. Not until they take that look in the mirror of discovery.

Sorry dude, I didn't mean to hang you up.

We all went/eventually bailed. Zero hit the zero in a big way. Went home; went down to my crib—cock firmly locked in my own hand.

*   *   *

Heading on to the day next; life went on as life does. I did what I did. Painted, played some guitar, did my nightly four mile run at the gym with the indoor track that I dig, rode my Italian racing bike deep into the depths of the night—I always pull out at eleven in the PM. And, that was that.

Maybe three in—three into the days since said party, I come home to a call on my telephone answering machine. The red light blinked. I pushed the button. It was Samantha. I smiled.

You know, in all honesty, it/the party, was one of those things/one of those situations where you meet people/you live the moment, but then it is all cast to the, *"Whatever,"* of life. My dick hadn't really been in hock as I had a

231

few babes on the line, so I didn't really think about calling either of the aforementioned ladies of desire, which I had met in that evening. But, with her calling me; the game was in play.

To make a long story short; I called her back, we set up a date. I went to pick her up. She lived in an apartment complex down in the LBC—the nice side of Long Beach. Not the junky side. Not the Cambodian side. Not the side that I normally frequent.

Now, I guess, I am supposed to tell you a little bit about her—her backstory, if you will. You know, the way all of those who write literature do. Do, in order to fill the pages of their books. So here I go... Iranian. Very pretty. Was twenty-six. Had hooked up with a dude; had a kid. A kid I never met.

Question: If a chick has a kid and you never meet it; does that kid really exist?

Date set. I hoped into my bad little *Porsche 356 SC,* headed a bit south down the PCH, and picked her up.

Now, for those of you who know me, or know of me. Me... Well, I like to hit nice restaurants. I mean it doesn't matter how much they cost; either on the high or the low side of the scale, but good food is good food. The problem is, most restaurants that serve good food; a least here in L.A. are on the expensive side of the photograph. And, they certainly aren't in the LBC or even in Redondo where I live. They are up in Beverly Hills, West

232

Hollywood, and the like. So, that was my destination.

As I wasn't quite sure how the date was going to play out, I didn't make reservations anywhere. I just went to Long Beach, found her building in the apartment complex; knocked on the door, was invited in, played nicey-nice, and then we were *out-a-there.* Her mother was babysitting the kid, so I was told.

Up to L.A., *central-city,* I cruised. The drive, (and she), was what the drive, (and she), was. You know how dates are... Mostly weird, which is why I don't like 'em and rarely go on 'em.

Where to take her? Well, as I had just met that girl at the same said party, that was a waitress at this one place I spoke of. (You remember the one I just describe). Let's go there! I can see what I can see. A reason to see her without calling her; etcetera, and so on...

Now, was that a fucked up idea? I don't know? I didn't think so. Not initially. So, I thought, and/or didn't think.

Anyway, we pull up; park and go inside. The *maître d'* set us right up with a table.

Then, there she was/is; the waitress. The blonde girl. The *dancin'* party go-er, into *Buffalo Stance.* I notice her out of the corner of my eye. But fuck, then came the reality setting in. She is to be our waitress.

She walks up, looks, realizes, who I am,

"What are you doing here?"

233

Then, she looks some more; studies who I am with.

"Weren't you at the party too?"

An uncomfortable moment passes,

"I didn't know you knew each other."

Referring to the girl/my date and I.
I chime in,

"We didn't. Now we do."

Then she chimes in...

"I thought you were going to call me?"

Uncomfortable, uncomfortable...
But, with and because of all that; I could tell, I knew, that I threw the major cock block on myself. Stupid... Stupid... Stupid!!!
The waitress girl felt like I was rubbing it in her face that she was a waitress. Rubbing her nose in it, that I had picked another over her.
In reality, it wasn't like that. No, not at all. I had enough cock... Oh, I mean enough love, for both of them.
But, it was what it was what it was. I had done what I had done. I fucked up. Fucked up big time. I didn't think/hadn't consider the implications. Typical of me; yeah?

Samantha, however, dug my scene even more. She thought I was *slappin'* the other bitch up-side the face. I was not....

Anyway, did as dinner does. I grabbed a bottle of nice Italian red wine off of the wine list. As dinner proceeded, in times that are times two. We ate, we spoke, we were uncomfortably served by the blonde waitress who dug Neneh Cherry; just like I.

Post and past, back in the car, driving south on the L.A. freeways, I tried to see if I was going to be able to get into Samantha's pants in the same said evening. Didn't really work out. Not that evening, at least.

But, we set a date, a time; tomorrow. There's always tomorrow...

The next day passed, as my days do. Doing what I do. I spent some time shopping, some time painting, some time fantasying about what was to *cum*. Oh, I mean come.

The evening rolled around. I got into my mode, into my car, and drove down to pick her up. I expected it to just be a so-lo pickup session again; as before. But, no. This time, there was a very-very gay guy in her crib.

Now, let me paraphrase here... I certainly have nothing against homo-sexuals. You are what you are. We are all dealt our destiny and then we each make the choice what to do about it. Gay is fine. But, I am not. Therefore, and as-such, I did not dig the fact that the moment I walked in, I could tell his, (her friend's), dick was getting hard over the sight of me. But, whatever...

As far as the chick goes, I was not really digging the scene. I was *thinkin'* that she must be a *Fag Hag* or something, as they obviously seemed very close. As such, and because of, there was a part of me that thought to just bail. But, being the gentleman that I am, I stayed on...

Anyway, the lollygagging went on for a few. We spoke, the dude and me, as she finalized her make-up or whatever she had to do off in the out-back/out-a-sight. He was a little drunk and way coming on to me. I was not happy being left in that situation.

In any case, she eventually came out from the netherworld of her whatever-world, ready to go. We headed for the door. She told me that she had to get something from her friends, (the gay guys), crib. Whatever...

We get to the door. She opens it. He stands behind me. He grabs my ass. I turn around.

"Don't ever do that again!"

I firmly tell him. He giggles.

We walk through the night, the three of us; from her place to his. He giggles some more.

Samantha knows I am not happy with *the sitch* and tries to chill me back. We get to his door, across the grassed and wooded apartment complex. I look at her. She looks at me. One of those moments that could/that should last forever. A moment of visual embrace where

236

your heart just melts and you fall in love with the perfection that is in front of your eyes. In doing so/while doing so, however, the guy had his moment. Again, he grabs my ass.

BAM! I turn. I punch him in the face. He goes down to the ground. He goes down hard.

"I warned you, mutha fucka!"

The guy looks up from the ground, holding his jaw. The truth be told, he's lucky I held back. Samantha goes to help the crying little bitch stand up.

In actuality, I figured that was that/there went the date/there went that glance of perfection/there went the chick—being a *Fag Hag* and all... But, it didn't. I guess she likes a real man. She helped him in. She got what she got in his apartment. We went out. Out to dinner and drinks.

The night proceeded very well. But, no; no pussy. Not that night...

I was a bit on the unhappy side of the situation. Not really liking what was going on. I didn't call her, day next. She did, however, call me; several times. I let her speak to the answering machine. But, as is the case with all dudes, I guess—all real men; the night rolls around and you want to get the *get-get;* you want get it on. I call her.

"Where you been?" She inquired. *"I miss you..."*
"Whatever..."

She had no one to watch her kid. I said bring 'em along. I can't do that; not yet anyway... So, went the conversation. So, went that the plans were made for tomorrow. Me, stuck with the four-mile run and health club, hoping for a new illusion to cross my field of vision to provided me with instantaneous, *no-hold-barred,* passion for the evening. None came my direction... I spent the night alone. I went to sleep, as always, listening to the waves of the ocean.

Day-next, we went to lunch. All be what it be. She then wanted to come over to my place. She wanted to see my library—stuck firmly against the wall on boards and brick mortar blocks. Right there, next to me; hundreds/thousands of books. They are there now, as I sit here and type.

Me, sure, I knew what it meant/what she wanted. She was an, *'On the third date,'* type of girl. I smiled. AOK with me.

Never did get it though? Why on the third date? Who set that rule? But, it is a rule long observed/long practiced. I just don't get it???

We, her and I, hit the crib. She sits on Mr. Couch. Didn't really look at the books. I pop a bottle of the grape; red, of course. We toast. We drink a glass. We have/experience our first kiss with the scent of Chianti on our lips. Perfect passion in the making.

We move to my bed. I undress her. Her body, golden in its coloration. Golden in its

238

Middle-Eastern heritage. Though she had a kid, her body; none the worse for the wear. Nothing noticeable.

We continue the kissing. My cock found its way inside of her. All was what it was, what it was.

Nothing so special, nothing so eminent to find its way into the realms of literature. Just was what it was what it was.

The one thing I did notice; amusingly, I guess... Amusing, for those of us who find these kind of things amusing. Is that as I went in and out, up and down, side-to-side, the stubble on her legs, did kind of scratch my legs. Rub me right or rub me wrong—depending on how you want to look at it.

I know a lot of women have complained about the same with my face once a few hours from my last shave have expired. But, this was the first time I had ever felt this from a women. I guess now I understand... Understand what the babes were *a-feeling*. Overall though, it was kinda sexy... Shaved leg stubble.

We did what we did and we were done. Like a gentleman, I took her to dinner. Then, took her home.

"Let's do something tomorrow! Okay?"

So came the words from her lips. What could I say but, *"Yes?"*

The day next arrived. Though not really in the mood, having had what I had—having experienced what she had to give, I got into my

239

356 and headed on down south to the LBC. I picked her up. But, then—then it began to happen. My car began to have a personality crisis.

Now, here's the thing for any of you who don't know. Classic cars, like my, *'64 Porsche 356 SC,* are great. They are beautiful. But, they have problems. They are old. They are hard to find parts for. They cost a lot of money to keep running. And, they can break down without notice.

So, as we motored down to the lunch I had planned at this cool little pizza joint in Laguna Beach, my car sputtered and spit.

Me, I wanted to go home and take care of the taking care of. She, had paid a babysitter. She wanted to hang.

I was in no mood, but I did follow through with the lunch. But, as I drove north, my car was having problems. I had to take it into my mechanic Al, to let him do what he do. I wanted to drop her off. She should have understood. She did not.

"I really like you. I want to be with you. I want to spend as much time with you as possible. Let's go make love again at your place."

So went her end of the conversation. Me, I have a tendency to get into a mood. A mood, where I just don't give a fuck about anybody or anything but me and mine. I was in such a said mood. I told her I had to bail.

240

"How much will it cost for me to spend more time with you," she asked.
"A million dollars."

She pulled out her checkbook. She wrote me a check. If only I could have cashed that check, all my woes would have been over. Of course, I could not. It would have bounced.

So, I took her home. I dropped her off. She was angry. She told me, if I dropped her off, I could never see her again. I told her that was fine.

So, that is the story of the girl named Samantha.

She had a kid. I never met the kid.

She had a fag friend that I knocked to the ground.

She had really stubbly/hairy legs that scratched me as we fucked.

Who won and who lost. Her? Me? I don't know??? It was just one of those things that was just one of those things. Had the cards been dealt differently, maybe we could have had something. Well... I guess we did have something. That something is spelled out here. But, in actuality/and in fact, (maybe), we could have had something more. Maybe... I don't know?

Maybe it was simply the gods of destiny that were telling me that I was walking down the wrong road, so they made my *356* break down. Maybe, I don't know that either???

And, that's the thing. No-body knows. We just do what we do what we do. We live our

241

lives; make our choices, and we are left dealing with the remains of those choices and/or their consequences.

L.A. 13

And, the nights they seem to go on forever and ever and ever and ever. Step out into the dream of whatever the key to destiny may hold and dish me up a plate of illusion. Yes, any flavor will do...

So, onto the so-called storyline...

Like, you know, I had been hitting this one gym on the local side of the photograph. For some reason or another, I had fallen into the regime of *hittin'* the club at like 10:30 PM or so, running my usual four miles, then hopping down to the jacuzzi to see what flavor(s) may be *a-callin'* me.

Anyway, I had been *rapin,'* on the Vietnamese side of the picture, with this sweet little babe of a local specimen. We had lined up this Friday night, *"Let's go dance session."* She suggested that we go to the club, workout, (because that was oh so important to her), and then hit out to the night. AOK. Fine with me.

But like, you know, how the hands of fate would have it... I like pulled in way late to the club. And, I guess she had bailed; figured that I had stood her up. I didn't have her number with me. So, a long story made short, it just didn't happen.

With nothing left to lose, I hit on to do what I usually do, when I'm not touching the goddess, in all her various shapes and sizes, in the mystic realms of the night, I did my gym session; hit the track to get my run on.

I did what I did. Then hit on down to the old locker room. There, I get the invite; direct from these two dudes on the serious side of geek, who I see around the club and once in a while speak to/with. They want to go and hit this bar and chug down and few.

I look at them. I look at me. Ithink, *"Are you fucking kidding me,"* But, with no other illusion at hand, and nothing really left to lose, I gave *'em* the AOK.

Now, I knew I was going to be out of my environment, as I really do not dig bars. But, never let it be said that I am not above *sippin'* a glass of the new illusion.

So, we bailed on out of the health spa. The one dude with his tee-shirt and way pot belly hanging out over the side of his belt. Real cool dude... The other *hombre* had his plaid Bermuda shorts on. Me, I'm in a baggy Italian suit. My normal attire. You can image what the three of us, (together), must have looked like...

We were to go and ride in the hefty homeboy's, like way old and funky 1970s, some sort of a junk mobile. Though I preferred to drive my own ride, it being a two-seater *Porsche,* there was no way that the three of us we going to fit in it—no way those two could take up the spare front seat. And, he knew where the place was. So, against my better judgment, I get in. We were going to ride, *bitch;* i.e. (three of us in the front seat), because it was a two-door and his front seats were broken and didn't flick forward to let

244

people get to the back seats. Me, I grabbed the outside spacing. But, I was not happy.

Anyway, long story, made long; we were *out-a-there.* Fatso was a bit worried about his one light on the head light side of the picture that was not *a-working. "They never give tickets for that,"* exclaims his friend. So, we drove on.

Approximately three minutes into our cruise, homeboy cranks up his stereo. Like, it was worth more than the whole fucking car. Like you know, the kind, where the earth moves due to all of the bass power. He was so impressed with himself. Me, I was thinking, *'What a mistake I had just made?'*

Just as he was pushing the buttons and playing with his stereo, the lights came *a-shinin'* in the mirror. It was COPS.

I sat there fucking laughing as they asked the guy why his stereo was so loud and then they gave him a ticket for his out-of-service headlight.

Fuck me, man. What had I gotten myself into?

Anyway, post all the ticket bullshit, we move on. The bar was set on the second floor of this building over on PCH, (Pacific Coast Highway), in the early parts of Manhattan Beach.

I'd driven by it a thousand times but never gave it any thought. I don't think I ever even ever noticed that there was bar up there.

We park. We climb the stairs. I try to back it up a bit, so it won't actually look like

I'm with those two, (for lack of a better word), geeks.

Inside, music was pumping and it, the place/space was full of all the trendy beach yuppies. Again, I was thinking, *'What had I gotten myself into?'*

But, just then; I mean I was only in the place for like a second or two and, at the end of the bar, I saw her. She was this ravishing beauty of a Goth. Dyed black hair, pale skin, horned rimmed glasses, dressed all in black.

What was she doing there? What was I doing there? It must be/has to be some sort of *karmic* destiny.

Immediately, I walk straight up to her, *"Hey..."*

Just as I do, the shit hits the fan. She apparently had been giving the bartender some shit. What/why, I didn't know. But, the bouncer walks up to her and another girl, (I'll get to her in a second), and tells them they have to leave. The bartended leans over and says something crude over the blasting music. She, (the Goth), throws her drink in his face. *Fuck! I am in love!*

The bouncer escorts her and her friend to the door. I look around. She's yanking and pulling and spitting fire. I check the scene. All there is are a bunch of beach yuppies. All the losers I would never have anything to say to; would never want to be seen with.

So me, I turn, I follow the girl(s) out the door.

She looks at me. I at her. Obvious

connection. The only people with any style in that entire fucking bar. Hell, probably the only people with any style in the whole South Bay.

"Can you go in and get my purse? I left it on the bar."

I smile. I laugh. I go back in to get her purse.

As I walk back in, the bouncer inquires, in all his manly-ness.

"You with her?"

I say nothing. I just walk back in. *'Cause* I know he does not want to meet Mr. Fist. And, if I said anything, it would just disintegrate to that level.

At the bar, I see a small black purse. I grab it. I walk out. I smile. I nod at the bouncer. I walk out, never to walk back into that shit hole again. I present her with her purse.

"So, what happened?" I inquire.

As it turns out, it was just another one of those asshole bartender *thAngs* and a girl in the wrong environment. It always amazed me, how girls either get hit on or harshly judged.

But, there she was, this beauty of Goth. With her, her sister, as it turned out. Younger by several years. Chubby, but very cutely chubby. She too, was dressed in black.

There we were, the three of us, standing

outside a bar on Pacific Coast Highway in Manhattan Beach, California. Each of us, totally out of place in our own way. We were the perfect team.

As I didn't have my ride with me, we moved towards the sister's ride. My babe, Victoria, was her name, she didn't even own a car. Such is life...

We climbed into the sister's 1964 brown *Chevy Nova,* and we drove off into eternity...

That night, we went about living one of the best nights I have ever known. Lived with two people I didn't even know. We drove around the *South Bay,* drinking, singing to songs on the radio, and just having one fucking great time!!!

At about three in the AM, we had to stop by their crib. They lived up in the northern section of *Redondo Beach.* They had to stop by to check on their brother. They asked if I wanted to go in, *"Sure. Why not?"*

They lived in just the typical apartment *thAng.* The three of them, two sisters, one brother. My babe's situation, a bit more complicated. But, I will get to that in a moment.

Inside, I sit on the couch. They go and speak with their brother; check on him.

Like some abstract force of energy from the distant realms of some ethereal plane, all I could see/all I could hear of him was constant coughing and laughter. You see, the guy, their brother, was dying from AIDS. He was close to the end. But, they took care of him. *Blood is thicker than water.*

248

Me, I sat there. I never met the guy. Never saw him. But, we were introduced thought the walls. He said, *"Hi,"* then he coughed.

We stayed there for a while; the two girls, the brother, and I. Then, it was back out to the streets.

We drove some more. We laughed some more. Then, we ended up in the large parking lot where my car remained. Remained from my leaving it there many hours the previous.

She, the sister, behind the wheel: turning and twisting and driving like a crazed mad woman through the empty lot. We were laughing, joking, living one of those moments of life that truly makes life worth living. Fuck, I mean there are so few...

But then... BAM! She hit something. You could hear metal on metal. SLAM! On go the breaks. Our laughing stops.

We get out.

We look.

Somehow/someway she had smashed into a wayward shopping cart. Oh, I forgot to tell you, some of the driving had been done with eyes closed. Closed, the way true mystics do it.

I helped her pull the cart from under her car as she backed up. I look/I checked. It had been more impact sound than damage. Her car was fine.

With this, and the light beginning to show in the eastern sky, the evening seemed to be coming to a close. They drove me over to my ride. My ride on the other side of the parking lot.

We spoke for a few more. The sister/the driver getting a bit tired. Me, the, *up-all-nighter,* that I am, still ready to go. So she, my newfound Goth-girl of exquisite beauty, we bid *adieu* to the sister. We get into my car. A new moment of perfection has begun. Begun at the hands of a couple of chubby geeks from the gym. *"Thanks guys!"* I never anticipated that I would be saying, *"Thanks,"* to guys like that.

The light of the morning began to pour in through the horizon as I got to know my new friend. I immediately felt very-very close to her. There we were, two very abstract individuals, lost/tossed/damned into the world of normality, where we did not belong.

Now, the truth being told, me being who I am and all, I had hope that her staying with me this AM would simply and immediately lead us to being intertwined, in the sexual sense of the word, back at my crib in the ASAP. Sorry, that's just who I am... But, I didn't push for it.

In worst case, I figured we could hit over to the 24/7 restaurant that I eat at all the time, *The Kettle* and chow down on some early AM *Break-Fast.*

"What do you want to do," I asked.
"Let's take a walk."

We got in my car, and she guided me over to this park at the far north end of

250

Redondo. A park that parallels the railroad tracks. We get out. She looks at me—at what I was wearing. She says,

"You probably don't want to get your clothes dirty?"

Believe me, whatever I am wearing, I am down/I am ready to go/to do whatever it takes to make life happen. I mean, you can replace clothing, but you cannot replace/relive the moments of life.

She looks at my shoes,

"What about your shoes?"
"No problem."

Now, just for the record here, and for the understandings passed down through the centuries/through the ages, when I am not wearing tennis shoes, which I am wearing most of the time with my suits, with my tuxedos, with my *what-evers,* I wear big clunky hard shoes. Now, this is an important point. So, listen tight, as it may save your life sometime.

Whenever you buy hard shoes, you need to buy *'em* with a rubber sole. The reason is, if you are wearing hard shoes with those slick soles; if a fight jumps off and you need to kick some ass and/or you need to book a scene in a hurry, they will cause you to slip and slide, and you may get jacked up.

Now, as somebody who's seen street warfare my entire life, and been in more than a few *rock 'em, sock 'em, tie ups,* you need to be able to substantiate yourself on the ground and you need to be able to move without fear of slippage. So, *never-never-ever* wear slippery-soled shoes.

Right now, what I'm *diggin'* is these shoes that you used to see the cops wearing back in the '60s and '70s. They are black, with like a saw tooth sole. Very cool, very clunky, and they grip like a *mutha fucka.* So, that's the story. Do with it what you will.

In any case, I was ready to take a walk.

She guided us up to and down the railroad tracks. It was cool. The early AM light just peaking over the horizon. The railroad tracks peering off, over, and into a million miles of nowhere. The city sprawled out to both—no, all four of our sides. And, her: her and I; two lost/lonely souls, walking our way into the promise of bliss in the *never-never-land* that never truly exists.

As we walked/as we talked, we pass a trailer park. She looks/she points,

"That's where I belong. Someday I hope to move into a trailer."

'Wow,' I thought. *'What a small life-dream. Easy to achieve in this day and age. But, who even has that dream anymore? That was from a different world/a different time. The 1950s, maybe even the 1960s. Then, but not now.'*

We walked on further, there was a

252

cemetery to our left. For those of you who know North Redondo, you know the one I'm *talkin'* about.

"I want to go there someday," she said, *"See how much graves cost. My sister, she died. I want her to have a place, even though we don't have her body."*

I could tell/I could feel it, this girl was broken/fractured/ruined, just like me/maybe even worse than me. She was damned to a world of death and the inability to live even the smallest of dreams.

One sister dead; OD'ed. One brother dying; AIDS. Her, walking down the railroad tracks with me. I may have just found my soul mate. Though I must admit, I do have a bit higher life aspiration than to end up, T.P.T., (Trailer Park Trash).

We walked a bit, and as they day began to come, the traffic began to move with more of a frequency, she decided it was time for her to go home. We got in my car. I drove her a few blocks away. Dropped her off, with the promise to communicate soon.

I drove from North Redondo towards the ocean. It took me maybe five minutes. I pulled up to my building, opened the security gate, drove into my parking spot, and parked. Out of the car, I walked to the stairs. I walked up the stairs, to the door that linked the outside of my building with the interior. Into the building I waltzed. I went down the hall. I found my door.

I stuck the key in the lock. I opened my door. I went inside. I threw my keys down on the kitchen counter. I took off my sport coat. I hung it on the coat rack. I kicked off my shoes. I went to the refrigerator, grabbed a *brau*. I sat down on Mr. Couch. I pounded the beer in three swigs. I got up. I threw the bottle in the trash. I walked to the bedroom. I lay down on the bed. I looked at the clock. It was 9:10 in the AM. I closed my eyes. With the sound of the waves pounding in my ears, I went to sleep.

*   *   *

It was maybe seven or so in the PM, and my phone rings. I pick it up. And yes, it was her, my Goth princess, Victoria.

'How perfect of a name for a Goth,' I thought, Victoria. It seems so Victorian, so gothic...

And yes, as promised, she had called. Yes, it was true; just like me, she was interested.

She asked me if I wanted to drive up to West Hollywood with her. As mentioned, she didn't have a car and all...

What was going on was that she had just bailed from an apartment she had on Santa Monica Boulevard. She wanted to go and pick up the last of her stuff. Then, we could hang out.

With nothing on my plate, I was happy to make the drive.

254

I hit over to her place in North Redondo and picked her up. Her sister was waitressing at a restaurant. Her brother, still down for the AIDS count in that hidden back bedroom.

We were out. The night was dark and cool. She, gothic beautiful. Just perfect passions for a white chick. Black clothing. Black hair. Black soul. Just my flavor.

We got into my ride and motored north. I asked about why she was moving out. Her answer was a two-part story.

Part Uno: It was just too noisy. I can dig that. I hate city noise, as well.

Part Dos: She has/had recently split up with her boyfriend. Ain't no *thAng* to me. What is over is over. But, what did strike me as a bit disconcerting in this *Part Dos* section of the convo. was the fact, (so the story goes), that she had gotten a *Restraining Order* against the dude. *"Why"* I inquired, *"Was he kicking your ass?"* The answer was, *"No."* She just wanted to make sure the *hombre* got the message that they were, in fact, done. So, she headed off to the courts, got the *Restraining Order,* and delivered it to him at his parent's house herself.

Now, here is one of those situations where you have to take a long hard look at a situation before you ever get involved in it—involved with said situation... I mean like I am of the firm belief that we all are shown a sign of *things-to-come* before they ever happen. Was this one of those signs? I mean, a

Restraining Order, whether true or false, is one of those things that stays on, what they call, *"Your Permanent Record,"* forever. I mean, for life... As you can image, this addition to her autobiography did put me in a bit of a quandary. But, she was hot and I was *dancin'* along. Never let it be said that I don't see things through to their limit.

We pull up at her place. It was one of those junky old dirty, off-white storefronts on Santa Monica where there are apartments up above. Not cool in any way. Just a location to live. But, only if you can take the traffic noise, which she apparently could not. And yes, there was a lot of that—traffic noise that is...

It wasn't in the section of S.M.B. where fags sell their ass or will suck your dick for a few dollars. No, it was a bit west of that. Over where S.M.B. is just junky.

Anyway, we get out of the ride. We go upstairs.

I quickly got the feeling that she maybe had bailed on the rent or something like that, because she was all cagey about checking everything out as she approached the door. And, cagier still when/while opening said door.

We go inside. It was dark. It was junky. It was kind of like one of those places where crazy people live who think that the aliens are attacking their brain, so they put a bunch of tinfoil on the windows and shit like that. I mean, her windows were all taped up with stuff, furniture pushed up against them. I was told, to dampen the noise.

256

But, I agreed, it was noisy as hell.

While there, I was kinda thinking that maybe I could scratch that itch and tap that ass right there. You know, I thought maybe she wanted it that way. Out with the old, in with the new, and all that... I thought maybe that is why she had invited me there. I thought... But, no such luck. It was just to get her stuff.

She dug around in the dark for a few. The electricity had been turned off. She was not happy. All that could be felt. She made it very obvious. But, she dug on and around, getting what she got. We were out the door. My dick still in my hand.

We packed her crap back into the back of my *356*. We drove off.

While driving, it was one of those feeling that her energy was so thick, it could be cut with a knife. I could see/I could feel, she was moving onto/away from something. But, that lost part of the past was haunting her. It wasn't her, *Restraining Order,* served boyfriend, she was almost jovial about that. It was something much deeper/darker/more haunting.

In any case, the night was young. And, West Hollywood is my scene. I dig the *nuevo-sheik* cafes and restaurants that line its streets. Not on Santa Monica Boulevard. But, on the better streets...

So, we headed off for a hundred dollar a plate meal and a hundred-dollar bottle of wine. We sit. We look at each other. We drink wine. We speak.

I could see she was, *down.* Not *down* like *down.* You know, not *down* like I'm *down.* She was *down,* in a different way. She was lost, out of her element. She had never been in a place like this. Never been, and she was the same age as me, twenty-nine.

In any case, I was glad to expose her to a new experience—a new realm.

Me, I was left with a new promise. I liked her. I liked her, a lot. She wasn't bullshit. She wasn't pretentious. She was *down.* Not *down* like me, Venchinzo, or my other soul buds. She was just *down.* Gothic on the verge of/rising from W.T., (White Trash).

Well... We all *gotta* come from somewhere...

Driving on the 405 back to the South Bay, I was *playin'* the game I always play,

"Wanna go for a walk on the beach."
"No, I hate the beach."

Oh no! The whole reason for my existence, *The Divine Mother Ocean.* And, she hates it! But, I've overcome worse obstacles than that on the road to lust/love/and the wherefores and the whatevers in between.

In any case, we did what I do. We had some late-night coffee, down South Bay way, spoke a word or three, and set-up a promise of *manyana.*

As I may have previously mentioned and/or alluded to, I didn't have too much going on right now/right here/right there/then in my

258

life, and I was way ready for a new illusion to pop into my field of vision.

So, I dropped her off, with the remainders of her belongs from her Santa Monica, B.L.V.D. apartment—back at the home/apartment of her sister, the waitress, and her brother, dying from AIDS.

Me, I went home. Dick in my hand, alone. Well, this isn't the first time.

Into my beach apartment, I hear the perfection of the waves crashing on the shore; tempting/promising/telling the entire story of creation, of love, of longing, of wanderlust. I thought to go and take a walk. I did not. Instead, I cracked open a bottle of the grape, went out on my midnight patio, with my bottle, with my glass; and, as I poured it down, I embraced the perfection of the meditation of the divine source of humanity; the mother ocean.

*   *   *

AM, it must have been about nine. The telephone next to my bed begins to ring. *"FUCK!"* I scream. It woke me out of a deep sleep.

I think to not answer it. It must be some fucked up telemarketer. Or, one of my babes over Asia way, not realizing what time it is here in *The States*. I knew that it could not be any of my *peeps*. No, not this early. They all know I hate to wake up before ten, eleven, twelve, or one; depending on the amount of drink consumed the night the previous. But, answer it I do...

It was her. It was Victoria. She tells me she doesn't sleep much; can't sleep—as she is haunted.

Me, on the other hand, I love sleep. Man, there is the whole other world in there. A different world from here. Not better/not worse/but different. And, I do love the different.

Mystics throughout time have tried/have attempted to define it—sleep. But, they cannot. It is all only their own impression of the impressionless. It is all their own interpretation of what they want it to be. But, sleep is, what sleep it. Like all mystical realms, it cannot/it will never be explanted—only speculated upon.

But, back to her, the girl/my girl. The one who couldn't sleep. I understood... Her sister up in the AM and going to work. Her brother hacking and coughing, dying from AIDS. Yeah, it had to be hard for her to sleep.

She asked me if I wanted to hook up. You know that I did...

I hung up, with the promise to pick her up ASAP. Yeah, I could tell that she had found what she was looking for; me. A new promised illusion. A new way out. A new and meaningful nothingness. You know, the kind that all the romance novels are written about. But, she... She: her and I, we were a bit different. We were two of the lost. Obviously, two of the damned. Caught/trapped into a reality that we had no hand in making. Cast to the realms of the world

260

we were could never truly be, whom we wanted to be/who we were. Her and I.

As I lay there, with the promise to get up, I began to realize that my head was spinning due to the alcohol consumed the night before. I hadn't slept long enough. No, not long enough to sleep it off. I had been awoken, way too soon. Way before my time.

But, with the promise of new illusion... I mean, FUCK, this obviously was getting serious in its own bizarre way. But, I guess that is the world I inhabit; bizarre. A world that so few can transverse. At least transverse with/and while maintaining enlightened consciousness. Remember, that is what I am about; I just take the path over to the left, in its transversion. A path very few can follow.

So and but, with the promises made, I knew I must drag myself from under the covers. But, for that one last moment of momentary perfection, I listen to the divine mother ocean. Listened in my laying. Listen in her moving. Movement, something which I must now do...

I get out of bed. Bam, I'm hit with that no blood to the brain cells, that instantaneous dizziness. Was it the alcohol still circulating in my system or my body/my blood cells, shutting down? I grabbed the dresser by my bed, to hold on; to stay erect; to remaining standing. But, as soon as it was there, it was gone.

As I sleep naked, I just made my way straight to the shower. Checked my look in the mirror as I walked by. As usual/as expected, I was a mess. My long hair all over the place. A three-day-old beard. And, the lost look of inner-knowledge trapped inside a human form; kept from emergence by the controlling hands of a world/of a society that has not the understanding/nor the care for the deeper realms of consciousness.

I slide open the shower door. Turned on the water. I got inside.

I love showers, man. There is just something right and perfect with them. You get the right temperature, the right space, and I can hang there for hours. Hell, back in my Hollywood, California adolescence, I used to climb into my shower, in my apartment building, on Hobart between Hollywood and Sunset Boulevard. I would turn off all the lights. It was in the way back of the apartment, so it was dark, no windows, and you could do that kind of thing. Yeah, it was pitch black. Me, I would sit there in my shower meditation. My mother thought I was wacking off. I was not. I would just sit in the base of the shower and become lost in the divine perfection.

In any case, that was then, this is now. I took a shower and tried to get my head to stop spinning. I got out. I dried off. I caught a shave.

Nude, I headed for the kitchen and my espresso machine. Took out the coffee beans. Poured them into the grinder. Ground them up. Put them in the espresso maker. Added the water. And, as it was brewing/steaming up, I hit the closet, grabbed some clothes. Put them on. I hit these long and baggy dark gray pants, via Italy, that I dig. A gray print shirt. I left it untucked, of course. A dark gray, with pinstripes, vest. And, I grabbed this gray, double breasted, sport coat.

So, that was that and this was this.

I hit the kitchen. Poured the two cups of espresso into a mug and shot it down. I went and grabbed three Bayer aspire. Popped 'em. I was set; ready to go. Got my big bulky shoes on. And me, I made it for the door.

I hit my *356* and I was off.

As I drove over to her crib, it was kinda strange, I thought. I mean, she lived so close; like five-ten minutes away. This is something that never seems to happen for me. But, here it was; destiny in the making/love for the taking/hearts for the breaking...

I parked, went up to her door, and knocked. She opened it; all gothic smiles. Dress in black; just the way all Goths should dress.

I hear the coughing, the dying of AIDS, in the background. She said, *"Bye,"* and we were gone.

Funny, she wanted to hit this other cemetery, not too far away. Remember, she wanted to look around for a gravesite. She didn't have any money but wanted to look anyway. Wanted to get a place for her sister to rest. RIP, even though the body was long gone—gone somewhere; to where, no one knew.

Now, don't get me wrong here, if you think I didn't see the strange coming on; believe me, I did. I mean, let's put the numbers together here. Dead sister. Dying brother. Apartment on *Fag Boulevard,* that she had to bail from. *Restraining Order* against her last dude. And now, here I was, driving her to another cemetery, to check out plots that she had no money to pay for, in my *1964 Porsche 356 SC.* Me, wearing a thousand dollars worth of clothing, a gold Rolex, Italian shoes that were upwards of five hundred dollars, and my dick in my hand, waiting to get me into all kinds/any kind of trouble.

But fuck, man, that first night; with me: her and her sister—it was fucking magic. And, our other time(s) *to-get-her,* they weren't bad either.

I don't know, maybe it is just me? I'm a fucking dreamer/a fucking believer. I believe in people. Believe that they can be more than they are. Something different/bigger/else. How many times have I been wrong?

Anyway, we did the cemetery. Equaling nothing, but some wasted time in my/in our lifetime(s): her's and mine. We did breakfast. And fuck, it was still on the short side of noon.

"Hey, you want to head back to my place? You look a little tired."

She did. She obviously knew what this all meant.

We pull up. We pull in. We get out. We walk. We get in. I open the door to *Love Crib Central.*

264

"Wow, you have a lot of books."

For the record, for those of you who don't know me, I have a wall of books in my place—floor to ceiling; wall-to-wall.

"The ocean's right out there."
"I know. I can hear it. I hate the ocean"

I go to open the drapes.

"Don't."

I smile.
Next comment,

"Wow, you have a lot of guitars. Do you play?"
"Obviously."
" I always wanted to learn."
"I'll teach you."

There was nothing left to say. It was time to do what we came to do.

"Yeah, I stayed up late. I'm kinda tired. You want to knock out for a few?"

I gave her the P.S.

"Don't worry you can trust me. If you can't trust me, who can you trust?"

Fuck, I don't even know how many women I've dished that line to?

265

But, she knew that I knew, what she knew was going to happen.

I throw my clothes off. I'm standing there nude. I go for her,

"You can't sleep in your clothes."

I began to undress her. Cautiously, she allows me.

I leave on her bra, her panties. Play it cool, you know.

I guide her towards the bed.

I get in first. Pull back the covers. She gets in.

Like all good *playas* I lay there for a time. Don't push the situation too hard. Let it/let her gel into the moment.

She looks at me. I at her. It is our time.

We kiss. One leads to the next and the next and the next.

Her tongue, it tasted like cigarettes. Oh, did I forget to mention, she smokes. Well, she is a Goth. I think all Goths smoke; don't they?

I hate cigarettes! I hate smokers! It is just a dirty habit. And, I especially hate to kiss smokers. It just tastes bad!

But she, the babe here, the one in question; I knew/I could see, she was so broken. Broken just like me. Broken in a different way though. So, I said *nada*. At least for/at least in this moment, I let her be who she be.

But, as I learned long ago, with my first serious babe, on the love shack side, in

266

Thailand; she was a smoker too. I learned that after you kiss for a few, the taste of cigarettes, it does dissipate. So...

We kissed for a long time. Locking toughs/touching souls. I took her bra off. White girl boobs. Not too big/not too small. They were okay.

Then, with my dick very hard, it was time to get down to business. I slipped off her panties.

I look/I see. I always want to know what I am about to dominate/to penetrate. I notice she had one of those trimmed down/shaved down pussies. You know, the way the trend is going now.

But, I don't know what it is or why? Why, all the girls, especially the white girls, seem to trim and to shave down the snatch *now-a-days*. Man, I just don't get it?

I mean, I dig that whole power bush scenario. Unshaved; something to get lost in. Something to let you know you're having sex. But, *the times they are a changing.'*

Now, to describe this situation for the *aficionado*. If this girl, my Goth little princess, was not shaved down, I mean that bush of hers would have gone way up. It would have been bush central—possibly the biggest bush I have ever encountered. I mean she did have some far-reaching nubs—way-way up her belly.

So, with my interests risen, if you catch my meaning, and I think that you do, I got to business.

She was wet. She was ready. So, I put it

267

in, just a bit/just for a second. And then, I pulled it out. Now, I hit that tradition a few times, just to get her *beggin.'*

Then, I power pile drive it in deep. Very deep. She liked what I had to give her.

For any of you who know me, you know, that I know, what I know how to do. I mean, between the years of *Tantra Yoga* and the years of power partying on the streets and in the gutter, (both here in *The States* and in the lost realms across the globe), I know how to give women what they want/what the need. And usually, I can get them to get their business done very fast. But, with her... I fucking worked. I mean, fuck, I was hitting that pussy for two, maybe three hours, nonstop. And *nothing, nada.* I mean the pussy got dry. I hit the lube, hit it some more, and all of the etcetera, and still *nada.*

She finally says to me,

"I can't cum. The doctor gave me this medicine, and it makes me not cum. I've never cum."
"What kind of medicine?"
"It's something for my problem."
"Problem? What kind of problem?"
"It's something to do with my emotions."

Well, fuck me! Let's add another number to the list of, *"What the fuck am I doing here?"* The bitch is on some fucking psych drugs!

268

Now, let's just think about this here for a minute. You're in a bitch—literally. You're fucking hard. You're fucking long. You're fucking 'em right. And, while you're in there; first she tells you, she can't *cum*. Okay, well I think I can fix that; I have before. But then, bitch tells you that she on psych drugs. All this, while dick is seriously still in motion.

Fuck it. I hit it for a few more and blew my rocks.

Post and past; me, being the gentleman that I am, I gave her the kiss, the hug, the cuddle, the love. You know, she's a fucking psycho, I didn't want to set her off.

So finally, it was our time to do what we had actually came there to do; sleep. From my lack of, and the lingering touches of a hangover, and my desire to mentally escape from said situation, I dosed off; pretty quick. I slept. Merged into that other and different realm. You know, the one I spoke of.

Maybe a half hour or so later, I open my eyes. Her eyes, wide open.

"I can't sleep with all this noise."

She was speaking of *The Divine Mother Ocean*. So, much for me crashing...

So, awake; though not really wishing to be. But, there she was. This nude form of a Goth-girl. Her dyed back hair and her remaining black pubes staring at me. Well, you know... Me, being who I am. I had to hit it one more time.

269

She was willing. And, so was I.

I, again, fucked her right. I fucked her hard.

Post, we get up and hit the shower, hit the streets. We do what we do. Living the nothing that only people who are out on the outskirts can understand. The world, the *nine-to-fivers* will never know. The normal, the indoctrinated, they can never understand. No, they can never know, the knowledge, the understanding(s), the feeling(s) of the lost. It is a world onto itself.

Now, you may ask, *"Why didn't I just ditch the bitch?"* I don't know, man? I know I should have. I guess... But, I dug her.

Yeah, she was fractured/broken. But, so am I. Me, I am just fractured/broken in a different way. Hell, call it my wanting to save her, make her and her life better; make her *cum*—let her know the feeling. Call it whatever. But, I liked her...

But, that's just me. I always fall for the broken/the damaged/the lost/and the alone.

*   *   *

A couple of days ticked on, as the days of life tend to do. We spent time together. Her: she and I.

Lost, yeah, she was lost. Dammed, yeah, she was dammed. But, I dug her. She was one of those lost souls, who was/is more than she could ever even understand. She was walking art in an artless world.

As Sunday rolled around, it was our first Sunday, post our meeting. Maybe a week deep, post the previously detailed, first insertion.

My bro, Saturday Jim's stepson was having a bike race over Manhattan Beach way. As was tradition, my attendance, complete with all my cameras, was expected.

Normally, I hit over to Saturday Jim's with whatever new babe I have in tow. It is almost like an inside joke. I bring *'em* over. Then, he or his lady nonchalantly takes a picture or me and her; her and I. Her, whatever new specimen I may have.

Man, I do not even know how many photos of me, (and them), they may have. But, there must be a lot...

But, this one, my gothic princess, well, I hadn't brought her over. No, not yet.

In any case, as she was my *New and Current, Main L.A. Babe,* I brought her along for the ride. The ride; to the bike race, you know.

So, on that Sunday, I drive through all the inside traffic, all the blocked off streets, trying to get to the appropriate parking lot.

Just a side note here... Now, me being an avid bike rider. Normally, I would have just avoid all the traffic and cruised over on my *Colnago.* But, Goth-girls are not that much into the doing-of-the-doing. So, her with no bike, well, that was not going to happen.

Anyway, with Victoria *ridin'* shotgun, I made my way through the crowds, driving my *356.* I pull up at the entrance to the parking lot.

271

I show the teenager who is staffing the gate, my Press Pass. But, he's too stupid to know what it means. I have to pay fifteen bucks for parking. I am not happy.

Inside the boundaries of the parked cars, I locate an empty parking space. I park.

Then, with my cameras over my shoulder; we: her and I, go out to where all the people who worship the sun dwell. Them, not me. Them, not her. Me, I hide from the sun whenever possible.

We find Saturday Jim, his lady, his daughter, (my godchild), his stepson, and even Saturday Jim's sister who is in tow for some nondescript reasoning(s). I introduce her. Her, my *New and Current, Main L.A. Babe.*

Saturday Jim's lady is unimpressed. She watches very closely as she, Victoria, plays with her daughter; my godchild. With all kinds of distaste in her voice,

"Where do you get these girls," she inquires.

She obviously just doesn't get the gothic vibe.

Saturday Jim's sister, however, immediately sees through the illusion.

"She is beautiful," she exclaims. *"Just look at that face. Look at those cheekbones..."*

Yeah, she saw it. She realized it. She pierced the illusion. Victoria just liked to dumb down. But, beyond all that, she was a stunning

272

beauty. Hiding from the world due to some, yet unrevealed, reasoning. Yeah, I too looked; yes, she was/is beautiful. Gothic perfection.

The bike race went as the races go. I took a bunch of photographs. Saturday Jim's stepson did not win. What else is new?

Then we, her and I, (Victoria), left.

Post the comments of both Saturday Jim's lady and his sister, my knowledge was reaffirmed that what I was seeing was true beauty. It was real. What I was feeling, love, was right.

Again, a few days danced on. Then, one night, Victoria took me over to her parent's home. It was an apartment on north side of Torrance. Torrance, a city in the South Bay of L.A., next to Redondo. The people who live there, live there for lifetimes; they are the children of the children of...

We walk inside. The parents were smoking. Victoria was smoking. There was country music on the stereo. Me, I was in hell. She took me, I guess, because she felt I had pasted any test that was given. That me, her and I, were on track for something. Something? But, what was, *"That something,"* remained the only question.

Post that session of the smoking, of the parents, of the country music, my mind started to shift.

"I hate county music," I exclaimed as we walked out the door. *"You took me into hell!"*

273

She was all sorry and shit. But, it was not enough. My mind/my feelings had shifted.

"You really need to quit smoking," I told her.

She told me, she couldn't. I let it go...

A couple of more days passed. Me, I was out of the moment/out of the mood; all the fantasy was lost.

I hit her pussy time and time again. It meant nothing. I got her to feel nothing.

I guess it must have been another week, because it was Sunday. It was the afternoon. We had just finished fucking. I remember studying her nude body. It was perfect, if she only would let it be perfect. Perfect for me, anyway.

I asked her if she would stop shaving *the beav*. She would not. She thought god had made her way too hairy. And, letting it go, even a little, would equal a massive explosion of hair.

Then, we got up. She lighted a smoke.

I mean this was my fucking apartment and she was doing the no-go of the no-go's— lighting a cigarette in it. In other words, things were not going my way.

I mean like, isn't that the foundation for a relationship? Things going your way. I mean, yeah and sure, things have to be going both of your ways. But, in those moments, when things aren't going your way, it is then that you have to speak up—say something.

"This is my world," I told her. *"And, I am only allowing you to be in it."*

Instead of questioning/contradicting, she, without a thought, says,

"Yes, I know. This is your world."

Her answer appeases me; at least for a moment.

We go and have a late lunch over at this high-end establishment in the Marina. As we stare out over and onto the boats, I start to ask questions. I had to know what was really up with her.

But, let me tell you, do not ask questions if you do not want to hear the answer(s). So, here it goes; you may want to skip this section.

As the story goes, when she was in high school, one of her teachers took her down to Mexico on a so-called field trip and raped her for a few days. He left her there. When she made her way back Stateside, her parents, being who and what they are, (W.T.) tried to do something; but nobody listened to them. Their voices and her screams were not heard.

I don't know, maybe they didn't scream loud enough? Because what they were told was that due to the fact that what happened took place in Mexico, there was nothing that they, (the police), could do. Mostly, it sounds like they, (the police), didn't give a shit; not about her, not about Victoria, not anyway.

275

I mean, if that had been my daughter and the police weren't going to do anything, I would have gone and cut that *mutha fucka's* dick off and then shoved it down his *mutha fuckin'* throat so he could choke on it. But, people are who they are.

In any case, there was obviously something deeper; more demonic to her life/to her childhood than that. I mean a whole family of children does not come out fucked up if there isn't something going on across the board. But, that story, I wasn't told. I probably would not have wanted to hear it, if I was to be told. But, I know, there was/is another story...

Anyway, things went on for a minute or two longer with her and I. But, her smoking got to me. And mostly, my not being able to either control her or fix her got to me more. So me, I did what I do, I played the arrogance card as a means to, *"Exit; stage left."*

"This is my world," remember?

I mean, really... What is arrogance? It is all based in a foundation of insecurity. So, in all my stupidly, I blew her off.

...Epilogue...

Maybe a year later, she came and called me from the call box at the door of my apartment building. It was winter for it was only like five o'clock and it was already completely dark. She wanted me to come down and take a walk with her. I did.

We walked along *The Strand* and spoke.

She had changed. Her hair was no longer long, straight, nor was it dyed black. It was light brown, a bit shorter, and much more styled. The clothing she wore, more contemporary and traditionally fashionable.

Though in truth, I was way more into the dark hidden beauty she had previously portrayed, but I could see that now the rest of the world would be allowed to see how truly beautiful she was.

We talked about what we had been doing, about what was going on with our lives. She told me about how her brother had passed away. How she was still living with her sister. She apologized to me that she was still smoking—that she had tried to quit, but so far, she could not.

As we walked, I began to think that she had come back to try again. …To make things work. To see if she could be what I had wanted her to be. I got lost in the illusion of that thought for a moment or three. But then, she asked me a question that came straight out of the stratosphere.

"I was wondering if you could get me some tranquilizers."
"What? How?"
"Well, I remember you telling me that you're a doctor."
"A Ph.D. Not an M.D."

"What's that?"

There it was. I had been handed the truth. She lived in a completely alien existence/lost in the abyss. Appearing to be of this place/of this time. But no, she was not. What we/what I had experienced was nothing more than an abstract mind fuck illusion. She wasn't even there. Somehow/someway, life had damned her to such a degree that I could not even comprehend; how she could not comprehend.

Though she appeared to be embracing/interacting with reality, she was not. She was *gone-daddy-gone;* somewhere else, pretending to be, but not actually being of this world. I felt very-very-very sad for her.

As we approached my building, I looked to see if the lights were still off in my apartment. If they were, that would mean that my chick, the one I was currently shacked-up with, would not yet be home. Me, being who I was/who I am, thought to go and bang one more piece off; for the annals of history/for literature. As she, this one-time Goth-girl was obviously more than willing... But, as we approached, I saw the lights turn on. Good thing, I guess. It would not have been too cool to be *hittin'* some pussy and have the new, *Main and Current L.A. Babe* walk in on said.

So me, I walked my one-time Goth-girl princess to her car. Oh, by the way, she now had a car. I told her I was sorry, but I couldn't get her any meds. I wasn't that kind of doctor.

I hugged her. I could smell the scent of cigarettes in her hair. She got in her car. She drove away. I walked away. And, that was that. Another one of those perfect illusions/perfect loves that could have been, but was not.

I walked up into my crib. I was greeted by my *Main and Current L.A. Babe.* She was/is beautiful. This sweet little Asian flower with long black hair and a spiral perm. Yeah, I love her... And, she loves me. When we go out, she hangs on so tight to me, it is like she is hanging on for her life/like she will never let me go.

Babes...

The nights they scream, and the days they dream, and life, like love poetry on a napkin, it means nothing at all.

Kisses and love, screams and dreams, and you just get so tired staying up all night/every night in love/making love, that you just gotta sleep all day.

So, the poetry does not get written, and the songs do not get played and/or the paintings do not get painted. The intensity of lack of accomplishment is kill.

But the feeling(s) in the arms of the babes... Ah, it answers all of those momentary addiction—those needs that lie.

Then, they bail out. The babes, you know. They have to go to work. They have to go to school. They have to make it home before their parents wake up and you're left all alone. The emptiness pounds as you stare into the blankness of off-white apartment, on the beach, walls.

So, I go slightly insane. I run outside to the morning. Well, more like the afternoon. I get my cappuccino, hang w/ the dudes, anything but the nothing of the alone. That isolation that becomes so apparent. That addiction of association felt; when your time has been so full-on.

But then, I go home as the night is

coming on—a million messages on my telephone answering machine. A moment, a choice, a purpose, a reason, who to choose tonight to fulfill the emptiness of nothing and a life where my biggest worry is to try to find a reason to get out of bed and where and when to go and have lunch.

It was a week, well actually, it was three days of that week: Tuesday, Wednesday, Thursday. Venchinzo and I, we had been *partyin'* and *clubin'* hard; way hard. We were like waiting for a reason to stop. But, there never was one in sight. We were waiting for a proposal to dream, to try to give us a purpose; a place of sanctuary of fulfillment—as monetary as that may be in both of our unfulfilled floundering lives. The nights, the babes, the clubs, they screamed to us.

Paraphrase in a paragraph... Like hey, there were a lot of other babes on the love-line, at the times/this time in my life. It's like life is never really in balance, you know—the all too real alone or the way far full-on. Anyway, where do I draw the definition for this tales of lust, love, god, and all of the things in-between. I guess I will do it/of the babe(s); met of and on these three nights in question.

Tuesday

Tuesday; step out, step in. It was this little place on the way *Heavy Metal* side of the picture, *The Cathouse.*

*   *   *

Excuse me for a moment, while I sit back into the nothing/everything of procrastination and play a song off this tape that my main babe in Kuala Lumpur gave me. A song by a guy name Chris Rhea. God, what was it now, more than a year ago.

She gave me a ring on the old *tele,* via the international lines, yesterday. The conversation was what it was... The same longing for me. The same promises of eternity. The same, *"When will I come back?"* The same... They all want the same. All the babes do. But, they never want to pay for it. The price is always the same. Me, I must pay for it/for everything. They want me. They want the illusion. They want the stupid promise of forever. And/plus they want me to pay for it. No fair, I think.

*   *   *

Song on the tape played, back to the, back-to; the subject at hand... It, (the tape), is one of those tapes, you know, where the whole thing sucks but there is just this one kill song on it. Yeah, I played it on this bad little yellow *Sony ghetto blaster* that's *sittin'* here on my drafting—strategically placed on the table in front of me.

Anyway...

Venchinzo and I pull on into this *Heavy Metal Church.* It's over there on the low side

282

of Highland in West Hollywood. If you're connected, maybe you know the place. Maybe not.

We kicked down a few of the *braus,* cruised the scene, scammed out the chicks in their miniskirts and leather jackets, and basically like, *"Woe, just flowed on into the vibes of the place, dude."*

We had been hanging downstairs, slid our way up the back-side, to the upstairs and in passing the bar, I have to admit I did make a bit of the old eye contact with this semi-fine babe of a chick on the Asian side of the photograph. Eye contact, met with full-on bitch glare back. Well hey, if they don't want to know then forget *'em.* We went and sat down; Venchinzo and I.

Maybe five into it, up she comes, planting herself down next to me. Her, this very same bitch of a babe, in tag with her was this *hoe lookin' Heavy Metal* blonde bimbo of a friend. Venchinzo and I naturally had already induced the buzz via the *al-co-hol* and I mean like, let's get serious here; we were laughing and having a fucking good time, just him and me.

It's like one of those things we do, you know. We have, like, our one main place staked out when we pull in early before the full-on crowd starts hitting, (about midnight), and we start dancing. Previous to all that, we like to kick back, drink a *Weiser* or three and discus whatever reality our, in the process of getting fucked up, minds like to throw out. I mean like, it was the same with his brother Saturday Jim back at our days at Hollywood High School. He and I, we had our wall. We would go and sit there on the ground, leaning way cool against it, every day. We even had our D.M., (Dead Meat), babes listed upon it. And like hey, if anyone wanted to pull up, they were *comin'* into our zone of excellence and they better be ready to be rejected if they were not welcome; were not wanted

Same with this club, Venchinzo and me; this was our turf.

So anyway, the babe and her friend pull up. Venchinzo goes to catch us another round.

"So, what are you guys laughing so hard about," asks the Asian girl.
"You wouldn't want to know," I answer.

The convo, well, it had been initiated. So, let's put the basic play into motion here. Play is as play was.

You know, I do the basic impress her and throw a bit of her native tongue her direction.

She couldn't believe it; a *la-way,* who could rap the Mandarin.

Yeah, she was from Taiwan too... Just like my *Former Main L.A. Squeeze.*

*   *   *

Sidebar here:
Man... *Dumpin'* her, *My Main and*

284

Central L.A. Babe via Taiwan, a few months back was the way far best thing I could have done. I mean since her, since the dumpage, there has been more babes than I even know what to do with. More than I can count. Life, hun?

*   *   *

So anyway, back to the story at hand... We spoke a bit; the two girls and I. She told me I looked like one of those typical L.A. *clubin'* sort of dudes. I think that was meant to be one of those playful insults. But, I mean, get real! Sure, I have long hair. I've had it most of my life. It's not a fashion statement, okay! It's just who I am. Sure, I have nine earrings, (at last count), in my ears. Again, I've had *'em* forever. But, like hey, I'm wearing a *Rolex.* I'm sprouting my bad, long baggy Italian suit. My shirt is way too big and way untucked, and my shoes way big and way chunky. This, while everyone else is seriously *chillin'* in their tight jeans, leather jackets, and cowboy boots. And, I'm not even gonna get to *talkin'* about what she was *a-wearin'.*

Anyway, a long story made long... Don't want to bore you here; you know. But, I played along with her. I mean, after all, I hadn't dipped my cookie in any babe via Taiwan in several months. At least none that I can remember.

Venchinzo comes back with the beer. The babe tells me she has to bail by 12:00 AM.

It was approaching…

So, I toss her my Thai business card, *"You can read Thai, can't you?"* She throws me her local number. She leaves.

Venchinzo and I kill the brews and hit the old *Heavy Metal* dance floor to whatever drunken and sensual feline momentary relief we may have found that evening. Truthfully, I don't quite remember. I woke up in the bed of *dos* babes, the next AM. The babes, still asleep.

How I got there; what we did, I just don't know? Obviously induced by the realms of the drink and whatever other narcotic poison may have found its way into my being.

Me, I just got up; got the old clothing on, (it lay there on the floor), and bailed. I caught a taxi. *"Redondo Beach, if you please."*

Wednesday

Venchinzo and I; first we went over to this, On-the-Boulevard, (Hollywood that is), Glam Slam of a gothic nightspot. I mean hey, I'm into that anemic look. The babes with the dyed black hair, the painted white faces. The new trend is the dudes wear dresses. No-go in my book. But, anyway and in any case, the place was like *dead's-ville, Daddy-O.*

And, I do mean like hey, this is verging on the 1990s and the times, as old Bob put it, *are a changing.'*

So, we bailed; hit on over to another B.L.V.D. The boulevard of the love punk fags and a club with live music that definitely fractured the old ear drums.

286

My hearing, none-too-good, from all the years of the *rock n' rollin,'* anyway. I mean, my ears they ring all the time. And, that is none-too-fun. But, with no place left to be, we chilled back, pounded more than a few brews and like, *Woe dude, we just checked it out.*

I was on. And, when I get on—look out...

"Yes," I said as a babe walked by.
"What?" she inquires.
"Yes."

She did say, *"Yes."* Which equals a moment or three of pure passion and generalized nothingness out in my ride. You know, by bad little *'64 Porsche 356 SC* does have a very big front seat when it is laid back, with lots O' leg room...

Oh yeah, I decided it was too much of who I am. So, I kept it. Unlike the detailing of the possible sale a few chapters back. And, I plan to continue keeping it; upkeep costs and all. Anyway, back to the in-car action...

Awh, how I do love sluts!

So, back inside, Venchinzo and I were pounding hard, when up comes this band straight out of what I guess was our era. They looked to be 1979/1980. Like hey, like woe, straight out of the *New Wave* dude.

It was four dudes, from other days, other bands; long gone past. In fact, a couple of *'em,* well they had some sort of minor local success eight years or ten years the previous. The funny

287

thing was/is that Venchinzo saw the guitar player and he recognized him. For him to remember anything that far back is virtually a fucking miracle. He reminded me, that I, for some drunken reason, was way pissed off at that loser, years back, and was going to jam him up at this little local club down Chinatown way, *Madame Wongs*. Back then, I went up, stared him down and told him, *"Why don't you catch the next train back to the sixties you fuckin' pussy."* That was back when we were very *Punk* and they were *rockin'* a sixties throwback vibe. Instead of facing me, the dude bailed to the dressing room and *pussed-up*. He wouldn't come out.

Funny, I had totally forgotten that situation. But reminded, I remembered it very well.

We, Venchinzo and I, were there at that club with our boys back in the day; Eddie, Joe, and Saturday Jim. But, of course, SJ, he was so fucked up he could barely move—as was virtually always the case...

I remembered... But, like hey, let bygones-be-bygones. I choose not to go up and remind the pussy of the situation, and finally get to jack him up.

So, the music pounded, here in the very late eighties, to the beat of the late sixties. Venchinzo and I, we were not particular amused.

Wait! Got to go grab another glass of the grape here. You see there is this babe due in about two hours. It now being about seven

288

thirty in the PM. In fact, she is the babe in which I am about to introduce you to.

Grape in hand. Back to the storyline. The storyline that occurred at the nightclub that night...

Standing there, in the distance was these two babes. Rather lost looking in admits all of the leather and teased hair.

Anyway, they were obviously *Ori-en-tal* on the *Kor-e-an* side of the view. So, like hey, what's a dude like me supposed to do? I slid on in.

I moved for the one, kill looking little babe. Waste length wavy hair. It was black, like all of the curses that haunt the realms of the night. She wore a high, tight, black, little mini-skirt. Yeah, I have become way more accepting of those as the years have trudged along.

Venchinzo slide on over to her friend. But she, the other one, didn't dig him. Leaned over to me and told me he was rude.

The bad little lad probably straight-up asked her to go out to my ride and fuck. Me, I *got-s* to say, when the boy gets a bit laced he isn't too tactful in his words. I mean like hey, with the Asian babes, not on the slut side of the picture, you have to play it a bit cool. But, anyway...

It was like in the old days, the Punk days. I used to have this van. *The Dodge Motor Inn* as we referred to it. Any key would open the driver's side door and yeah, I guess my bros did use it a bit. If you catch my meaning, and I think that you do.

Anyway, that van was like this music; the music we were listening to—blasting music that was from an era, long-long ago.

The music continued to get worse. I asked the babes if they wanted to book and go and hit *Canter's*.

One of the babes, the babe who Venchinzo was attempting to romance, asked, *"Can you leave your friend here?"* Of course, I could not! So, I laid the babe, the other babe, the babe I was *rapin'* up, my number via my business card.

I mean hey, like if they want to know what they were missing and what they will be missing they can place the old call my direction.

But, I did walk away with the promise of a call, day next. Day next, Thanksgiving...

So, the music was way bad. We said our goodbye's. Me and my homeboy, we bailed on out and into the night.

I dropped him off at his crib and headed on home, once again, in my full-on L.A. paranoia of the cops again busting me for *a duce*. I mean like hey, I was a bit juiced up.

Thursday

Day three, Thursday... The same location but the club, a different title.

You know, that is what has been happening to the club scene here in L.A. post the decline of the full-on live music venues. I mean like, the structure(s) rent themselves out, like a whore in heat to whatever promoter can come up with the bucks for the bill. So now, the clubs they come, the clubs they go. Though the foundational locations, they stay the same.

Prior to the club we had to go put in a little, *have dinner,* family session, at Saturday Jim's. Where, I must admit, that I did partake of a bit of the grape. Oh yes... I mean, it was Thanksgiving 1989 and all...

While there, the once very bad, Saturday Jim, had to give us his <u>now</u> family man rap,

"Aren't you guys ever going to grow up? I'm going to pick you two up in the morgue one of these days."
"With smiles on out faces," Venchinzo chimed in.

And now, for a moment of remembrance...

Yeah, we have not even really had one of those infamous *Jimmy Jam Sessions* in quite a long while. I mean, fuck! Saturday Jim used to party...

The last time was pushing almost a year back, when his wife wanted a new garage door and the bad S.J. said, *"No-go."*

Well, it was one of those L.A. *Santana* windy days, and so she had the bad German lad, Wolfgang, from down the street, pound on and knock down the garage door. The wife used to know him and his wife in Germany. She, S.J.'s wife, was/is from Holland, via Germany, you know.

Anyway, when Saturday Jim got home,

she told him it was the wind that knocked the garage door down. But, I mean like him way being no dummy, he took a look, he knew what happened, and, well, he got more than *kinda* pissed.

It's like, I jokingly told the bad lad Wolfgang, when the story of how the garage door came down was being told, *"I guess god carries a hammer."*

If I may present a side note here...

Wolfgang is one very bad lad. One of those dying breed of real men. Like when he wakes up in the morning, his wife pours him a glass of the breakfast of champions; whiskey and water. He downs that, then he goes out to warm up the car. She slices him up another glass and then goes and opens the gate for him. As he is backing up, he hands her the glass and is off to his day of employment. Pure poetry.

But that night, the one I am actually *takin'* about, Saturday Jim and I did begin to wet our lips. He was pissed. So, we poured long and hard.

One of the funny stages of the evening was that his stepdaughter's boyfriend leans in and tries to climb on board the, *get the drink on train with us.* But, I do mean like, *"Look out!"* When serious drinking *mutha fucka* like Saturday Jim, Venchinzo, or I climb on the party wagon, if you are not full-on, you better step back.

I mean like, S.J. was pouring the drinks. And, he was *pourin'* 'em heavy. It was like the old days back at Hollywood High School when

292

we: S.J. and I, used to bail out for *The Val* on the weekends and crib up at our friend's house. We would stay up all night and pour any alcoholic/alchemic conjunction we could find into the blender and drink it on down. We would spend the weekends FUCKED UP! And, those two words are meant to be in capital letters. Then, we'd show up at school on Monday morning, smelling of the stench of the drink and of the long weekend, lived too hard.

Few people, I believe, ever partied as hard as we did in the high school years...

Anyway, that night, Saturday Jim's stepdaughter's boyfriend, just couldn't hang. We warned him! He eventually got too fucked up and bailed on. And, as I am told, he spent the night making love to the toilet bowl, as he barfed it all up.

S.J. and I, well, we partied on...

Now, Saturday Jim has some of the biggest and badest Rottweiler dogs I have ever seen. And this night, S.J., post us *gettin'* totally toasted, he decided that he wanted to go out and sleep with 'em in their doghouse. This, on a cold and drunken, L.A., winter's night.

What was I supposed to do? It was his house/his desire, so I let him.

So, he went outside to the backyard to crib down. Me, being the nice guy that I am, I naturally locked the sliding glass door, after he left. I mean hey, I didn't want anyone to break in or anything like that. Then, I went and turned off the lights. You know, I didn't want to waste electricity. I mean you have to conserve energy to help save the planet; right?

A few minutes later, comes this quiet knock upon the door,

"Big guy... Big guy... Let me in. Big guy, it's cold out here!"

I sat there in hysteria for a few, laughing my drunken guts out as he continued to quietly knock. Finally, I let him back in.

Saturday Jim, well he passed out on the floor. Me, I straight-shot and killed the last of the bottle of Vodka we were drinking and slid it on over to my home away from home; S.J.'s couch.

Another day, another dollar...

*   *   *

Back to the real story, the one I'm *talkin'* about; here and now.

Venchinzo and I bailed S.J.'s crib, post getting our eats and our drink and our lecture. *"Thanks for the hospitality..."* We headed back to the fag side of the B.L.V.D. in West Hollywood; onto the night at the nightclub aforementioned mentioned.

Unlike the night before, the club it was pumping with all of the shallow mindless masses that tend to inhabit these realms. It was full-on fashion passion.

In some ways, we were out of place, Venchinzo and I. Both of us much deeper minded then our partying or our lack of

294

accomplishments in life would reveal.

Inside, we pulled up to the bar and kicked down a *Weiser*. Well, better make that three.

Pulling up next to me was this semi fine babe of an Asian chick; obviously on the Japanese side of the photograph. She was with a couple of dudes that looked like fags; straight off the *Booty Boulevard.*

But, she was semi-fine. I mean hey, what could a guy like me do? I had to rap a little of her native tongue her direction. She did dig it. The faggot(s) didn't. But, who the fuck cares! Fuck '*em!*

We danced a bit, her and I. Then, we went back to chill. I left her with her fag *lookin'* friends and went and threw back another *Weiser* or three with Venchinzo.

While I was *dancin'* with the new flower of passion, this sweet person of a female friend of mine had entered the club. I guess, I had invited her. I don't know? I'm kind of like that, you know. I say things I don't really mean. I say them to be nice.

Anyway, she's a friend introduced to me by an old lover—this Japanese via Hawaii chick who lives in a big bucks McMansion with her parents. I had met her maybe four/five years the previous. Venchinzo and I had hit up a Punk nightclub over W.L.A. way. Catching the last gulp of anything that was left from that/our era. Anyway, there she was with two friends. She was fucking beautiful. She had a great body and a great fully hired pussy. Plus, she was a great fuck. I was really into her; for a minute, maybe two. But, she was just fucking insane. And, not in a good way. She just wanted to sit around; *day-in-and-day-out,* with me. She was happy to do nothing, forever... Just fuck, eat, and hang out. I guess that's how you can be when you don't have art burning a hole through your inner being and your parents are paying your bills.

But, in any case, I had to cut her loose. She just killed my life/my creativity.

Then, right here/a few months back, she called me and told me about her friend. This chick, the one of which I now speak. The one who, I guess, I invited to the nightclub.

Now, this girl is very nice. I like her a lot. On our first meet, we just hung out at her apartment in South Pasadena and talked for hours. After that, sometimes we would just hang out there, at her apartment, and drink coffee. Sometimes we would go out and eat.

Though this girl really digs me and wanted much-much more/wanted me to take it/take her to the next level. And though, I thought she was very nice, very pretty, and we got on very well; there was one issue that my shallow-self could not get past. The girl is maybe a hundred pounds, maybe more, overweight.

As the story goes, her uncle had fucked with her in her childhood. She was half German/half Mexican. It was the Mexican side of the photograph that had done the *messin.'*

296

I don't know how many times I have heard a similar story from girls of the Latin heritage. But, what I do know is that it is fucked up! Men doing that to little kids. I think all those *mutha fuckas* should be hung by their nuts, their dicks chopped off, and then throw them into prison with a bunch of hardcore sodomites.

You know, a kid never really gets over something like that happening. It fucks *'em* for life. And, from a psychological perspective, girls, once this has happened, from a deeply hidden place in their brain, do things like put on big weight so men will not be attracted to them. Yet, in the conscious mind, they still hope/seek love. This was her case/this girl's/my friend.

Anyway, she had cruised into the club. Saw me. Came over. And, hung with Venchinzo and I. I bought her a drink.

But me, my mind was on the love action available in that new form of the Japanese sweetheart, I had just met. My eyes were glued. I know she, my friend, could see it/feel it.

Venchinzo though, he fucking man-ed up. That *mutha fucka* went and danced with her; my overweight friend. He made her feel special. He made her feel not alone. *Thank you my-man!*

Me, in all my shallowness, (though I liked her a lot), I could not bring myself to do it.

Anyway, she knew where my mind was. Understood, how she never had a chance/how we: her and I, would never be together. She got back from the dance floor, said her goodbyes, and went home.

Me, now I had my chance. My chance was back; uninterrupted. I was back on the prowl for the Japanese babe in question.

As the story goes. One of the *homosexual* looking *mutha fuckas* actually wasn't. He was just a *fuckin'* Aussie.

He had apparently got pissed at her, (the Japanese chick), dancing with me and all, complete with the *look-of-love* in her eyes; shining my direction. He told her, *"Fuck you."*

So, post my brew and my watching Venchinzo dance with my overweight friend in question, I waltzed back over to her and saw her; she had tears running down her face.

You see, *"Fuck you,"* is just not something you tell a Japanese babe. I told one of mine that once and she cried for three days.

Like, here in L.A., it's no big deal. I mean like somebody says, *"Fuck you,"* to me, and it's like, *"Fuck you too."* No big *thAng.* But, to a Japanese babe, it is, *not-too-nice.*

So, she stood there for a long time; literally crying on my shoulder. I mean like, everyone was walking by, fully looking at me; like I was the one that had done the dirty deed. The whole thing kind of pissed me off.

By the time I had gotten the babe calmed down, I was all geared up to go and kick the fag *lookin'* Aussies ass. But unfortunately, (or fortunate for him), he had gotten thrown out just prior to that for pissing in the sink in the

298

bathroom.

Fuckin' Aussies...

Well, the babe had my number. She was going to call.

So, I guess that is the set-up of the story, like the old Mod Squad T.V. series you know: *"One white, one black, one blonde."* Here it was, *"One Chinese, one Korean, one Japanese."*

Tuesday, Hui Quing
Wednesday, Joung Yee
Thursday, Mariko

Like Saturday Jim says, *"Where the fuck do these people think up these names?"*

Well probably, on the deep side of the far side, out in the out-back of Asia, they probably think John is a weird handle.

Stage Two—Part Two

Wednesday called first, on Thursday. But, I was out. She left a message on my answering machine. I called her back on Friday.

Tuesday called a week or so later. She was trying to play it cool. I was cooler, I didn't care...I let her call me a second time.

Thursday, called on Saturday. I was busy until Wednesday next. But, we did hook up.

And, that's how the story goes...

Now, for the details:

The Wednesday Girl...

"Well, like fully hey, why don't we, like, go out, you know."

So says, Joung Yee.

Joung Yee... There she was, this kill babe, *par excellence,* of a decade and a year younger than me, who spoke even way more L.A. then I did.

As she spoke... As she inquired as to our going out... For a moment, no two, I pondered the age difference, the lifestyle difference, and/or the possibilities of actually living a dream. But, I only pondered it for a moment.

Even though I generally find no interest in women more than a year or so my junior, I said, *"Yes."*

So me... Well, I headed on down the 405 freeway south. Headed for the O.C., Orange County on the *Gutenberg-Richter Scale,* and her abode of *livein'* with the family. I picked her up.

We only had a few hours, for she had to be to work in the afternoon. With no place and no further full-on density to dive into, I offered to take her lunch. She agreed.

Now, my previously mentioned, *Main L.A. Squeeze via the Taiwan,* being from O.C. herself, had introduced me to this little outdoor way, far-good, Mexican restaurant in the vicinity. The only problem being, I just vaguely remembered where it was.

300

So we, the new squeeze and I, we went for a drive here and there, in the open-ness of my Jeep style object. My bad *356* was down for the temporary count.

Look, but no find, as we tried to locate the said subject of the restaurant. Finally, I just said, *"Fuck it."* I mean we only had a couple of hours, and she didn't know where it was either...

I mobiled on down to this way cool, outdoor restaurant, on the side of King's Harbor, over here by my crib. We ate and all of the etc...

Did she understand or appreciate the price? I think not.

Anyway, post the initial lunch; a suggestion of a walk upon the wintering beach. So, we motored a block or so over. I parked my bad ride in my parking spot.

I mean, you know, just for the possible, in case, that I could give her the old convincing line of, *"Like hey, want to see my apartment?"*

So, we walked... We spoke. We laughed. All along that, oh so poetic ocean. You know, the one, that one; you have seen in all of the movies upon the late-night television screen.

Back from the walk, we sat down in the afternoon sun on the beach and hey, we even held hands for a time. But then, it was time for her to be off to work. Me, being the gentleman that I am; I, of course, drove her back to her home.

One date led to another and another and another. Then, I took her to one of those underground nightclubs which I frequent. It was dark, walls painted black. The people there were dark, (not in skin color, but in temperament/personality). Their hair was dyed black. The club, its name was, *Séance*.

The club, however, had undergone one of the infamous L.A. scene changes. What was once the full-on happening Saturday night Goth place to be, just two weeks the previous, was now sparely populated and in the vogue of meaninglessness. So, as it goes...

But anyway... How do I tell this story?

Well, I took her out several times, to all of those way, *"Neat-O,"* as she put it, underground type of haunts that I hang out in/at. Took her to the late-night restaurants that only the true bohemians know of and the coffee houses of the dark, the artsy, and the dismal. Me, always being the perfect gentleman, I never putting the move on her. She was so pretty, so young, so sweet.

Anyway, post one of our sessions, maybe four, five, or six, deep, I was driving her home in the area of the 3:00 AM and, out of nowhere, she exclaims,

"You know, I'm not a virgin or anything..."

She proceeds to tell of the six before me and how she really likes me and how she wanted to, *"Do it,"* with me.

Like I told her,

*"Damn, I have been too much of a gentleman!
You should have told all of this to me earlier."*

So anyway, she had to be home before
her mother woke up and there was little else
which I could do but give her the old invite to
come over morning time,

*"Why don't you wake me up on your way to
work,"* I concluded the evening with.

A kiss goodnight and all of the
possibilities of the poetry of being alone. I
drove home saying to myself, *'Well, fuck me.'*
I did this, as I once again realized that dudes
just do not want to hear about all those who
have walked through the fields before them.
We just don't want to know!
So, to all you chicks out there; listen
tight... Don't tell guys, your guy/your man
about your dick-list—about who has done you
or how many have done you in the previous
past. Men just don't want to know!
I went to sleep with more than a dream
of possibility and the knowledge that she had
to be to work in the ten of the AM and there
was no way in the world that she would chill
on by to give me that early morning call of the
wake me/it up.
7:00 AM. Well, fuck me again! Post just
a few hours of sleep. The telephone rings,

*"Hi, it's me. I'm downstairs. Can you let me
in?"*

With that, she came up to my apartment. I opened the door. She walked straight back to my bed. There, we would experience our first real kiss. Then, we made our first love.

We're *doin'* it. She *cums*. She starts to cry.

"Why you crying?"
"I never felt that before."

So, the six before me; well, they may have known what they had, but they didn't know how to use.

This wasn't the first time that happened... The first *cum,* that is. And, if luck holds, it won't be the last.

Even now, as I sit here, it has been several hours since I last held her nude, perfect, and hard body, next to mine. I mean our session(s) have continued... Yeah, I'm even popping a woody at just the thought of all of her perfection.

The perfection of the Wednesday Girl. That's her story...

The Thursday Girl...

Not so artistic, as the previously describe venture into the realms of the abyss of lust/love. Let's see, if I can wrap it up in a paragraph or so...

Thirty-one, just like me. Here from Japan; pushing five years. Just got done *cribbin'* with a nineteen-year-old—for a year,

304

so I am told.

I smiled as she told me that. All the youthful hormones and all... He probably gave it to her good, and often; but probably two strikes and he was out. If you catch my meaning and I think that you do...

Then, of course, there was that *faggy lookin'* Aussie, previously detailed. But, back to the story at hand—hers and mine.

First date. First walk on the beach. First kiss. Equals our first fuck in my love crib. Nothing really to write home about.

Well, this is my home, where I am writing; right now.

She could tell I was not really all that satisfied/all that inspired. Told me that she would try to make me, *"Feel better,"* the next time. She would try to, *"Do it,"* better, next time.

"Would there even be a next time," was the question reverberating in my brain. I mean, was there a point? But, the thought did cross my mind, *"That right! It is your job to please your man. So, get down to business."* And, I did appreciate her caring enough to care.

Overall, she was way fully serious. Never liked to loosen up. Said, she liked it that way.

She did have a seriously bushy pussy thought. I mean thick. I dig *'em* that way.

About a week post said session, I was sleeping. It was 8:00 AM in the morning of this Saturday. The telephone rings.

"This is the BLANK Hospital. Miriko Yamahiro has been in a serious car accident. Both of her legs were broken. She apparently was drunk, fell asleep at the wheel of her car, and smashed it into a wall. The reason we are calling you is that she wrote your number down as the person to contact in case of emergency."

My mind was fuzzy. It was early and I was still drunk from the night before. Venchinzo and I had partied hard at *The Rainbow*.

God, that place is full of losers! It is always the last resort! But, they do pour their drinks strong and there is always a *shit-load* of *Heavy Metal* chicks to choose from.

In any case, I wasn't quite sure what name the dude, on the other end of the line, had said. And/as, I had been *bangin'* this one babe, who had almost the same name as Miriko, and I had just recently found out that I had got her knocked up and I wasn't sure if she had dropped the kid yet, via the old pregnancy termination process.

(Remember... Why do you think Saturday Jim titled my dick, *"Dirty Harry?"* He shoots no blanks).

So anyway, there was no way in hell I even wanted to get near her if it was the one that may still be *a-carryin'* my child...

But, I was a nice guy about it. You know me; I'm always so caring and so concerned.

"Is she okay," I inquire.

306

"Yes, she is very lucid, and she will eventually be fine. But, she needs someone to translate for her and wants you to come and talk for her."

I play it cool/play it like I care. I say, *"Okay."* Then, the dude chimes up again,

"Oh, by the way, her bill, thus far, has been $10,344.00. Could you please bring that amount with you when you come?"
"Be right there."

Yeah right! I rolled over and went back to sleep.

*   *   *

Now, if I can give you a little PS; sidebar to a side note here...

So, Venchinzo and myself were out *clubin'* maybe a week or so later. It was Sunday night. We hit this half live music/half dance music—separated in two separate rooms, of course; place over on Santa Monica, B.L.V.D., on Sunday nights.

It was not on the sell their booty, fag section, of the boulevard. It was more over towards the Hollywood ghetto. We hit there because they served up free burgers; grilled on an outdoor grill.

I mean hey, not only could we get our drink on, our dance on, possibly get our dicks wet, and maybe listen to some decent live

307

music, but we could also get our eats on.

So, it is the Sunday night place to be. At least as long as it lasts.

Anyway, this evening, the one I am speaking about, we walked out of the door(s) of the venue with our dicks in out hand; *nothin'* equaling *nothin.'* But me, I had this great idea. A great drunken idea at two in the AM. I would drive us over the hospitable were my Thursday chick was laid up, recuperating from her injuries and would perform the great stunt of *hittin'* that big bushy pussy in her hospitable bed.

Venchinzo was drunk. He didn't care. So, off we drove.

Now, the hospitable, (which shall remain nameless), was over on the East L.A. side of the photograph. For those of you who know L.A., then you will probably know of where I speak. It is the sanctuary where all those who have no insurance end up. Remember the bill they tried to hit me with?

Through my drunken stupor, it was a bit hard to find; for I had seen it, (from the freeway), kind knew where it was; but didn't really know how to get to it. But, Somehow/someway we pulled up, parked the car, and we walked towards the door.

Now, as you can expect, it being about three in the AM by this point, the hospitable was on lockdown. It was dark. It was closed up. But, Venchinzo and I made our way straight for the front door. *En route,* we had the great idea to bringing the chick some flowers. So, we picked some plants; ripping them from the ground of the hospitable garden. We went straight through the front door, waved at the security guard, and walked straight past him like we were supposed to be there. The flowers/plants dripping dirt in our hands.

I knew the floor she was on; the ward she was in, because she had been calling and calling my answering machine. I, of course, never picked up. We made it to the floor. The plants, dripping dirt, and falling apart left a trail being us. A trail of breadcrumbs, if you will.

As we walked, trying to find the room, they truly started to annoy me; the flowers that is. In all the drunken perfection of the moment, I just tossed them on the hospitable floor.

Now, keep in mind, the hospitable was dark. The lights were low. The injured, the dying, the insane were all supposed to be asleep. I guess they were.

We walk past the nighttime nursing station, ignoring the nurse. She looked up. She looked at us. You could see the wonderment in her eyes. We kept walking. Walked, just like we owned the place.

We must have presented quite a site. Our long hair. Our drunken meandering.

I was dressed in a black sport coat and black baggy pants. Venchinzo wore torn jeans and a leather motorcycle jacket. We walked on...

Somehow/someway, we found her ward; my Thursday Girl. As this is the poor-people hospitable, it was a ward where she was housed. There were a lot of the injured and the dying in the room with her.

I made my way in. Venchinzo held vigil outside. I guess he didn't want to watch as I was *a-doin'* my *thAng*. If you catch my meaning.

I wandered around until I found her. There she was, all broken and Japanese, covered in a white sheet, in a white room, in a steel hospitable bed. Her long black hair etched her being into the lost realms of this lost night. She was the perfect object of perfection. The perfect form of desire. The ideal embodiment of the goddess. Abstract flawlessness, in all her brokenness beauty. She had casts on both of her legs.

I saw her. Knew what I had come there to do. I began to pull back her sheet. As I did, I stroked her hair. I kissed her. I looked and I knew that I could love her. Yes, just as I could love anyone—any perfectly broken piece of perfection; just like her/just like me.

Yes, it was her. Yes, I could love her. If only I would let myself. We: her and I, could live in the *never-never-land* of love forever; *forever-and-ever*. Yes, we could. If only I would allow myself to feel. Feel what everyone else feels. If only I could allow myself to believe. Allow myself to be seduced by the believing. The believing that it is all real. That life is real. That love is real. That the promises of *forever-and-ever* mean something. I knew it. I looked at her. She was beautiful. I had it. I

310

had her. She could be the one. She could be the, *"It Girl."* Broken/damage, just like me. Forever lost, in the lost. Yes, there she was. She was just like me. My perfect reflection. It could be forever, her and I; if I could/would only let it. But, I could not. I am who I am. I cannot believe the lie. I know, because I have tried.

I pull her sheets back. Her eyes slowly open. She looked at me. She speaks to me in Japanese,

"Are you a dream? Are you an angel?"

I smile. I was going to tell her that I was. In Japanese, of course. Then, I was going to do what I had come here/gone there to do. But, the moment was stopped.

I hear Venchinzo speaking in the hall.

"We are going on tour tomorrow. We have to catch our flight at 6:00 AM. He has to see her. This is his last chance!"

Where he came up with that, I do not know. But god, that was one fucking great line.

I looked at my Thursday Girl. Her beauty. My lust. My dick was rock solid and ready. But, all I could do was to kiss her on the cheek. I knew I wasn't going to get to do what I had come to achieve. So, I pulled the sheet back over her. I smiled. I walked away. Walked towards the conversation.

By the time I got there, Venchinzo had

the security guard wrapped around his finger. Venchinzo, unlike me, is a very personable guy.

As I walked up, the security guard was actually apologizing to me that it wasn't visiting hours. He actually offered to pull her bed out into the hallway, so we could visit. But, I figured *hittin'* the pussy out there wouldn't be that doable. So, I declined. Said, *"Thanks."* Walked on

Normally, that being a fucking massive hospitable, I would have never known how to find my way out. But, we had left a trail of breadcrumbs. Remember? Dirt and pieces from the plants we picked.

I laughed as we walked towards the door. The dirt, the plants, the flowers, were strung all the way through the hospital.

We made the door. Got to my car. I dropped Venchinzo off at his place. I drove home. It was getting light—the sun was rising in the eastern sky as I approached the ocean and saw her/heard her/embraced all of her absoluteness. Her, *The Divine Mother Ocean.*

This is my life...

The Tuesday Girl...

Now, the Tuesday girl, Hui Quing; well, her story is a bit more involved. Could it be more involved than the last one? I don't know?

Anyway, she called up my machine, as stated, a week plus later, asking if I still remembered her. We made plans, made a date and she was way ashamed, or whatever, of where she lived over there next to Monterey Park in Rosemead. She didn't want me to pick her up. She wanted to meet me. *"Sure. Whatever..."* So, we set the meet for a *rendezvous* at this Japanese restaurant in Little Tokyo.

Post my traditional, yearly, go cut down the Christmas tree, on the far side of Semi Valley, session with Saturday Jim and his daughter, I was *leavin'* his crib and geared up for the go.

I did my basic and/or traditional pick up the dozen log stemmed roses. The babe at the shop was digging my scene. So, I got her number. Never did call that little white bread type of thing though. I guess, maybe, I should have???

I hit over to restaurant where we were to meet in Little Tokyo. She was late; way late. And, I am not one to wait for anybody. So, I bailed.

I did a little drive through the downtown, checked out what I could see, and headed on home.

On my machine, I was greeted with the, *"I have to help my mother. I'm going to be late."* And then, all of the full-ons, *"I'm sorry."* Which basically means nothing, right? But she did try... I'll give her that.

Now, via the message(s), I was asked to call. So, what the fuck, I did. Her brother gave me the scoop and said that she was going to be waiting for me in this restaurant. Waiting, until I arrived.

Now, let's put the numbers here together... I had an *Eight-P* meet with the chick. I got there at 8:00 PM. I'm a punctual guy...

She wasn't there. I chilled for twenty. Still not there. I left. I drove around downtown, looking for any new illusion that may be found. Found nothing... That was maybe another twenty or so. I headed back to my crib in Redondo; which had to take me forty-five. Now, If I were to head back to Little Tokyo, it would take me another forty-five. Would she still be there, waiting all that time?

Well, leave it to me to play the hand to the fullest. I drove back on downtown.

Now, my mind played all the scenarios in my head as I drove. If she was still there, I had fully expected her to be sitting at the sushi bar drinking, conversing, and playing it full-on with all the local hang out sort of dudes. I had my whole pain formulated to such an occurrence, if such said occurrence, occurred.

I pull up. I pull in. Got a parking space on the street pretty much right in front of the place. I walk towards/walk in; pretty much expecting the worst. Either no babe, or a babe *hangin'* with *homeys*.

Through the doors, I make my entrance. Immediately, I see her. There she sat. Sitting solo at a table, nursing a beer. Or, should I say it in Japanese, *"Biru,"* as it was a Japanese restaurant and all... Though she is, as mentioned, Chinese.

The guy, the owner/the waiter, whatever

314

he was very excited to see me.

"She been waiting long time," he jokingly exclaims.

Like it was my fucking fault or something! Whatever...

On first glance, I realized that I remembered her to be a bit more beautiful than what I was seeing here/there. But then, that night; the night I met her, I was a little lit up; *drinkin'* the *Weisers* and tequila shots and all...

With all of the apologies out of the way. They mean nothing, I must again say. We were on to off and all of that sort of stuff in-between.

There she was; ten, maybe fifteen pounds, overweight. Chinese, via Taiwan. Grew up in New York. And, though she had been *livin'* in L.A. for eight years, she was still sprouting that New York accent. I guess it gave her form and identification in a generic sort of world. Nothing to me.

She was rude. She was a bitch. She had a full-on attitude. Just like all New York *hoes* do. I liked it.

She didn't want to go dancing. I figured she probably didn't know how.

She told me she wanted to get a boob job, a nose job, her eyes done, and all of the etcetera. I told her that she didn't any of that. I lied...

She wanted to be like a banana, you know. She even claimed that. Said she's white on the inside, yellow on the outside. I guess it

315

is hard trying to find acceptance in a world which you feel separated from.

"Let's go have a drink and talk."

Or, like she said, *"Tolk."* You know, New York accent and all.

Now, going and having a drink that is just not an L.A. thing to do. I mean, like sure, we go out to dinner, go out *clubin,'* and stuff. But, a drink... Fuck, I didn't even know where to take her.

So, I guess that's the basis. I guess I should have seen it all right then, right there, but...

We did a few basic meet-and-greet one another's. She always came late.

Now me, as stated in the previous, I am one punctual person. If I say that I'm going to be there, I am there. But, for whatever foolish reason, I played along. I guess it was just the allure or the chase/the promise of the catch. Or, maybe I just didn't have anything better to do on the nights we met. But, for some reason, I kinda dug her. In that weird, *'I don't really want her,'* sort of way.

Hell, I even bought her this one carat sapphire ring.

Me, I was out *doin'* my X-mas shopping, saw it, and thought, *"What the fuck?"*

When I gave it to her, I played it all cool, like I do. Just threw it her direction over dinner

316

at a Malibu beach restaurant. She picked the place. I didn't really dig it. Sawdust on the floor and all. How that is supposed to give a place ambiance is beyond me.

She tried to turn it down. But, you could see in her eyes, she wanted it. Well, she got it. Whatever...

We played along for the few weeks through Christmas. Went and had drinks at high-end bars and cocktail lounges that I didn't even know existed. Just not my scene. But, it was a unique experience; experiencing all these new places, in and of its own way.

At one point, she gave me the story/her story; she used to be, *"A bit promiscuous,"* back in her NY days, so she said. She hadn't been *hittin'* any since she moved to L.A., however. Well, that was all well and good. It had been eight years since she had been dicked. I guess her pussy was clean. But, in actuality, it was all a big, *'Whatever,'* to me.

But now, I at least had a mission. Let's reopen those floodgates.

New Years Eve, 1989. I had a date with my Wednesday girl, some other chick, and her, my Tuesday girl, Hui Quing. The reality is, one woman has never been enough for me. That being said, Hui Quing, she won the lotto. I guess the other two sat home waiting for me. So I have been told. Such is life...

I knew this was the night. I had a feeling. We had been hanging and it was just time. She didn't want to go out. I can dig it. New Years Eve is one of those weird holidays; too many

317

zero drunks and the etcetera in the clubs and out on the roads and stuff. So, we chilled at my place. Sat back, got drunk, snorted some coke, and at about two in the AM, she tells me she is getting tired, she should go.

Now, this is/has long been the play that many a woman has laid down my direction. Be it a nap, be it a late night; be it a whatever... Tired means we are going to do the deed. So, of course, I play the nice guy.

"Oh, if you're tired, you should stay here. If you can't trust me, who can you trust?"

Which leads to her assertion that we are not going to have sex, just sleep together.

"Of course..."

We hop in bed. Me, my typical naked self. I strip on down. She had her bra and pantyhose on.

I play it cool. I actually dosed off for a few. But, then I wake and it is on... There was no effect. We had our first actually kiss in that moment. Yes, it is true, we actually had not kissed up until that point in time.

The kiss leads to the touch, to the feel, to the bra removal, to the pantyhose removal.

As mentioned, she was a few over. But, you know, every now and then it is kind of fun to hit 'em when they are a few over.

The nakedness led to the doing. The doing led to her *cuming*—more than once.

318

She was no expert, no great sexual master, but what she was—was an active participant.

It was good. Good for what it was.

So, after about an hour plus at the post, we completed our completion(s), and we slid off to sleep. Her in my arms. The ocean waves caressing my ear.

In the AM, we wake up. I think the first wake up is always the hardest. I mean the two bodies are living by such different schedules. Someone always wakes up first and then wonders what to do. Well, in this case, it was me to be the first awake. But/and, I knew just what to do, if you catch my meaning.

What a great way to begin a new decade, the 1990s. After having sealed the 80s with a kiss.

So, we did it once. We did it twice. In fact, I guess it had been so long for her, all she wanted to do, (all day), was to lie around and do it again and again and again and again and again. That was fine with me.

If my count was right, we hit fourteen times. I think that was some new record for me; at least with the same girl. And, you never know, it might have been for her, as well. Probably...

That's the great thing about *Tantra Yoga,* you can do it and do it and do it again. And, you never have to *cum* unless you want to.

But, I digress... So, we did it a lot that day, January 1st, 1990.

We had a few more dates after that eventful New Years Day. I took her to some of the restaurants I like in Beverly Hills and West Hollywood. On one such occasion, however, the relationship met its maker.

Now, she had actually warmed up to my knowing where she lived. I mean, in actuality, the place, her house, was not all that bad. She should have tried coming up the way I did, if she thinks where she lived was negatory in any way shape or form. In any case, I had picked her up, drove her to this little *shi-shi* Italian place, over on 3rd Street, off of La Cienega; that had just opened up.

Actually, I was kind of weirded out by what she was wearing: white fringe cowboy boots and a glistening white mini dress. I don't know what she was thinking. I mean, it did not look good! And, it did accentuate the chub in her legs.

Anyway, we cruised up in the vicinity of the restaurant in question. They had a valet, but I saw a parking spot across the street. So, I grabbed it. Good thing. But, I'll explain that in just a moment.

I got out, walked around the car, opened the door for her, and, as no traffic was approaching, we slowly made our way across the street, near the center of the block.

So, in we go. The host sits us down at a table. I look over the wine list and order a nice bottle of the *Pinot Grigio.*

Now, I'm not really into white wines. I'm into the dark stuff; red. You know, like all

320

the good winos. But, she liked it light. So me, being the gentleman that I am, I played along.

While we were waiting for the bottle to arrive, she tells me, in all her NY feminine bitchness. You know, the attitude she had that I kind of dug. Yeah, she told me that she was going to hit Vegas over the weekend.

"Cool," I said. *"I'll come with you."*

But, *"No,"* was the clear and present answer in that matter-of-fact New York accented way of stating what was being said. Claimed that she was going to visit a friend—a male friend.

Now, whether this was one of those chick tests, a straight-up fuck you, or whatever... I do not know? But, anybody who knows me, knows, I don't play that. There was nothing to say.

I reached back, gathered my long, black wool coat from the back of my chair. I put it on over my dark blue, double-breasted, *Armani* suit. I gave her that one last look as I began to stand up. She grabbed my hand.

"Don't go."

I said nothing and continued my motion.

"I love you," comes echoing in through my peripheral hearing.

I walk towards the door. I opened the door. I'm out the door.

I could feel the cool breeze of the Los Angeles, California Wintertime blow across my face. I could feel it caress my hair, as it moved in the wind.

I walked to the edge of the sidewalk. The two Mexican *valets* looked at me. I smiled. I nodded.

I looked to the left. I looked to the right. There were no cars coming.

With my coat and my long blonde hair blowing in the soft evening wind, I made my way: slowly/coolly across the street. I climb into my *1964, Porsche 356 SC.* I drove off into the night.